TIDES *of the* HEART

TIDES of the HEART

THE MAVERICK KEY SERIES

MARGOT KEENE

Published by Gulf Stream Fiction, an imprint of
Margot Keene Publishing LLC

Edited by Jennifer Herrington
Cover Design, illustrations, and book formatting by Ashley Santoro

eBook ISBN: 978-1-967133-05-5
Paperback ISBN: 978-1-967133-06-2
Hardback ISBN: 978-1-967133-07-9

Library of Congress Control Number: 2026903818

For permissions, inquiries, or more information:
contact@margotkeene.com

<u>The Maverick Key Series</u>

The Carter's Drop Trilogy

Maverick Key: Hearts on the Line

Tides of the Heart

The Heart's True North

AUTHOR'S NOTE:

Maverick Key and Carter's Drop are fictional locations at the heart of the Maverick Key Series. Nestled off South Florida's Gulf Coast, near Naples, Florida, these settings serve as vibrant, immersive backdrops that blend the best of Florida's coastal beauty, charm, and mystery.

While the diving sequences are based on the author's research into actual practices and aim for realism, some aspects have been fictionalized for storytelling. All advanced diving technology in this story is fictional.

DEDICATION

Daddy—thank you for loving the sea.

Water, water, every where,
And all the boards did shrink;
Water, water, every where,
Nor any drop to drink.

—

The Rime of the Ancient Mariner
Samuel Taylor Coleridge

MAVERICK KEY

Carter's Drop

Coastguard Station

Maddie's Cove

Tiki Beach

Dive Club

Gulfstream Marina

Driftwood Inn & Cottage

Cemetary

Richter's Beach House

Old Town

Police Station

General Store

Spock's Ice

City Hall

Naples, Florida

Castle Light Bridgecauseway

Looper Motel

MOTEL

Coconut Grill Cafe

Lazyshores Park

Beach Drive

Sanddollar Dive Bar

Sunset Strand

The Blue Fin

Lighthouse

Carter's Drop Survey Volume 4
Cartography by: Scott Rickter
Passage Length Surveyed: 3896 feet
Maximum Depth on Sonar: 450 feet (150m)

Carter's Drop

The Megaron (21)
210 ft.
P. 400
XX
240 ft.
The Torches
End of Line
P. 1425
Hecate
XX
Main
25
Entrance
25ft.

Mapped
Sonar Plan
Unexplored

Legend

25	Depth at Floor
(3)	Floor to Ceiling
P.80	Distance from entrance
r	Restriction
x	Major restriction
xx	Blocked
///	Slope

CHAPTER 1

The Turning Tide, years ago

I know who I am.

A Sarasota boy who spent most of high school in college classrooms and touched ground in distant places around the world before most kids got the chance to leave their backyard. One who's on a fast track for a direct-entry PhD in marine geosciences. The youngest in my field.

There's a rush and a peace I find while I'm swimming underwater. And yeah, I write poetry because what I see makes me feel things.

I promised my father on the day he died that I'd take care of my mother and sister and always try to do what was right.

And so far, I have.

I'm disciplined. Responsible. Focused.

So how the hell did I let myself get talked into this?

"You promised me one last adventure," she teased this morning.

"Sorry, Cat."

"You've got what, five hundred and something dives logged already? I think we'll be okay. Anyway, this is our last chance to get those pictures."

I knew it was a bad idea. But I went along with it anyway.

"I'm in charge. If I call it, we're done."

"Deal."

The St. Augustine West Start Field Study Program wraps up next week, and we won't get another chance to photograph the wreck. So we loaded up and took the boat out this morning. Since we're both student divers taking part in the excavation, there's nothing unusual about this. Except that we're diving unauthorized on our Sunday off.

If we get caught, we're going to be in a shitload of trouble. It could cost me my transfer to Miami.

For what?

Now, we're swimming above a skeleton of rotted timber covered with colonies of coral and sea sponge. Once a proud member of the Spanish Treasure Fleet, the galleon now rests over forty feet underwater. Dozens of snappers, amberjack, and sheepshead scatter away as we approach the remnants of the carpenter's chest we found on our last dive. The ship's carpenter would have been respected and enjoyed the privilege of his own cabin.

His job—keep the ship afloat.

My dive buddy and partner in crime, Cathy, is midship on the GoPro, trying to get as close as possible to the chest area without entering the unstable structure. The chest itself has been reduced to splinters, but scattered across the floor lie rulers, ax handles, and a brace and bit—centuries-old wooden tools, still recognizable connections to the past.

After I take some overview photos at the stern, I check on Cathy.

Her enthusiasm is getting the better of her. She's way too close.

I tap my tank to get her attention and flatten my hand, pointing down. *Slow down.* After my third attempt, she circles her thumb and index finger to acknowledge my command.

OK.

The tension in my chest loosens. I'm not a fan of being in charge of someone else's safety. It adds too many variables. The riskiest? The other person's free will.

She gives me a wicked smile.

Before I can react, she squeezes between two beams of the ship to get a few feet closer to the artifacts.

Damn it, Cathy.

Annoyed, I signal for her to stop and turn around. But she's not looking at me.

That's when I notice the glint of threadbare fishing line knotted throughout the area.

Oh no.

Seconds stretch into slow motion. To get her attention, I call out through my regulator, letting out a muffled sound followed by a stream of bubbles.

I motion to her with my fist. *Danger. Stop.*

When she turns, it's too late. Already in the thick of it, she's immediately snarled in yards of nylon. Her eyes burst open, and she tries to move toward me, which tightens the lines. Disoriented, she hits the inflator. Her BCD expands with air, jerking her into a vertical position.

Oh shit.

She screams, spitting out her mouthpiece. A rush of air explodes from her mouth as her arms wave wildly, reaching for it.

This is how divers die.

I go still and try not to panic. Then I close the distance.

Her breaths burst out in short, hammering jets, tearing through the water. The sound is savage, like a desperate animal trying to survive. My vision narrows.

Careful not to get entangled myself, I approach her as fast as I can. Her arms flail, and she hits my face, driving my teeth into the walls of my mouth. I swallow hard, ignoring the sharp, metallic taste of blood. She's going to die or get me killed if she doesn't calm down.

I focus on her, grab her wrist and the regulator, and force the mouthpiece back between her teeth, holding it until she seals her lips around it. Then, I shove the inflator hose down. It stops her rise, but she's in trouble and knows it. Her eyes blink open, and she stares at me blankly, her pupils blown wide. I push away my fear. Right now, I can't think about her little brother Michael, or Peanut, the Yorkshire Terrier she's had since she was a teenager.

Carefully anchoring myself to a timber, I signal for her to calm down and pull her close until her mask is inches from mine. Her breathing's still erratic, but she's taking in a few deeper inhales and trying to regain control.

I hold her steady until she stills and lets out one controlled breath. Once she's breathing with a steady rhythm, I take the line cutter out of my pocket and show her I'm going to cut her out. She nods.

I move behind her and pause.

Where do I begin?

So she knows I'm still with her, I keep one hand on her waist and start at the tank valve. I work my way through the lines around her equipment, arms, and legs. When I come back up, I realize I'm going to have to cut through portions of her hair.

This will hurt. Her and me. The last thing I want to do is destroy her beautiful hair. I know it will grow back, but… There's no real choice, so I do it.

Clumps of line and strands of hair float around us, their intrusion a brief distraction to the schools of wrasses and damselfish swimming nearby. After cutting the last knot of line, I gently adjust her forward and confirm she's free.

We stay still for a moment until Cathy's ready to head back. At a safe distance from the wreck, she throws her arms around me, muttering something through her mouthpiece.

I cradle her head and let her hold me until she's able to swim.

Back on the deck, we're silent as we get ready for the ride back to the field house. I take the helm, and she sits beside me.

"I really fucked up," she whispers.

Yeah, she fucked up, and I was stupid enough to let it happen because I listened to my hormones and not my head. I could have gotten someone killed and thrown away years of hard work and sacrifice for a few hours of fun.

Not my proudest moment.

My father's face flashes behind my eyes as disappointment washes over me. Pulling out the titanium dive knife he gave me after my open-water certification—I rub my thumb across the blade and read the engraving.

Son, be brave. Be free.

A reminder. After every achievement, every win, that's what he'd say. It was his way of telling me—I'm proud of you, son.

I grip the throttle and ease the boat forward.

What would Dad tell me right now if he were still alive?

He'd probably have just kicked me in the ass.

I promise to do better, Dad.

"Will you forgive me? Still friends?" Cathy asks.

I lean over and brush my fingers across her face, running them through her choppy, shortened hair. She looks up, tears in her eyes. I give her a reassuring smile. "Yeah. We're good."

She moves back to Virginia next week and will graduate in the fall. It's time for her to focus on the rest of her life, and the same goes for me.

The engines drone and the wind carries across the water. I take another deep breath of the salty air, letting my muscles relax.

There's no sense in dwelling on mistakes.

My next stop—Miami.

SoBe, Miami Beach.

An intoxicating tang of salt, sea breeze, and sunscreen fills the humid afternoon air. There's nothing I love more than the ocean. That said, sharing the beach with about a million other people at the same time isn't my idea of fun. I've been in Miami for eight months now, and this is my first day off. My buddy Mark demanded it.

My suggestion was Key Biscayne. I wanted to check out Neptune Memorial Reef and take some pictures of the artificial reef designed to resemble the lost city of Atlantis. I'd packed my gear and was ready to go. But Mark pushed for Lummus Park, so here we are.

Bright, sandy, and loud. Mark fits right in. Already lit on the vodka he's been sneaking into his tumbler. Drinking's not my thing. It makes you stupid. Takes away all the control you have over what's going on around you.

After weaving through the crowds, we snatch a small open spot next to the blue and yellow Art Deco lifeguard stand. I drop the cooler and bag on the sand.

Mark whistles. I sigh, glancing in the direction he's looking. Who is it now? We've been here for fifteen minutes, and Mark's already got four girls lined up to ask out.

"Nice. I'm adding her to the list."

I follow his gaze. The lifeguard's pretty, blonde, and about our age.

"Highly fuckable." He tilts his head in her direction. "You want that one? I'm feeling generous."

He's drunk.

"Take it easy."

"Hey, I'm just a concerned friend. When's the last time you got laid?"

I ignore his question. The last time was with Cathy in St. Augustine. But I don't miss it. That wreck fiasco taught me a valuable lesson. Stay focused. My adviser has been warning me that the committee is skeptical of my dissertation topic. A few members are reserving their judgment, and I need to sell them at the draft review.

The rest of my life's a blur. There's no time for anything else. I've decided that this beach day is the last time I'm going to let anyone talk me into doing anything for a while.

Stay focused.

"Shit. Look at her." He gazes toward a beautiful girl who's dipping her toes into the waves. "She's going to be the lucky lady tonight." Smirking, he walks off.

Stopping him, I take his tumbler and drop it next to the cooler. "Time to cut you off."

He laughs and heads over to the girl. Making his standard introduction, he gets her to smile and agree to whatever it is he's selling her.

Hopefully, she's smart enough to keep her distance when he makes his move. Leaving him to it, I stretch out on the sand.

Closing my eyes, I let myself enjoy the heat. I'm dozing off when a light, citrusy vanilla scent drifts toward me.

My face turns cool, and I hear a camera shutter.

When I open my eyes, I see the blonde lifeguard standing over me. She's putting something away in her hip pack.

Did she just take a picture of me?

Close up, she's a vision. Fair skin warmed by a golden undertone. White-blonde hair and clear blue eyes that shimmer in the sun. A light dusting of sand clings to her like glitter, catching the light. She's... bright. I glance at the lifeguard stand and see that another guard has replaced her.

"Where's your friend?" she asks.

"Who? Mark?"

"He's been drinking." Hands on her hips, her face is serious, as if she's scolding a child. This is going to be fun. I sit up.

She spots the tumbler. Picks it up and sniffs.

"Vodka." She pours what's left of the liquid onto the sand, closes the lid, then puts it back in its place.

"Alcohol is prohibited on the beach."

"Sure." Smiling, I try to look innocent. Which I kind of am. "I'll make sure he knows. Anything else I need to tell him?"

She sits down beside me and stares at the sand, then bites down on her lip. Curious now, I watch as she looks up, then down, then back to me.

"You're Nathan Carter."

"That's me." Now I'm *really* curious.

"Hi." She stares and waits.

"Hi?"

"I'm nervous."

I try to stop myself from smiling. And I'm dying to know what she's going to say. "Don't be. Just spit it out."

"I need a student mentor." She pauses again, then clears her throat and sits up straighter. "I'm majoring in marine biology."

"Oh yeah? We have something in common. My mother is a marine biologist. Both my parents were," I say. I think of my mom and my little sister, Mads. A pang of guilt hits me. I'm here, focusing on my future, while they're home alone. But Mads is sixteen now, and Mom had insisted.

Her mouth curves, the tension draining from her face, replaced by a cautious openness that hadn't been there before.

Who is this girl anyway?

"I'm curious—why are you asking me to mentor you? Have we met?" I know we haven't. How could I forget if we had?

"No… I've heard you're the smartest, the best—I want to learn from the best."

My mind goes blank. I'm clueless about what to say. Is she really asking me to mentor her? Because I have zero time for that.

"Will you teach me? I won't disappoint you. I'm the hardest worker you'll find."

"Hmmm." I'm so intrigued, I almost say yes.

But I'm going to have a little fun with her first. "Before I commit, I have to know you're a serious student." I give her a firm stare. I'm struck by her eyes. They're unnerving. Like mirrors.

"Can you explain diel vertical migration?"

She nods enthusiastically, and I can tell she's about to spill out all the textbook knowledge she's sure to have on the subject. I raise my hand. "Wait a sec. Teach me like I'm a little boy with no knowledge of marine biology."

Rose-colored plumes flow up her neck.

Got her.

She's going to need to think about her answer. Good.

Clutching my hand, she clears her throat. I stare at our clasped hands.

"So, have you heard about how birds, butterflies, and fish—like salmon—all leave their homes in big groups and move over long distances each year to find food and shelter or to have their babies?"

"I think so."

"Well… those are called animal migrations, and they're super important in the cycle of life. Did you know the biggest mass migration in the whole wide world happens every single day in the ocean?"

Most people I've met talk with their hands when they're explaining something they're enthusiastic about, as if to occupy them while they search for the right words. Not her. Her body is still.

But her face is the most expressive I've ever seen. Alive. As though there is no gatekeeping of her thoughts and emotions. A verse from my favorite poem comes to mind: *"A mind at peace with all below…"*

"No. Tell me more."

"At night, when it's dark, billions of little sea creatures all swim up to the surface of the ocean so they can eat. Then, when the daylight comes, they swim back to the deep to hide from the bigger creatures that want to eat them."

She's a good teacher. I'm mesmerized by the cadence of her voice and how the words glide out of her lips, their color a hue I've only seen in my mother's garden.

"That's cool."

"It sure is. And it's important for the health of the entire ocean—to speed up circulation and keep everyone fed. Every creature, large and small, plays a big part in our world."

"How do they know how to do that?"

"They don't. Their bodies are made to do it." She pauses for effect. "Nothing's random. Everything has a purpose."

Her naivety both touches me and surprises me. It's a beautiful thought, but does she believe it? Do I?

"Are you a philosophy major too?"

Her face falls, and her lips tremble.

Shit, Nathan. I squeeze her hand, surprised to see I'm still holding it.

"Hey," I say softly, "let me put you out of your misery. A+. You've got yourself a mentor."

She shakes my hand as if she's going to yank it off. "Thank you, Nathan… thank you so much." When she pulls away, I hold on a little tighter. I want to talk to her some more.

A shrill whistle cuts through the noise of the crowd. In an instant, she's running off. What the? I didn't get her name. Several lifeguards are rushing to the waves. A beachgoer must have gotten themselves into some trouble. The woman Mark had been hitting on is standing in front of the crowd, screaming. Oh no. Mark.

They've already got him pulled out by the time I get there. He's sprawled, arms spread wide, until they roll him onto his side. The blonde girl is crouched, leaning over him, gently touching the sides of his face.

"You're safe now, Mark. My name's Crystal, and I'm here to help."

"Thank you." He grasps her hand and pulls it toward him. That's when it occurs to me. I just volunteered a shitload of time—time I don't have—to mentor a freshman.

Oh well. Time is relative.

And I think I'm gonna be learning as much from her as she will be from me.

SEVEN YEARS LATER

THE MAVERICK KEY REGISTER

Dr. Nathan Carter, 28, Renowned Marine Archaeologist, Presumed Dead After Cave Diving Incident

Dr. Carter was reported missing thirty miles off the coast of Maverick Key while conducting a solo cave dive in the sinkhole—a blue hole—he discovered seven months ago. Carter was accompanied on the dive by his boat captain and friend, Mark Glassier, who alerted authorities after Carter failed to surface within his designated safety window.

Following an extensive search led by technical divers trained in specialized body recovery, efforts were suspended late Wednesday. Investigators cited the extreme danger posed by continued attempts to navigate the underwater cave passages.

Lead investigator Reeves stated, "After consulting with multiple experts, we've concluded that there's no chance of survival, and it's too dangerous to continue entry into the unexplored sections of the caves. It's with regret that we suspend all recovery efforts indefinitely."

Colleagues refer to Dr. Carter as a prodigy and a humble genius, crediting his discovery of the blue hole as one of the most significant marine archaeological finds of the century.

Born in Sarasota, Florida, Dr. Carter was the beloved son of the late Christopher Carter and Natalie Carter, both respected marine biologists whose work strongly influenced his early passion for ocean exploration. He earned his Ph.D. in marine geosciences from the University of Miami. He is survived by his mother, Natalie Carter (49), and his sister, Maddie Carter (23).

Nathan was unmarried and had no children.

SIX YEARS LATER

THE MAVERICK KEY REGISTER

Mystery Solved? Local Legend, Dr. Nathan Carter, Allegedly Murdered by Longtime Friend

The years-old mystery surrounding the disappearance of renowned local archaeologist, Dr. Nathan Carter, might have a resolution after a tragic series of events has left three more people dead.

Authorities confirm that Maddie Carter, a Maverick Key resident and Dr. Carter's sister, was kidnapped Thursday morning while investigating new evidence suggesting her brother's death was not accidental.

Lead investigator Detective Daniels explains, "Local diver, Scott Rickter, reported an assault at his home in which his dog was wounded and his girlfriend, Maddie Carter, was kidnapped. Shortly afterward, Scott received an anonymous tip that Mark Glassier had taken Maddie into the underwater caves of the Carter's Drop blue hole. Scott Rickter and Maddie's friend, Wes Harrington, then attempted a high-risk rescue in the caves. Thankfully, Scott was able to get Maddie out safely. Regrettably, Wes Harrington perished in the caves when he took a wrong turn and was pulled into a siphon."

In a statement given to investigators, Maddie Carter alleges that prior to his death, Glassier confessed to murdering both Dr. Nathan Carter and Dr. Elaine Fischer. She claims he provided no motive in his confession.

The body of Mark Glassier was recovered on Saturday.

An investigation into the deaths of Dr. Nathan Carter, Dr. Elaine Fischer, Wes Harrington, and Mark Glassier is underway.

CHAPTER 2

The Widow

The air is thick today. A heavy, invisible weight that digs into the pores of your skin like fingers and pulls you toward the ground. I'd like to say I'm used to it. It's what you expect in southern Florida. But some things are impossible to get used to. You learn to accept them because they're unchangeable. Like the setting sun and the pull of the morning tide.

"Hey, Crystal. You think they're gonna shut down Coral Fang?" Fred's anxious voice carries through the breeze. He wraps rope around the bollards as he docks his boat, the *Reefing Around*. "That'll cost us this season's snorkeling income."

Fred's right to worry. Around here, everything runs on ecotourism and the beaches. All year long. Any downtime, and the financial hit can be brutal. To supplement his income, Fred also runs a water taxi service for the city's Department of Coastal Resources. He's been taking me out to the reef daily for the last few weeks to investigate some recent coral deterioration reported by local divers. With today's samples, I think I've gotten all the information I need.

Fred squints at the shoreline, his bagged eyes weary. "The tide is wrong."

I follow his gaze over the water. He's right. The tide is *wrong*. Waves fold too far up the beach, licking at sand that should still be dry. Damn. I want to reassure him, but the data is troublesome. Trends are clear, and it's time to submit my report through the Office of Marine Research and Conservation. Coral stress response. Unusual channel flow. Subtle but noticeable signals. Like so many things in Maverick Key, it makes no sense.

But it's happening.

"I'll have Darcy run these samples stat and supervise the results myself." Picking up my case and dive bag, I walk to the stern. "But Fred, I'm so sorry. I don't like what I see. Something's warming the water to temperatures that aren't sustainable for coral. Unchecked, these changes could be detrimental to the reef."

Fred helps me step onto the dock. I get a whiff of sun-dried pine and diesel. Comforting and familiar, but it doesn't calm my unease.

"I don't have to tell you that times are hard around here. If there's anything you can do…" He doesn't meet my eyes.

The consequences of my findings for Fred and for others like him weigh on my mind. I love my job, but I also care about the people in this town, and I don't want to be a part of anything that makes their lives harder.

"I'll do what I can." His face relaxes a bit, but he knows I have very little say in what will happen.

Before I reach the car, I glance back at the shore one last time. Growing up in the foster care system, I never put down roots in any place or person. The only stabilizing force I had back then was the connection I created with the ocean. It became my home. I never imagined I'd love anything more.

I was wrong.

But it was my first love, and I'll do whatever I can to protect it. This is serious, and we may be running out of time to reverse whatever's ailing the ocean. I'll go straight to the lab to be sure, but I already know no one's going to be able to get into the waters surrounding Coral Fang or Carter's Drop until we find a solution.

After more than a year of sensational news stories, outsiders, and murder, Maverick Key may be about to get even more attention.

It's been a long afternoon. As much as I wanted to be wrong, the lab results came back as I predicted. My boss and I have another meeting lined up later tonight to brief county leaders. Now there will be days of navigating red tape. And sadly, the people who'll be most affected will be the last to know and won't have much time to react.

While I'm supposed to keep my mouth shut for the moment, there's one person I can't keep this from.

When I reach the Maverick Key Dive Club, I pull in beside a silver Land Rover I've never seen before. The windows are tinted, but I can make out what appears to be someone sitting inside.

I read the license plate: Washington, D.C. *TAXATION WITHOUT REPRESENTATION*

We always get a throng of out-of-state visitors in December. I'm sure it's one of them eager to get their kids swim lessons before beach day.

As I step inside onto the pool deck, I smell the chlorine.

Four little children are in the pool, paddling their way from one side to the other. Maddie and Sandy watch attentively, ready to move in at a moment's notice, but keeping enough of a distance to encourage the little swimmers.

I wait near the door as they finish up and their proud parents help them dry off.

After the last family leaves, Maddie calls me over.

"There she is! Miss Assistant Director of Environmental & Coastal Resources... come join us, fancy pants. Cool off."

Maddie leans back on her arms at the pool's edge. Her belly is bigger than the rest of her now. She's overdue, but it hasn't slowed her down one bit. My recent promotion is exciting. It's what I've been working for—for how long? All my life? Now, three days in, I'm already challenged with a crisis.

Maddie and her husband Scott have worked so hard on their dive club and the Carter's Drop cave exploration. I don't want to give them this news.

"Sorry, can't do it today. I need to head back to City Hall and get ready for another late night." Walking by the desk, I see Maddie's brand-new pink scuba tanks. A birthday gift from Scott. There's a smiling green elephant painted on each one.

"They're right there, but I can't use them," she grumbles.

She can't dive until after the baby comes.

"I've done everything I can think of to induce labor—pineapples, long walks, lots of sex—it's no use. But I guess the good news is, I can float around without breaking a sweat."

Sandy laughs and gets out of the pool. "Gotta go, girls, Clint's taking me to dinner." She pulls her strawberry-blonde curls back in a tie and waves goodbye.

"See you Saturday," Maddie says.

Sandy is Maddie's assistant. She helps with the club's swim lessons and with Maddie's veterinarian house calls. She met Maddie after her boyfriend, Clint, started working for Scott as a boat captain. Clint and Sandy are young, sweet, and deeply in love. I remember what that felt like.

Don't think about that right now, Crystal.

Turning back to Maddie, I point to the tanks. "Don't worry. Christopher will be here before you know it. Then you won't have any time to eat, sleep, or take showers, let alone dive."

Frowning, she sticks out her tongue. "That's not very nice."

Christopher is named after Maddie and Nathan's father.

Nathan.

The thought of him knocks me off-center.

Instead of pushing the memory away, I let myself imagine him for a moment. That day at Lummus Park. It wasn't the first time I'd noticed him, but it was the first time he'd seen *me*. He was walking along the shoreline. His chiseled chin in profile against the horizon, golden-brown hair aglow with the highlights of the fading sun. My dreamer. And the most brilliant man I've ever known.

Dr. Nathan Carter. Natalie's father.

My husband.

Clutching the platinum wedding bands and engagement ring that lie against my neck, I sigh. It's been over six years since he's been gone, and I still love him just as much.

Until recently, only Maddie and Scott knew Nathan and I were married. It was a secret. One I agreed to keep because Nathan asked me to. He insisted no one could know who I was to him. That it was important. As much as I asked him to share the reasons with me, he refused. It's the one thing we ever fought about. He was so damn stubborn. Nathan carried his secrets to the grave. Leaving me alone, his hidden widow with a broken heart.

Then I married Mark, our *friend*. Burying the past that I shared with Nathan. Mark promised to take care of my unborn child and me until I could get back on my feet. Blinded by grief, I trusted him. I'd known him for as long as I'd known Nathan. At least I'd thought so.

Why couldn't I have seen what should have been so obvious from the beginning?

Now they're both dead, and I'm still Crystal Glassier. Keeping Mark's name for Natalie's sake and because of my uncertainty about what Nathan was hiding.

Mark.

When he died, and I learned what he did to Nathan, I gave the monster's rings to a women's shelter and threw away his ashes.

I despise my last name.

In my heart, I'll always be Crystal Carter.

"Hey..." Maddie's raised voice draws me from my thoughts.

"Where'd you go?"

"Sorry, there's a lot on my mind. That's actually why I stopped by." I take out the lab report. "The coral in the waters surrounding the Key is showing signs of bleaching. Something's causing the water surrounding the island to heat abnormally. We've got to figure this out quickly, Maddie."

Maddie's face drops.

I point to the symbiont density counts and the chlorophyll concentration.

Maddie gives me a puzzled look.

"Unfortunately, to reduce the stress on the coral as much as we can now, we need to shut down aquatic activity near the reef. It'll happen soon. Before the end of the week."

"No," she says, closing her eyes. "We were just getting back to normal."

"I'm so sorry. I know Scott and his team were getting ready to restart the dives into Carter's Drop, but they may have to wait a little while."

Maddie blows out a puff of air and shakes her head. "Yeah, but more than that, it's going to cause some bigger problems. Dr. Phenias Clark arrives any day now, and Garrett's head is going to explode if he doesn't have any progress he can share."

"Who?"

"Dr. Phenias Clark."

The name sounds familiar, but I can't place it.

"He's taking over all of Elaine's responsibilities and more. Clark has earned a reputation as a maverick in the scientific community. He works across several fields and does his own thing. According to Hannah, the rumor is he's a JASON. Whatever that is."

That gives me pause. I'm familiar with the advisory group of elite scientists. They're often consulted by the government for urgent, complex problems, but they insist on complete independence from state influence. Why is one of their members getting involved with the Carter's Drop blue hole? As much as they may try, their research is never completely independent. Someone powerful is always watching.

"What's his field?" I ask.

"Get this. Deep theoretical science in materials, quantum mechanics, and archaeology. That's an odd combination, isn't it?"

I keep listening as she explains what she's learned. But my thoughts are racing, thinking of all the connections Nathan had with others like Dr. Clark.

"If they're still trying to explore and chart the caves in the Drop, they don't need someone like Clark. Have they changed their goals?"

"Nothing that Garrett has shared. Scott thinks they're after rare earth or something." She frowns. "But the university hasn't trusted Garrett to run things alone since the beginning. Even less so after the murders. Do you think this is about what Nathan found?"

"The stone?" I ask.

"There's no explanation for it. Carved symbols in a language no one's recorded, and it generates heat on its own. What could it be?"

"It's got to be radioactive."

Maddie told me about the stone last year, but I didn't think too much of it. Nathan had never mentioned it to me, and it's been in police custody since they found it among the things that Mark stole from Nathan.

"It's the *only* thing that makes any sense. And even that's a stretch." I add.

This new information about Dr. Clark concerns me. There's got to be more than archaeological research at stake to get his kind of attention.

"It's going to get dramatic around here fast if these guys are told the project is on hold again. Garrett's already in a foul mood because his daughter's coming here to the inn. Geesh. He's going to be intolerable."

"I didn't know he had a daughter," I say. "Why in the world is he upset?"

"Well… she's not exactly coming here to visit *him*. A film producer has hired her to film the Drop. She's a nature documentarian. Garrett's out of his mind. He's been plotting all week about ways to sabotage her. I feel bad. He's convinced it's too dangerous for her to dive in the caves."

"For a father, it is, isn't it?"

Maddie pulls herself out of the pool. "Yeah. I'll try not to get involved, but with Garrett…"

"Good luck."

"Right."

She wraps a towel around her waist and hobbles over to the desk, yanking open her snack drawer—packed to the brim with granola bars, dried fruit, and jerky. "I'm starving. Want one?"

"No thanks." I laugh, remembering those days of cravings and swollen feet.

"You and Natalie are still coming to the picnic on Saturday, right?"

"There's no way she'll let me miss it."

"Good. It's gonna be a lot of fun. I'm bringing corn casserole. Sandy's bringing fruit salad, and Hannah's got the honey-cut ham."

"Natalie's baking chocolate chip cookies."

"Perfect! Let her know Aunt Maddie can't wait."

My alarm bleeps. It's time to get back to work.

"They're closing the investigation," Maddie blurts out as I say goodbye. "I'm sorry. They're about to return Nathan's belongings."

"Oh." Her words hit me like rocks, obliterating the fragile walls I'd built to keep the grief contained. "They've cleared you, right?" I ask.

"Self-defense," she says. "They believe me."

I shiver as I picture Maddie in the underwater caves of Carter's Drop, dragged deep into them where Mark thought no one would ever find her. When she got too close to the truth about what he did to Nathan, he tried to silence her. She escaped. He didn't.

"They officially ruled Nathan and Elaine's deaths as homicides." Maddie adds, "No conclusions about Mark's motives. I don't think they care about why he did it since he's… gone." She stops.

"At least it's over," I say. "Thank you for keeping me out of it." Maddie didn't tell the police about Mark's motive because his motive was me. He had wanted what his best friend had, and he killed for it.

"As soon as they release Nathan's things, I'll give them to you. They belong with you."

"Thanks." I swallow the ball in my throat. Turning my head away, I try to will back the tears that are teetering at the edge of my lashes. Quickly brushing away the ones that escape, I turn back. Shouldn't I want to have more of Nathan's things, to hold on to more pieces of him? But I don't. I don't want any more reminders of the man I've lost.

"And this." She pulls a leather-bound notebook out of her desk drawer. Dark brown with a wraparound strap and deckle-edge paper. I recognize it right away—Nathan's personal journal.

Slowly, I take it from her. "His diary."

She gazes at me with sad brown eyes. Carter's eyes. The same ones that Nathan and Natalie share with her.

Even years later, we both still struggle with Nathan's loss. Some days it's a quiet echo of pain, woven into the joys of life. On other days, it's as fresh a wound as the moment I knew he was never coming back.

After we hug, I leave with the journal in my hands.

Why does it feel like he's not gone?

There's a cold part of me that can't forgive him. I begged him not to go. For me. For Natalie. He dived that day anyway. But the part of me that still beats hot with the love I never lost can't blame him. He died being true to who he was, and I know he did everything right.

Evil had him in its sights. It was out of his hands.

The parking lot is empty except for Maddie's Honda Civic and the Land Rover I parked next to when I came in. Strange. Maybe it's someone waiting for someone at the marina. As I fumble with the door to my car, I feel a breeze brush against my skin, raising the hairs on the back of my neck.

It's not windy today. I turn my head to look over my shoulder, expecting to see someone.

No one's there.

CHAPTER 3

The Stranger

For a guy with no memory of the man he used to be, I spend a hell of a lot of time in my head. After I park my car in the small gravel lot, I take off my lanyard and glance at the ID badge.

Elliot Trevor.

I toss it into the center console and stare at the busted gray door through the windshield. I'm on a month-to-month tenancy-at-will agreement with the company that hired me to clean vacation rentals on Maverick Key. The room's cramped, and the bathroom reeks of mildew, but the bed is soft, and there's not too much noise at night. It's a short walk to the beach. Not bad for someone who only has a few dollars to his name and barely had the means for the car ride here.

One thing I am is resourceful.

I'll get something a little nicer when I can.

I spend a few more minutes thinking of every place and face I've seen since I got to the island. Wondering whether any of them hold a clue about my past. Not finding any answers, I get out and grab the cleaning caddy to restock it for tomorrow. The crumbling quadplex must have been built a hundred years ago. I open the door and walk in—there's no lock. Inside, I put down the caddy and spend a few minutes fiddling with the door to get it to close. There's a trick I've been using that's been working well. But this time it's just done. I give up, move a chair in front of the door, and head straight to the bathroom.

As far as first days on the job go, this one wasn't bad. My first assignment was a beach house. Renters hadn't used it in years. There was a lot of dust and square footage, but not much else to worry about. Still, I'm filthy, and my bones ache. I ignore the scratched, peeling mirror and toss my dirty clothes into a basket near the door. After I brush my teeth, I step into the shower and turn the handle. Frigid water trickles over my head. The pressure sucks, and there's no hot water. But I don't care. I like the sting. It makes me feel something. I tug on the leather band around my neck, making sure it's still there. I never take it off.

Stop it, Elliot. Stop fixating on that dream. On *her*.

I've been on Maverick Key for a few nights. I'm not sure what I expected, but I thought there'd be… something. When I read that newspaper article about the Key back in Miami, I felt… recognition. I was so certain I'd been here before. But when I crossed over the Castle Light Bridge causeway and saw the island's tranquil landscape, nothing seemed familiar—or even real. A beautiful mirage.

I towel off and pull on a clean pair of boxers, checking my phone. There's one message from Karen.

Elliot! How was the first day on the job? We miss you so much. 😭

Karen misses me. The rest of my friends in Miami? I doubt they're too worried about me. I like Karen, but I'm too fixated on my problems to be a good friend to anyone right now.

Went well. Just tired. Going to bed.

I watch the cursor blink for a few seconds. She wants to chat, to be the supportive friend, but she knows me well enough to let it go.

K, rest up! You know I'm here if you wanna talk.♡

Relieved to be off the hook, I put away the phone. But not without a pang of guilt. I should care enough to be more grateful. But I don't care enough because I'm empty.

I opened my eyes almost seven years ago. Waking up and feeling intact, able to recognize what was going on around me, only to find my mind fractured. As much as I searched, I couldn't find anything. No name, no memory. Early on, I tried to reclaim my life. The hospital staff helped me heal, but had no information about where I might have come from. My only belonging was the leather band I wear around my neck.

An anchor to the past that I lived and lost.

My nurses explained to me I'd been pulled from the sea and stripped. Admitted to the hospital for weeks, I was treated for severe sun exposure, dehydration, and muscle deterioration. Investigators suspected drug runners conducting illicit activities might have found me in the water and dumped me near the shore as a mercy instead of getting involved.

The police fingerprinted and interviewed me, labeling me a *John Doe*, but nothing ever panned out. My social worker helped me for months—then years—working with the police to search for any sign of who I was. When that hope faded, they helped me establish a new identity. I got a delayed birth certificate through the courts, enabling me to get all the documentation I required to function. Everything I needed for a fresh start.

Being *Elliot Trevor* was my key to holding a place in society. But it became a prison, with freedom an elusive goal. It was giving up.

The life I remember has been a journey of discovering all the things I already know how to do. Knowledge and skill without experience. Retrograde amnesia. I can drive. I know how to use cell phones and computers and speak Italian, French, and German. Operating a boat and scuba diving—check. I'm an expert. What I don't know is everything that came before the day I woke up in that hospital bed in Miami.

That newspaper gave me hope. Now, finding nothing here and being away from the familiar faces and my routines is unsettling. Should I call Dr. Paulson?

I think back to one of our earliest counseling sessions.

"Real men remember who they are. Who they loved. Who they buried," I said.

"You're acting like your past disappeared," Dr. Paulson said. He tapped his pen once on the notebook and pointed it at me. "It didn't. You did."

He set the pen down and snapped his fingers. "Instincts. Know-how. The engine that made you *you* is still running under the hood. You didn't lose it. You've just lost access to the road."

I'd wanted to believe him.

He slid a piece of paper across the desk. "I want you to answer some questions."

I glanced at them and scoffed. "The hell, Doc? Do I sleep with the door open or closed?"

"I know they seem small. But you don't need memory to answer them. Patterns emerge. Experience. Training. Preferences…"

"What's the point?"

"The point," he said, locking his gaze on mine. "Is that you don't get to decide you're a nobody. You can build a future."

"Doc. I know you mean well, but that's horseshit." I laughed bitterly. "You don't know me. I picked the first random name that popped into my head. I could be a drug dealer for all you know. The hospital gave me a job as a janitor that pays for the roof over my head. I'm a fucking charity case."

Undeterred, he pressed on.

"Then stop waiting," he said, cutting a hand through the air. "Build something new. Or don't. Just own it."

"Yeah…" I stared at the black-and-white photo of the Eiffel Tower behind him. "I'm never getting my memories back, am I?"

He gave me a sympathetic look, but to his credit, didn't lie.

"The longer it's been, the lower the odds of a full recovery." He paused and gave me a small smile. "But it's still possible. Rare. But it's happened."

His brows drew together. "If we can just find the right triggers," he continued. "You've mentioned recurring dreams. Are you still having them?"

"Every night. They're more like fantasies."

"There's a chance they're connected to your past. Hold on to them. Just don't let them keep you from moving forward."

Right. My future.

Dr. Paulson's a good guy. But he couldn't help me.

No. There's a reason I'm here—a reason I read that newspaper article about Maverick Key in that small breakroom in Miami.

The clock on the motel room wall thrums. 2:40 a.m.

I grab the remote and turn on the television. Sometimes watching something helps me fall asleep. Scrolling through the satellite channels, nothing catches my interest, and I can feel myself getting more restless. I pick up my notebook and flip through the pages. Dr. Paulson suggested keeping a diary, but using it feels instinctual. Like I would have done it anyway. I use it to capture and organize all the little things that feel familiar. On good nights, it helps me steady my thoughts.

But not tonight.

Damn it.

I toss it onto the nightstand, then put on some clothes and shoes. The beach is only a couple of blocks away, and I need to see it. I'm going for a run.

The sand is unrecognizable, a charcoal landscape lit by the stars in a moonless sky and a few stray lights from distant buildings. It's nearly impossible to tell where the shoreline meets the sea.

Three a.m.

No one else is out here. Most insomniacs are plagued with racing thoughts and fear. For me, it's a beautiful dream.

Her.

I'm terrified one night I'll fall asleep and she won't be there.

But if I can get to the point of pure exhaustion…

I jog. The sand is firm. Great for running. At first, it feels good. Numbness and fatigue melt into a pleasant, warm heat that flows through my body, and all my senses awaken. I can taste the salt, feel the breeze, and smell the ocean. Exhilarated, I push harder, letting the crash of the waves help me find a rhythm to my strides. Pebbles of sweat form at my temples. They're tactile, cool—proof I'm still awake.

Go harder!

Okay. Let's do it.

My lungs are burning now, and my short breaths hurt. The pain screams at me, reminding me that I need oxygen to live. Warning me not to push too far. I ignore it and run harder. As hard as I can. There's the lighthouse ahead. It's about four miles from the motel. Have I climbed the stairs and looked out over the ocean? I really want to do that.

Without warning, my muscles lock. They're refusing to continue with this insanity. Forcing me down, regardless of whether I choose to stop.

Good.

I collapse a few feet from the sea. A sweet release with no control. No responsibility. Waves wash over me and then retreat, repeating the motion again and again. Stretching my arms across the cool sand, I ignore the tears running down my face. They'll blend in with my sweat.

Finally. My breathing slows, and I let go.

It's time to see her again.

Sleep takes over.

I toss my wetsuit into the soak bucket and grab the labeled Whirl-Pak bags sitting in the cockpit to put them in the box on deck. We've just finished a recon dive and have been cataloging samples for the past hour. We're running behind and need to get the skiff back to shore. The field log will have to wait. Shoot. I misplaced the iron samples. "Can you hand me…"

"It's break time!"

Playful laughter rings out through the air, followed by a loud splash.

I glance up to see her swimming away at a breakneck pace. She's already about seven meters away.

"What the hell do you think you're doing?" I take off my shirt to join her. Hesitating, I open my mouth to call her name. But I realize I don't know it. "Get back on the boat. We've still got a ton of work left to do, and we're already running late."

"Hey, I'm the boss this time—remember? You told me so."

"We've got to head back to the dock. We're about to lose daylight. Come on."

She's got to be close to fifteen meters away now. Her bright silver-blonde hair looks darker when it's wet and lies flat against her head. Still, I can see her blue eyes from here. Shining. I know her face.

"Relax, sailor. I can see you fidgeting from here. I promise we'll get our work done."

"Well, boss—my other boss won't be pleased if I miss ETR. There's already no chance I'll get the field log in today."

"Since we're already late. We'll just be a little later, right? Fifteen minutes?"

"So, you're gonna make me come get you?"

I'm speaking to her back. She's ignoring me. Damn it. I turn around to retrieve the anchor when I notice movement in the water. Heading toward her.

A dorsal fin.

"Come back!"

"What is it?" Her back is still turned to me.

Panicked, I jump in. The fin is circling her now, getting closer with each pass. "Stay still! You need to stay still!" She turns back to me with a confused look.

More fins. At least six. Oh my God.

I swim harder.

What the…?

A small gray head pops out of the surface and whistles.

Well, shoot. Dolphins.

Slowing my strokes, I watch as the dolphin who first approached swims to her side and hovers. She bobs up and down in the water, prompting the dolphin to mimic her. Like a dutiful student, it follows her lead.

I stiffen when it nudges her with its rostrum.

"Don't worry," she calls out, giggling when it bumps her shoulder as it swims by again. "They're gentle." She strokes its skin.

Another one jumps into the air and swims up beside her. A young bull rolls to his side, exposing a flipper.

"Okay, little guy. Can you tell me your name?"

Chirps.

"Michael. That's a nice name…" The dolphin jumps. "What's that? I see. You want to play?"

More chirps.

"Let's play, then." She stretches out her arms.

Both dolphins rush off and then circle back, approaching her from behind. As they pass, she gently grasps the bottom of both of their fins, and they pull forward, taking her for a ride in large circles. I stop swimming and watch. She continues to talk to them as they make soft clicks and whistles in response. I want so badly to remember her name.

Something brushes past me. I turn to see two fins circling behind me.

"Hey there. Me too?" That's cool.

Stretching my arms, I catch on as they glide by and gently hold on to their soft, slick fins. Ready to let go if they get spooked, I let myself enjoy the ride.

Now we're both gliding through the ocean, carried by these intelligent creatures. I'm having so much fun, I forget—I don't know who I am.

It's only a few more minutes before the dolphins get bored and swim off. Leaving us in their wake.

"Wow, has that ever happened?" I ask.

She's grinning from ear to ear, and I can see the scarlet blush on the skin of her neck and cheeks. "I know. Wow! No, I don't think so. Not in the wild. I think that's going to be a once-in-a-lifetime thing for us. I'm still shaking." She lets herself laugh. So carefree. So beautiful.

We're only a few feet away, and I can see the beads of water on her face, the soft curve of her sweet mouth. Those eyes that match the sky.

My blood is rushing through my veins when we swim up to each other. There are no words. As if she can see my thoughts and wants the same thing, she eases closer. There's nothing in my life I've wanted as much as to touch her.

She's not yours.

Yes. She is.

I pull her into me and kiss her.

Combing her fingers through my hair, she exhales a soft puff of air. A jolt of electricity shoots through my lungs, bursting through my chest. I deepen the kiss. She tastes of sun, salt, and honey.

When we finally break apart, our gazes meet.

In an instant, all joy evaporates. "I'm dreaming, aren't I?"

"Yes. But this is real." She pulls me back into the kiss. And I believe her. Please stay. When I open my eyes, she's staring at me. She's still here. Her large pupils are pebbles in the sea of her irises. She blinks and moves her eyes toward the boat. I follow her gaze and see a calm ocean. No boat. But there's something else out there. I sense it. Deep below the surface.

When I turn back, she's gone.

No.

Like clockwork, this wakes me up.

With effort, I open my eyes. Blinking at the light, I glance at my watch—it's 7:20. Slowly, I stand and brush off some of the sand that's matted into my clothes and legs. A passerby on his morning run looks in my direction with concern. I wave to reassure him I'm fine and harmless, then walk back to the motel.

She always comes back to me, and she always leaves.

And I've got to be at my next job by nine a.m.

CHAPTER 4

The Widow

I ease the car onto a narrow stretch of grassy beach roped off for parking. The Maverick Key Lighthouse looms ahead of us. At one hundred, it's the oldest surviving structure on the island. Today, the town is celebrating its centennial with a cookout complete with dozens of picnic tables, a live Southern rock band, games, and plenty of food.

I cut off the engine and step out with Natalie. The whitewashed tower casts a long shadow over the crowd. Once, it guided sailors through reefs and shoals. Now it features a gift shop and daily tours.

We grab our things.

"Momma, can I have a cookie? *Pleeeease.*"

"Since you asked so nicely, yes. But just one."

Smiling, she carefully lifts the plastic wrap and takes the cookie out of the bowl. While she eats it, I stare out at the beach. The ocean is eerily calm, but it's breathing. Dozens of small patches of ripples bloom across the murky surface. A floor of shattered glass.

A muffled curse drifts from the rusty blue Prius parked beside us. A man shifts unsteadily, trying to balance several containers of food he's pulled from the back seat all at once. He's thin, tall, and… striking. I wince at the impending food disaster. Certain it's moments away.

"Here, let me help you with those." I move quickly, grabbing a few of the dishes. Deviled eggs, rolls, and a veggie platter, all pre-packaged from the Maverick Key General Store.

Startled, he loses his footing and scrambles to catch himself, dropping a container of colorful cupcakes. After he regains his composure, he's left clutching a plate of tea sandwiches.

His gaze fixes on the ground, staring at the sand-covered icing.

"Ohhh dear." His accent is clipped, crisp—distinctly British.

He sets the sandwiches on top of his car and takes off his glasses, rubbing his eyes and the dark skin of his forehead with a handkerchief. This brings my attention to the expensive, tailored charcoal suit he's wearing. Not exactly beach attire, and even in the late fall, the temperatures in the afternoons hover in the eighties. He's going to die in this heat.

"I must look like a clown." He smiles as he puts his glasses back on and extends his hand. "Finn."

He looks like he's in his late thirties, maybe early forties. Uptight? Maybe geek chic. I shake his hand and introduce myself.

"Thanks for the help. I was hoping to make a good impression." He gestures to the stacks of food. "May have gone a bit overboard."

"Are you new to the Key?"

"I flew into Naples last night. I'm staying at the Driftwood Inn and Cottages. When I heard about the celebration, I thought I'd pop by and introduce myself to some of the town's residents."

Ah, he's one of Maddie's new guests. Either the scientist or a member of the film crew.

"How long are you planning to stay?"

"That depends."

I raise my eyebrows, holding his gaze. There's a curious pause, like he's deciding how much to share.

The corner of his mouth flicks up. "Apologies for sounding so cryptic. Habit of mine. I'm consulting with Dr. Garrett Harlow to study the objects Dr. Nathan Carter recovered from the blue hole. And oversee the continued exploration and cartographic mapping of the cave system."

I bite back a smile. With an explanation like that, he's definitely the scientist.

"Dr. Phineas Clark?"

"Just Finn," he says with gentle eyes.

I like him. He's kind of awkward, but Nathan had a quirky side too—if not as pronounced as Finn's. I have a soft spot for charming nerds, so he's already won me over.

We gather up the remaining food and walk to the buffet. Tables are brimming over with covered dishes of all shapes and sizes. I'm not surprised to see Maddie already dipping into a full plate at the other end. I wave and start arranging our dishes with Finn's help.

Natalie tugs on my shirt. "Can I play with my friends, Momma?"

"Sure, sweetie." I watch her run off with a group of other first graders.

As I prepare the serving tongs, I gaze over the lighthouse green where volunteers have laid out all the activities and tables for the picnic. Most of my friends and family are here. Hannah and Jamie are in the middle of the lawn tossing beanbags at a cornhole while Scott and Garrett stand nearby, absorbed in a heated discussion.

Typical for them.

I'm not a fan of Dr. Garrett Harlow. After Nathan died, he swooped in to take credit for all his work, and he's just a rotten human being, just one notch above a criminal as far as I'm concerned. He's also the guy in charge of the Carter's Drop project—a renowned archaeologist commissioned by university funders. Scott runs the dives and doesn't put up with any nonsense from Garrett or anyone else.

They're only a couple of yards away, close enough for me to hear what they're saying.

"Scott, you've got all the divers you need. My answer's still no. How many times is this going to come up?" Garrett huffs in irritation. "Wes Harrington stays dead. Or he goes to jail."

I haven't thought of Wes in a while. His fake *drowning in a siphon* last year is the worst-kept secret on the island. The rest of the world believes he died in the caves attempting to rescue Maddie from Mark. But he's alive and well. Where? No one knows. Once a popular urban explorer with a massive social media following, he's now invisible.

He's also kind. After he found out about Natalie and me last year, he called me from one of his burner phones. We spoke for almost half an hour about Nathan and our daughter. He offered his help if I ever needed it. He loved Nathan, and I hope I get a chance to meet him one day.

"If you want to move at the speed you're asking for, we need every cave diver we can get," Scott says. "Wes has experience in the Drop. We need him to cover more ground."

"Then get the divers you need. BUT NO WES."

Scott says something under his breath and stomps off, joining Liam and Margaret at the picnic tables. He pulls out a seat and motions over to Maddie. Maddie's been making laps around the buffet and picnic tables, helping everyone get what they need.

"Give me just a minute," she calls out to him, giving him a flirty shake of her hips and belly.

Maddie's eyes light up when she turns her attention back to Finn and me. But before she can speak, Garrett spots Finn, pushes his way through us, and extends his hand.

Finn accepts it with a measured shake, his expression polite and confident.

"Dr. Clark. Welcome to Maverick Key. I trust the accommodations at the inn were satisfactory. Ms. Connor keeps the rooms clean and provides a decent breakfast each morning. Worth the price if you don't care about frills."

I stop myself from rolling my eyes. Maddie and I are used to him. If he weren't politely hostile, we'd wonder what was wrong. Finn, apparently, is a quick study—he doesn't react at all.

Finn clears his throat. "Well, um. Yes. Very comfortable. Feels like home." His gaze flicks to Maddie. "I appreciate the welcome."

Garrett continues without missing a beat. "Very good. If you have time after lunch, I'd like to bring you up to speed on the work I've supervised. I've prepared some detailed field reports that should capture your interest."

"Brilliant," Finn says, smoothing the fabric near his watch. "I'm eager to jump right in. Would it be possible to see the stone Nathan found first?"

Garrett frowns. "No. The police still won't release it. They're dragging their feet, saying they need to keep it as evidence until they finish investigating that crazy murderer, Mark Glassier. It's ridiculous."

I stiffen at his callous mention of Mark's name and look for Natalie, hoping she's out of earshot. Relief spreads through me when I spot the kids several meters away, preoccupied with building sandcastles.

Finn's hand settles on my arm, his brows drawing together. "You okay?"

"Yeah."

He turns his attention back to Garrett, who's still talking—explaining how the dives into Carter's Drop are planned to resume next week. I feel awful knowing that their plans are about to fall apart. My boss hasn't given me the green light to tell anyone what's going on yet, but I'll have to say something soon, before they get too far along.

I hate keeping secrets.

A motorcycle engine roars nearby, drowning out Garrett's voice. We all look over and see a sleek red cruiser pull up a few feet away from the buffet. At the seat, a young woman removes her helmet, freeing long, dark sable hair, which cascades over her shoulders. She parks and jumps off the bike, walking toward us. Her short denim cutoffs and fuchsia-colored cropped tank scream for attention while warning *Don't mess with me*. As she approaches, I see that her left arm is adorned with a beautifully elaborate tattoo of a temple garden in vibrant colors, and she's wearing a golden ring shaped like a curled cat with jade eyes. I've never seen her before. She walks straight to a horrified Garrett, arms outstretched.

"Hi, Daddy Dearest."

He goes pale as she gives him a warm hug.

"Sidney."

"Miss me?"

Stiff, he sniffs and straightens, inching back and out from her arms. He points to the roped area. "The designated parking is right over there."

She waves her hand, dismissing his concern. "I'm not staying long. Just wanted to stop by to say hello. Meet the neighbors."

She greets the rest of us. She's incredibly poised and confident. Miss Sidney Harlow, or *Sid,* as she asks to be called.

She looks like she's still in her early twenties. For someone so young, she carries herself with effortless grace, a quality that usually takes decades to develop. Her job filming documentaries has taken her around the world, from Africa to Mexico, and she's earned a reputation for provocative underwater cinematography. Fans call her the *Diva of the Deep*.

There's a resemblance. Garrett has the same dark sable hair as Sid's—his is flecked with gray strands. They have dark brown eyes, expressive, with a naughty glimmer. Both attractive, Sid's face is fresh and open, while Garrett's is lined from years of scowls and smirks.

"We'll catch up more at dinner, Sidney," Garrett cuts into her introductions. "Where the setting is more appropriate." Garrett glances at us anxiously.

"Isn't this a picnic?" She looks around. "Seems like as good a place as any for casual chit-chat."

He looks unwell.

"Okay, Daddy Dearest," she says and laughs. "Dinner it is. But since I'm already here, I'm going to check this place out." She softly squeezes Garrett's shoulder and turns.

His hand lifts, then drops. "Wait. Does your mother… does she know you're here? And what you'll be doing?"

"Course she does." She lifts one shoulder casually. "She asked me to tell you she said hi and told me to have fun." Her grin widens. "She also told me to get kick-ass footage of those caves—and don't die." She meets Garrett's stare without blinking.

"Dave said hi, too." She walks off to the picnic tables, leaving her bike.

Frustrated and mumbling something under his breath about Sid's mother not doing her job, Garrett excuses himself and leaves without another word.

Now it's just Finn and me. Where did Maddie go?

I spot her at the beach, cradling a crying Natalie in her arms. All the other children are gone.

"Excuse me," I tell Finn.

When I get to her, she looks up at me with her bright brown eyes.

"Sweetie, what's wrong?"

"Timmy told me..." She glances at the smashed sandcastle and sniffles, putting her head on Maddie's shoulder.

"Her friend told her there isn't any such thing as time travel," Maddie explains. "She wants to study physics and build a time machine one day." She brushes the hair out of Natalie's face.

"Timmy's mean." Her little voice is high and strained. "He said Stephen Hawking said it's impossible." She looks back down. "Mr. Hawking knew everything."

"Well..." Finn walks up from behind and crouches down beside Natalie. He doesn't seem to notice or care that he's getting his designer suit dirty. "That's not entirely true. Hawking, like most scientists, accepted that time travel into the future was proven by the laws of physics. And while he didn't believe it allowed for the possibility of time travel into the past, he acknowledged he couldn't claim so with certainty."

Natalie's eyes brighten. He smiles and picks up a giant conch shell lying next to the sandcastle, its walls now smashed in after the boys pretended to be raiding pirates and destroyed it.

"What's this?" He points to the pile of sand.

"That was my time machine. Timmy smashed it."

Finn's mouth curves as he points to the ocean. "See those waves?" Now full of crashing surf, the earlier slack is gone.

She nods.

"They're created by wind blowing across the ocean's surface, the air and water transferring energy. They flow in the wind's direction until the coastline bends them toward shore. You never see them flow the other way."

"And if you're a surfer..." He holds up the shell. "We can't push the waves back to ride them again. That's how time feels to us. One direction.

Every ride is different." He stretches out his arm, moving the shell to illustrate the flow of a wave.

"But if we imagine, just for a moment, that there's a magic tunnel beneath the surface—a shortcut that bypasses the longer surface and returns us to where the wave's energy is still moving..." He turns the shell in his hand. "Then we could repeat the same ride."

"That's a wormhole," Natalie states with pride.

He laughs. "Yes." He hands the shell to her. "You're very smart. Put this to your ear and tell me what you hear."

"It's the ocean." She smiles, looking up, her eyes shining.

"Some believe time has an echo. That the imprint of the past never disappears. Just like this shell remembers the ocean."

Quiet for a moment, she looks at the shell and then back to Finn. "Do *you* believe time travel is possible?"

He considers her question. "Yes. I do." Then he gives her a serious look, softened by his eyes. "But it will be a heavy burden for anyone who learns how."

"Maybe someone already knows and is keeping it a secret," she says.

He laughs. "Anything's possible."

She beams and gives him a hug before running off to her friends with Maddie following behind her.

I pull back the hair the wind has blown loose, wrapping it around my ear. "Thank you for that."

"She dreams big."

"She gets that from her father."

He gives me a long look, then he glances upward. "I know what it's like to want to revisit the past. To see if you can change it." He rubs his face, squinting his eyes.

I'm sure he has his share of past regrets. Don't we all?

"It's too bad that science doesn't like paradoxes. Exploring the possibility of revisiting what has already occurred…" He shakes his head. "We all dream of it. But it's not something we serious scientists can entertain."

His gaze drifts to Natalie, running in the distance, laughing as she plays.

He turns back to me, his voice soft. "She's Nathan's?"

I catch my breath. How did he… "Yes."

"Maybe she'll be the one to figure it all out one day."

CHAPTER 5

The Widow

What a crazy afternoon at the picnic. In the middle of the balloon toss, Maddie's water broke. We all watched as a frantic Scott rushed her off to the hospital in Naples. Less than two hours later, Christopher Malencai Rickter made his grand entrance into the world.

Scott sent me a selfie. Little Christopher, wrapped in his striped blanket, rests between his smiling parents. Natalie and I are keeping their dogs, Denver and Ding, for the night. We'll stop by and visit the new family in the morning.

After putting Natalie to bed and feeding the dogs, I sit down on the couch and look at the coffee table. A cup of oolong tea, old photos, and Nathan's diary rest on top.

Am I ready for this?

I unclasp the chain around my neck and remove the three rings, staring at them in my hands. We never wore our rings in public. Despite all those secrets, we lost each other anyway.

I turn the engagement ring between my fingers. An elegant two-carat princess-cut solitary stone set in platinum.

The day he gave it to me comes back in sharp detail. We'd taken a spontaneous day trip to Fort Myers and gone from store to store. I always loved those days because we could be ourselves in public. We could laugh. Kiss.

After a caramel latte and way too many cookies, we walked into the last place, and I knew instantly which one I wanted.

"Pick the diamond you've always dreamed of. No *starter* ring. I want you to have the one that means forever to you."

Growing up with very little taught me to be frugal, but not this time. I gave myself permission to indulge and chose the ring that felt the most like us. The one I'd never want to replace.

"Can I try that one?" I asked.

The jeweler unlocked the case, lifted the ring, and handed it to Nathan.

Nathan stared at it for a moment, then at me, his eyes filled with excitement and maybe terror. Then he dropped to one knee and slid it onto my finger. His hands were trembling. He was anchoring us to eternity.

"What do you think?" My voice was thin and high. I stretched out my hand, turning it from side to side.

He kissed my hand and stood, locking his gaze with mine. "Mrs. Carter, I promise to love and protect you for the rest of my life."

In that moment, I believed him.

He held my ring hand and touched my cheek with his other. Gazing at me from head to toe, he moved his hand to my waist. I'd worn my navy blue velvet button-down dress with matching heels. His favorite.

"I'll never forget the way you look right now." He pulled the camera out of my bag and handed it to the jeweler. "Can you take our picture?"

Before the snap, he grasped my face and brushed his lips against mine. Then, he trailed his lips up my jawline and cheek before gently tugging my earlobe with his teeth.

It tickled, making me giggle.

"Love you," he whispered, then pulled me in. "Now smile."

Our lives were perfect. I didn't care how fragile perfection could be.

After we picked out his band, we drove back to his cottage—our home. Although I'm sure Ms. Connor suspected something might be up, she never asked us about it and fiercely guarded Nathan's privacy. That night was the first time we made love wearing our rings. We were already married, and I wasn't on birth control.

"I thought you wanted to keep me a secret. If we keep doing that, sailor—you're going to have two of us to keep hidden."

He'd taken a deep breath and kissed me. "We'll figure it out."

"Just tell me."

"The less you know right now, the safer you'll be."

"That doesn't make any sense, Nathan. You're going to get me pregnant. That's a fact. It's going to be *really* hard to keep a baby secret. What's your plan?" I'd gazed at my ring, waiting for him to respond. "I can call my doctor and get a…"

"No." His jaw ticked, nostrils flaring.

We'd talked about it. He knew about my past and wanted to give me a family of my own, having experienced what it was like to be a part of a loving one. It's like we were living in two realities, and they didn't reconcile.

"We'll figure it out. I'll think of something." He reached for me then and held me to his chest, rubbing my back. "Let's get some sleep, Mrs. Carter."

Not too long after that beautiful day, I was pregnant.

Nathan, I miss you.

I caress each ring once more and kiss them before putting them back around my neck.

Then, I pick up the journal.

I've never read Nathan's private words before. He'd write them down before bed from time to time, but I didn't need to read them because I had him. After he disappeared, I hid it in the nightstand drawer by our bed in the cottage. I couldn't open it.

But this time, I do.

The first entries reflect a boy's handwriting and thoughts. Despite their simplicity, the sentences reveal his sharp mind, his thirst for knowledge, and his desire to delve into the ocean's mysteries.

> *Mads learned to swim today, and I got a Game Boy.*
> *I got to meet Dr. Langston on our boat, and he told me about diving in Spain. It was wild. I'm definitely doing that one day.*
> *Dad grounded me. He said I can't go diving for a week because I went past the buoys. It wasn't even that far.*

Even then, he couldn't resist pushing farther than he should.

When I reach the entries written when he was fifteen, I'm struck by the sudden shift in his internal thoughts. No longer short bursts of observation about external events, they become longer, more introspective—centered on his own emerging research and his thoughts on his family, on love, on his future.

He was worried about his dad, who was showing signs of a brain tumor, which would soon claim him. He admired his parents' love. But he'd convinced himself that love wouldn't be for him because his destiny was underwater.

I continue to burn through the pages, recognizing so much of the man I knew. He was so stubborn, but so easy to bend when it came to matters of his heart.

And he was wrong about love.

The way he loved me.

Quietly. Fiercely. As if loving me was the safest place he'd ever known and also his greatest risk. I remember every breath, every touch, every moment.

It's when I get to his college years in Miami that I stop. I'm going to make an appearance soon, and I don't think I can bear to read his first impression of me.

Not right now.

I put the diary back on the table and lay back on the couch. Despite all the pain, I'm grateful. Our time together was good. And there's Natalie.

Closing my eyes, I drift off to sleep until I hear Denver's low growl.

Startled, I make my way to the kitchen. Ding's underneath the table, his shaggy coat spread across the floor, tail wagging furiously. Denver peers out the window.

"What is it, boy?"

He lets out a single bark and then continues his growl. As a Belgian Malinois, he's trained to guard. It might be a long night if every noise outside puts him on edge.

The yard appears well lit from the window.

"I can't see anything past the road from here. Let me get a flashlight and check it out." He runs to me, barking furiously. "It's okay, I'll be careful. You can come with me."

Skeptical, he grumbles, but reluctantly lets me go, trotting along beside me.

I open the door slowly and walk out. There's nothing unusual out here. However, something has toppled the garbage cans over. That happens sometimes with all the animals running around the neighborhood. I walk over and start picking up the trash, using the tips of my fingers. Denver stands by my side, scanning the periphery.

"It was probably a raccoon."

He snarls, unconvinced.

I brush my hands on my pants and look up. A man stands in the distance, staring at me. He's about sixty years old, with an average build and a trim beard. I don't recognize him. When he notices my attention, he moves forward, and his mouth opens as if to speak.

A shiver runs through me. Denver charges toward him, barking as if he's going to tear him apart.

The man jumps, startled, then turns and darts down the street. He disappears after he makes a sharp turn through the yard of the house at the end of the cul-de-sac. Denver closes in on him rapidly until I can't see either of them.

Anxiously, I wait for Denver to return, moving backward and closer to the door as each minute passes.

I tremble as I think of the man's stare. He was watching me.

A few minutes later, Denver returns and runs back to me, nudging me on the leg. Bending down, I reach my hands out to him. "Thank you for protecting me." He nuzzles his face into my hands.

Inside, I bolt the front door and double-check the back. Should I call the police? What do I tell them? More importantly, what can they do? Easing her bedroom door open, I check on Natalie. She's safe, curled around her stuffie. Her chest rises and falls in a slow, almost imperceptible rhythm. I linger, counting her breaths until my own steadies.

This is the second time this week I've felt as if I were being watched. Already filled with dread over what's happening to the ocean, I can't help but wonder if the dangers Nathan was so worried about have caught up with me.

CHAPTER 6

The Widow

As I study the walls, an uncomfortable pins-and-needles sensation crawls over my skin.

Natalie and I start the long walk down the hospital corridors. We're here to visit Maddie, Scott, and Christopher. As we make our way to their room, I remember my own stay here years ago.

The first of several visits.

I force myself forward.

Natalie was born on a rare chilly night in December. I remember wearing a brown sweater and working on her nursery late into the night. The primary color of her room was rose pink, and I had her changing station, crib, and rocker perfectly arranged. Ready to go. On her dresser, *Goodnight Moon* and a small stuffed dog, Brownie, waited for her. Brownie was the only belonging I still had from my childhood. Growing up, I'd shared all my secrets with him, as I imagined Natalie would too someday.

Mark had been on duty, so when my water broke, I drove to Naples Comprehensive Health and checked myself in without bothering him. Mark's parents lived in New Mexico, and he was an only child, so neither of us had any family nearby.

Would anything have been different if we had?

I didn't want to seem ungrateful, but our charade was making me feel uneasy. Our mutual work friends at City Hall were all thrilled for the happy young couple, who were about to become parents for the first time. What they didn't know was that we were platonic—no sex, no kissing, just friends. They couldn't know that the baby we were awaiting belonged to one of Mark's oldest friends.

When it became clear Nathan was gone, Mark was the only one there for me. He knew that Nathan and I were married. And as Nathan's friend, I thought he was grieving too. He drove me to my doctor appointments, helped me pay my bills, and gave me a place to live.

I did worry he might misread my need as something else—we'd dated long ago, before Nathan. But I thought it was a mutually awkward experience for both of us. Was it really the same for him as it was for me? He assured me he just wanted friendship, offered me a ring, and promised to take care of Natalie and me until I was ready to move on. After that, he said, he'd let me go. He made it sound simple and practical. All he wanted to do was help.

I said yes, and at first, I felt safe. It was as if Nathan had left his best friend behind to watch over us since he couldn't. The desperate part of me had taken Mark's offer to take care of us without thinking about the consequences. He was our friend. He was safe. I had no family and no one else, and I made little money of my own.

But as the months passed, Mark grew a little too accustomed to his role as my pretend husband. He stopped knocking. His hand brushed mine as we crossed paths, and he would linger a little too long, a little too close when we were both in the house. No matter where I was when he was around, I felt his gaze. I'd known then that I would need to find a way out as soon as possible, for both our sakes.

After I reached the hospital, I was in full-blown labor. The whole time, I'd imagined Nathan by my side and how he would have wiped my brow and held my hand during the delivery. The doctor put our little girl on my chest, and she lifted her tiny head.

It was then that I knew I'd never love anyone more.

I nursed and cradled her all night. Crying. Laughing. And Nathan was with me the whole time. Talking to me, playing with his daughter. Everything I did that night, we did together. Even if he wasn't really there.

It was too soon to tell which one of us she looked like, but I imagined her with golden-brown hair and eyes. I let her go only when the nurse came by to check on her and insisted that I get some rest.

The next morning, Mark walked into the room. I smiled and excitedly told him about Natalie. A chill ran up my spine when he looked at me and glared. He didn't respond. Instead, he walked to the bassinet. I sat up and started to get out of bed. Afraid he would… what? hurt her? But he just looked down at her and stared. She lifted her little arms and cooed at him.

"She looks like you."

His face showed no emotion when he turned and walked out the door without another word.

Less than two weeks later, I visited the hospital for the second time.

For secondary postpartum hemorrhage.

I knew the truth of what had happened. Of what Mark did. But I was confused, shattered, and trapped.

He hurt and took more from me during our marriage, but not what mattered most. And over time, I learned to work around him, and to work on myself, my career, and my plan to get away from him.

But then, when Maddie arrived in Maverick Key, fate took care of Mark for me.

Now, my body is mine, and it no longer braces at every shift in the room, every male voice. I'm still healing. But I'm stronger, and it's this little girl who's given me that strength.

I shake off the memories and tighten my grip on Natalie's hand.

A lot has changed in our lives, but the halls of this hospital haven't.

We reach the room we're looking for.

Scott's in the corner, cradling Christopher. He's a tall, muscular ex-Navy SEAL. It's adorable seeing him hold his tiny baby. But as he does with most things, he holds him with confidence and seems to be a natural.

Natalie rushes to Maddie, wrapping her arms around her. Maddie squeezes her and kisses her cheek.

"You look good. Tired?" I ask her. Her face is flushed, and her swollen eyes have dark circles under them.

"A li'l bit," she laughs.

Her best friend stayed with them last night, but I don't see her. "Where's Hannah?"

"Getting me breakfast. Nat, go see your cousin," Maddie says.

Natalie hesitates, then walks over to Scott and stares at Christopher.

"Want to hold him?" he asks.

"Will he break?"

"Nah… he's a tough guy. Come over here." He pats the couch. "We'll do this together."

She sits and listens as Scott shows her how to hold a baby. Christopher coos, his little arms jerking as Natalie carefully cradles him. She looks up at Scott, uncertain.

"He wants a kiss," Scott says.

Natalie bends down and softly presses her lips against Christopher's forehead.

I lift my phone and take a picture.

"You know…" Scott explains. "You're the older cousin. The two of you are the first kids of this generation in the family. He'll be watching you to learn how to act, what to try, and who to trust. That's a big responsibility."

"I can do it," Natalie says. "Cuz I love him." She places her pinky finger in Christopher's hand and giggles when he clutches it.

After they finish playing, I step closer and take him from her. His weight settles into my arms and feels so good. He's a Rickter, and a Carter too. Our little family is growing.

"Your Uncle Nathan's here too," I tell him as he falls asleep. "And he'll be watching over you. He's so proud." Christopher's mouth twitches into a tiny reflex smile, and I smile back.

I hold him a little longer before handing him back to Scott.

Stacks of notebooks and other items sit next to Maddie's bed.

"Nathan's things. They released them." She frowns. "Not the stone, though. Seems Dr. Clark got clearance from the authorities to take it into his possession."

"I think the stone is why he's here," I say. "He's a materials expert. Maybe he'll find answers."

I move to Maddie's side and rub my hands over the journals. More of Nathan's handwriting and drawings are inside. He preferred the feel of writing his thoughts. To touch ideas physically. I'd watched him sometimes.

He was slow, methodical, and careful to think before committing words to paper.

And his poems… When Maddie and I met after Mark's death, she gave me the poem she'd found in Nathan's things.

Between waves, a memory sings
Whispers of a touch
The sea calls, but it will not claim
I hear her

It wasn't the first note he'd written to me. Before we were together, he'd sneak into my backpack and stick Post-its on my notebooks with quotes and stray bits of wisdom from philosophers and his favorite poets. Words meant to keep me focused. To teach.

After we admitted what we felt, they turned into love notes and short poems he wrote me himself. I'd find them in my purse at work and tucked under his side of the blanket after he'd left for the day. The one Maddie found must have been his last. He never got the chance to hide it for me.

The pain of missing him has settled deep in my bones. It's never going to go away.

"Take them, Crystal."

"I'm sorry. I don't think I can."

"Why not?"

I don't want to upset Maddie, but she and I are so different in how we handle loss. She's relentlessly driven to find answers, to comb over every clue. Me. I want peace. To move on with Natalie. I've accepted that he's gone.

"The police lost Nathan's encrypted note."

I flinch. "What?"

"They claim they never had it."

Maddie and Nathan created a language as kids to send each other *secret* messages for fun. She'd found a note he'd written in this code, but she didn't have time to decipher it before Mark stole it. Nathan wanted to keep a secret that no one other than Maddie could uncover.

I swallow the lump in my throat.

"Someone is lying," she adds. "They told me they had it right after Mark died and that they'd give it to me when they finished."

Natalie tugs on my shirt. "Momma, can we go to the beach now?" I glance at the clock—10:30 a.m. I promised Natalie we'd stop by the beach so she could look for seashells.

"Just a minute, sweetie."

I think of the man last night and the constant feeling of being watched. Then there's Finn. And the stone. Could either of these men be digging into Nathan's secrets? I don't believe in coincidences.

Maddie needs to focus on her family right now.

"Let me know how I can help," I tell her.

"You focus on that new job of yours and find us some answers about how to save the coral. Ms. Connor's at the beach house. She'll help me with Christopher."

"Who's going to keep up the inn?"

Maddie inherited the Driftwood Inn and Cottages from Nathan, and since she moved in with Scott, Ms. Connor has resumed running the day-to-day operations, including homemade breakfasts.

"We called around and found some help," she says. "Someone to clean and make simple breakfasts for the guests. He starts today."

Another stranger. "Who is he?"

"No idea. Ms. Connor is working with an agency. They're paying for his lodging at the old Cooper Motel." She grimaces. "That place is a dangerous dump. No one should be sleeping there."

The door opens.

"I got you the last one," a cheerful voice calls out. Hannah.

She hands Maddie a paper bag and strolls straight over to Scott and Christopher, gesturing to Scott to hand him over.

"Is it blueberry?" Maddie pulls out a muffin.

"I had to fight for it." Hannah winks.

Maddie picks up where she left off about the newcomer. "He'll stay in the housekeeper's suite. Ms. Connor left him a key and some instructions so he could get started."

"Did they give you a name?" I ask.

Maddie shrugs.

"He just moved here from Miami," Hannah says. She makes a bubble face, and Christopher stretches his little hand toward her, brushing her bright red hair with his fingers. She blows him a kiss.

"Miami. That's a long way to move for a cleaning job. Any idea why he's here?" I ask.

Maddie shakes her head. "Nope."

"I'll get the scoop when I check in on him later today," Hannah says.

"Momma…"

"That's my cue." I hug Maddie. "Love you."

Scott gives Maddie a kiss and gathers up the notebooks. We follow him to the car.

"It's going to be a nice afternoon for a boat ride," Scott says, pointing at the sky. His crew is doing some routine maintenance on the ship this afternoon. They're getting things ready to restart the cave dives.

I absentmindedly count the journals as we walk, noting their colors and textures. Meaningless thoughts. Anything to avoid thinking of them lying in the closet with the rest of Nathan's dusty things.

Despite myself, I need answers. I want to trust Finn, but his reasons for being here are murky at best. I'll talk to him and see what I can find out before worrying anyone else.

I close the trunk and drive us to the beach.

CHAPTER 7

The Stranger

After cleaning the Driftwood's tiny one-bedroom cottage, I walk back to the inn to get started on the rooms upstairs. Today's my first day on this new live-in assignment. When I checked in with my boss this morning, he told me the owner, Maddie Rickter, had offered me a room so I could work and sleep here, and she added a five-hundred-dollar bonus. I make a mental note to pick up something small at the store and thank her as soon as I see her.

Most of the guests have left for the day, but a few men and women are gathered in the living room watching television and talking. Listening to bits and pieces of their conversation, I've gathered that they're a documentary crew here to film Carter's Drop, an underwater blue hole that lies about thirty miles offshore.

Carter's Drop.

It fascinates me.

When I first arrived on the Key, I picked up a few brochures at the general store, eager to explore the island. One pamphlet caught my attention right away: *Carter's Drop, the sinkhole that put Maverick Key on the map*. It chronicled the two prior exploration attempts and the controversy surrounding the man who discovered it.

Cave explorer and archaeologist Dr. Nathan Carter. Maddie's brother.

In the brochure photo, he's wearing scuba gear and a mask, one hand lifted in a casual wave to whoever's behind the camera. Even through the mask, his smile is unmistakable. Self-assured, carefree. A man comfortable in his own skin.

The article described his discovery, the subsequent beginning of a caving expedition, and his disappearance more than six years ago.

About the time I washed up in Miami.

According to the article, he'd been conducting unsupervised night dives when he failed to surface from one of them. Presumed to have drowned, he was lost somewhere deep in the caves. It turns out a friend of his, Mark Glassier, sabotaged his dive equipment. And then there were more murders last year after this guy tried to cover up his crime. The university funding the project temporarily put the expedition to map the caves on hold due to the controversy. It's been nearly a year, and they're preparing to restart it.

Interesting.

I've done a lot of scuba diving with my friends in Miami. Not cave diving yet, but I've explored a few wrecks closed-circuit on rebreathers. When I took the required training to get certified, most of it came easily. I didn't have to think. I knew what to do.

Cave diving is a different animal, but I've watched vlogs, talked to friends who dive caves, and I know everything about it. I had already planned to do it when I lived in Miami, but it's expensive. It must have been part of my life. I feel a small spark of excitement. Exploring Carter's Drop is something I can do. It fits.

A woman's voice rings out from the hallway. She doesn't notice me as she joins the group in the living room.

"Y'all are growing sprouts." She's carrying gear, cameras, and dive bags. "We may be in a holding pattern on the Drop, but we can still get lots of supplemental footage of the local wildlife."

"Sid, you had us down three hours longer than we planned the other day. There's probably a hotline out there for reporting this kind of abuse," one man says.

"Nonsense," she replies. "You think it's bad now? You won't know what to do with the sixteen-hour days we're about to pull. I need to work y'all up to it… because I care."

This girl looks like she's just graduated, and she's already leading a film crew into underwater caves? Impressive. Like the others, she's wearing swimwear and pull-up shorts. They're about to dive.

There's grumbling, but they all gather up their equipment stacked against the living room wall and follow her to the door. That's when she notices me.

"Hi there. Sorry if we disturbed you. Are you staying here too?"

"Yeah, I'm moving in tonight. I'm the housekeeper. Elliot Trevor."

I'm going to go for it. You don't get anything if you don't ask.

"I just got to town and am doing cleaning jobs to make ends meet. What I'm really interested in is diving. I heard you guys talking. You're filming Carter's Drop?"

She looks at me closer, hesitant but curious. "Yes, we're coordinating with Scott Rickter's dive team. They're mapping the caves—we're making the movie."

They're obviously in a hurry. I'd better spit it out and see where it lands. "I know this is a long shot, but is there any chance I could get signed on as a volunteer for the shoot?"

"You're certified for caves?"

"Yes," I lie. I'll figure that out later.

She glances past me toward the door, then back again. "Well, it's not something I'd usually agree to on the fly like this, but we do need more hands. Had a guy quit yesterday."

"Jeremy took the bribe we all got from Garrett," an older, red-headed man adds. The rest of the group laughs.

"That's because Jeremy has no balls. And I only need crewmates who have balls." She gives a short nod to the other women. "She-balls are perfectly acceptable." Her eyes sweep the room. "Anyone else missing their balls?"

They all snap into mock seriousness. They love her.

"I've got balls." Seems like an easy enough prerequisite to me.

She looks at me again for a long minute. Uh oh. I don't think I've impressed her.

"All right, I'll give you a try if everything you're telling me checks out." She purses her lips. "Get all your documentation together. We'll talk it over with Scott tonight. He's got the final say."

She heads for the door, her crew falling in behind her.

I stand there, stunned.

Did I really just land a cave-diving job with a film crew?

I'll clean the upstairs rooms after lunch. What I need to do right now is find a place where I can think and figure out how to get the cave certification quickly.

I drive until I find the sign for Sunset Strand, the locals' favorite beach. It's not too far from the lighthouse. I park in the sandlot and grab my sandwich. Being the weekend, it's packed. Swarms of people crowd the beach—swimming, playing, and lounging. There's barely an inch to move. I consider leaving. But I'm already here.

After weaving through the crowds, I finally find a spot where I can sit. While eating my peanut butter sandwich, I take it all in. Maverick Key is beautiful. Even if I don't find any answers, it's been worth it to come here. If I can get this gig with Sid, I'm going to stay. I hate to bail on Maddie so fast, but I can still help with the inn's chores and breakfasts.

Soft, bright sand stretches along clear turquoise shallows that blend into a vibrant blue-green ocean. Today's waves are gentle ripples, nearly invisible except for the light froth of sea foam brushed onto the shore. Gulf waters are calm in general, but as a barrier island, the Key does get choppier surf more frequently than its nearest neighbor, Naples, FL.

I try to envision this place without the crowds.

The noise of the beach drifts away. Then, a wave of nostalgia washes over me. I've been here before. This place matters to me. I push into the corners of my mind, sifting through the landscape, searching for anything I might recognize.

Getting up to walk it off, a beach ball rockets across my face. Barely dodging it, I stumble and catch myself in the sand a few feet away from a woman lying on a blue beach towel. She's wearing sunglasses that cover her eyes, but then she raises them to her head, and I can see her face. Eyes closed, she looks like she's dreaming. And it looks like a good dream. There's a small smile, just lifting one corner of her rose-colored mouth, and her skin is flushed. She opens her mouth slightly, relaxing. Her blonde hair is tied in a loose bun, and she's fair, her skin lit with a golden undertone.

I can't believe what I'm seeing. Trying to get myself to calm down, I ignore the pounding in my chest and force myself to breathe.

What the hell?

It's *her*. It must be.

Shocked, I stare silently, begging her to open her eyes. She looks exactly like the woman from my dream. If I can see those blue orbs, I'll be certain.

Unsure of how much time has gone by, I continue to stare until a little girl with bright blonde curls runs up to the woman. She shouts and points in my direction. Terrified she'll see me gawking like this, I turn and dart back to the car.

"Wait!" I hear her call to me. But I keep walking. It's too soon.

Sitting in the car, I debate whether I should go back to her now or try to find out who she is later. She might have answers about my identity. What if it's *her*?

CHAPTER 8

The Widow

Sunset Strand is the beach to visit on Maverick Key. Eight miles long, it spans most of the island's southern coast. Warm, soft muslin-colored sand darkens to deeper taupe with the tide, and tiny shell fragments sparkle in the sun. The water begins as a soft aquamarine near the shoreline, deepening to a rich blue like a clear sky slides into a summer storm.

I love this beach.

Natalie inspects the dunes as soon as we arrive to make sure no one has disturbed the ropes or tossed trash into the hills. Last month, she learned about our city's dune conservation efforts and is doing her part.

We find a stretch of sand that isn't too crowded and spread out our beach blanket. A vibrant logo of Maverick Key's lighthouse, framed by palms, decorates the soft fabric. Hannah gave it to Natalie for Christmas last year, and she's already asking what she's getting this time.

With the big day only a few weeks away, the town is bustling with festive decorations and activities, including a holiday bonfire and a movie night on the beach, which is coming up in a couple of weeks. Maddie and Hannah have already invited us along.

Traditions and routines are important, even when there's a gaping hole in your heart.

We eat our ham sandwiches made from the picnic leftovers, then Natalie runs toward the water with her bucket and shovel to look for shells.

I lie back on the towel and stretch out. Usually, on an afternoon off like this, I'd grab a paperback and get in some reading. But today I can't focus. My thoughts are too scattered, too unsettled. I push my glasses up onto my head and let the sun wash over my face.

I close my eyes.

The first thing that pops into my head is a team of Clydesdales pulling wagons through the snow. This makes me laugh. Snow. I've never even seen real snow. What a strange, beautiful thing it would be to see snow on the beach.

Now I turn my thoughts to the past.

Some memories come to you in fragments. Jolts of nostalgia or pain. Others, permanent ones, fill with such rich detail they develop like a photograph. The moment Nathan told me he loved me for the first time is one of those moments.

His brows raised in question. The quiver of his lips. The smell of his skin.

His eyes…

Unforgettable.

It was on Sunset Strand, years ago, that my life changed. That all the empty spaces in my heart were filled, and I found my home.

I let myself daydream and remember the day we swam with dolphins…

L'heure bleue.

The blue hour.

We're over an hour and a half late when we return to the docks from our field excursion. I was expecting Nathan to scold me for not taking work seriously and not following the rules. Instead, he's quiet. Not in a melancholy way, but in that way you get when you know something is about to change. He's nervous. And I am too.

I mean, we swam with freaking dolphins today! I'd done it before during my stint at the Dolphin Research Center on Grassy Key, but wild dolphins just don't do that.

But they did today.

"It's too late to get it in. I'll get my excuses ready," he says as we step onto the dock. But I know him, and I know he's going to get that damn log done tonight. He's letting me off the hook.

"I'll help you."

He smiles, and we drive to The Blue Fin to work on the report.

Hours later, after we finish, he walks me home. The sky is ultramarine. The blue hour. Sunrise is coming.

"Are you thinking the same thing I'm thinking?" he asks, his sideways smile wide and mischievous.

"I am." I grin and take his hand, then pull him towards the Sunset Strand access walk.

Carrying my sandals, I let myself enjoy the coolness of the sand against my feet. We stop at the tide line and sit.

I don't think there's any place you can feel closer to eternity than an empty beach before sunrise. Even out at sea, surrounded by the water, it's not the same. On the beach, where it's just you and the ocean, you stand in the in-between. The lemniscate. And if you let go of everything else and just exist in the moment, you can sense the infinite.

I watch Nathan and laugh as he rolls onto his belly and puts his chin on his crossed arms. He's my best friend. I moved all the way to Maverick Key for him. To stay close to his brilliance and… to be near him. In my heart, I've always wanted more than friendship.

I join him, and we both gaze toward the water.

"I'm proud of your work on this project," Nathan says, staring ahead.

"You're an excellent teacher."

I'm still looking at the water when I feel the gentle softness of his fingers brush across my cheek and turn me toward him. I lean in, hesitating before returning his gaze. Light golden-brown eyes. Warm and sharp. I know that look. Cautious but determined.

He's going to bring it up.

That kiss earlier came out of nowhere. How many years have we known each other? Worked side by side. Laughed. Played. Slept in the same tent. It never occurred to me he might have dreamed of something more.

Just like me.

Nathan threads his fingers through my hair, his face open. His expression is one I've seen a million times before, but I never recognized it for what it is. "Crystal, today…"

There's a ding from my cell phone.

His gaze stays fixed on me as I check the message.

Mark.

Are you home? I'm thinking about you.

Ugh. How do I tell Mark this little trial of ours isn't working? I've been putting it off for weeks. But now—after that kiss—I've got to tell him today.

Nathan stiffens, and then he pushes himself upright.

"Everything okay?" he asks.

"It's nothing." I send a quick response to Mark's text.

Nathan doesn't press. But I know he doesn't believe me. He forces a smile. "How's your new job with the city going?"

I've been so absorbed in Nathan's latest project that my position as an entry-level technician at town hall slipped my mind.

"Mr. Stevenson tells me I'm doing well. He may have even hinted that I'm top of the class."

I can't stop smiling. Mr. Stevenson didn't hint. He flat-out told me I'm the best. "Turtle nesting surveys begin next week."

He grins and clasps my hand. "That's no surprise to me. They know they're lucky to have the most talented marine biologist in the field right here on the island."

"Spoken like a true best friend," I say and laugh. "I'm still learning. There's a long road ahead before I can claim to be that good."

His face changes. He's finished with the warmup—now he's going to bring it up.

He turns his eyes away from me and faces the water. "Mark told me things are getting more… serious between you two."

I feel a flash of anger and confusion. How could Mark say something like that to Nathan?

Other than a few awkward kisses, we've been friends at best. The dates are getting less frequent—our conversations are drier. It's not going to work. After all these years of being in Nathan's orbit, we tried to find something in each other.

But all I've found with Mark is disappointment.

Nathan rubs his face and the back of his neck. "Crystal, hell," he says as he stares at the sand. One of his hands is closed tightly, holding on to something inside. "I was *way* out of line today." He swallows and blinks his eyes.

I touch my lips and turn my gaze toward the distant shore, catching the silhouette of a ship sailing home. Long seconds pass by as I follow its steady trek across the horizon.

"Don't," I whisper. "I was there too."

And it's the happiest, most confusing moment of my life so far.

"Do you love him?" he blurts out, squeezing the object in his hand tighter.

"What's in your hand?"

He opens it, showing me the shell. A pink Dinocardium robustum. Whorls of darker rose trace the ridges. The hinge is broken cleanly, leaving two perfect halves. Each one is shaped like a heart.

"I don't think I've ever seen a cockle shaped like that." I brush my fingers across it and shiver when I feel his skin. Everything is in slow motion. "It's pretty."

"I found it while I was in Belize."

"And you brought it here with you today?"

His face flushes, and my stomach flips.

"Take it." His voice is breathy and low. He puts one half in my palm and closes his hand around mine.

I freeze. He's just given me his…

"Nathan, I don't love him. I…"

"Wait." He pulls me onto his lap, facing me toward him.

Instinctively, I close my thighs around his waist, and I lean into his chest.

He pulls me closer. Takes a few breaths. Opens his mouth to speak, then closes it.

We stare.

If either of us says it, everything's going to be different.

He puts his arms around me and rests his face against my shoulder. His heartbeat and the rapid rise and fall of his chest comfort me and scare me at the same time. His hair smells like the sea. Like the sky after a storm. I hold him and kiss his temple.

"Crystal. I don't expect anything from you. Never. It's just." He pulls his face up and fixes his eyes on mine.

My heart jumps. He's going to be the one to say it first.

"It's no secret after that kiss today, but I need to say it… I love you. I've loved you for a very long time."

He releases the pressure from his arms and waits.

I want him to know everything I know. To feel this in his bones, like I do.

My hands shake as I clutch his collar and pull him to me. Just like he kissed me earlier out in the ocean, I kiss him back with all that I have inside. Every unspoken word, every stolen gaze, every second of silent restraint collapses into this one moment.

And after all those years, that's all it takes.

We're consumed by flame, like the cobalt blaze of Kaweah Ijen.

All over each other, we roll through the sand, not concerned with consequences or anyone else's feelings. Only each other's. Only the way this feels.

He trails his hands across my body, feeling his way through secret places…exploring. When he rolls on top of me, I feel him. Scared for just a moment, I hold my breath and squeeze my eyes shut.

"Crystal, you feel too good. Tell me to stop." He's already pulled down my shorts and is working on his.

"No," I gasp.

Why is he stopping?

"Don't stop."

His brows raise.

"I'm just answering you. Please don't stop."

He leans in to kiss me again as the sun rises, spilling amber light across the beach. Snickers drift from behind us. We're not alone.

We burst out laughing.

He shakes his head as if he can't believe what just happened. I can't believe it either. It's so confusing. And wonderful.

"Oh well. They say sex on the beach is overrated, anyway." He gently pulls my pants back up and moves back a few inches, trying to calm himself down. "Let's go back to my cottage. We can take showers. If you still want…"

"Nathan… I'm a virgin." I lower my eyes, embarrassed.

He squeezes and rubs my thigh. Smiling. "I know."

"Aren't you disappointed?"

"No. Never." He cups my face and kisses me softly. "Who do you want to be tomorrow?" he asks, grazing my lips.

I go still and lose a few beats of my heart when the corner of his mouth turns up the tiniest bit. He's fighting that damn lopsided smile of his.

What I want is to be yours.

I run my fingers through his hair and bring his face closer to mine, breathing him in. I can't speak anymore. I just want to be closer.

He stops holding back his grin and lets it go wide, kissing me passionately one more time. Then takes my hand and stands.

"Wait…" I pull out my phone and snuggle in beside him. "This is important." I wink.

Wrapping an arm around his waist, I pose us for the selfie.

Snap.

Then we race to his cottage…

Loud chatter on the beach startles me, and reluctantly I pull myself out of my daydream, keeping my eyes closed as the rest of the memory plays out like a movie. I want to finish this one. So I push myself back into his cottage—back into his arms.

He took his time with me, exploring every inch of my body with his fingers and mouth. I was always told not to expect to enjoy my first time, but I did. Sure, there was a little pain and discomfort, but they were nothing compared to being worshipped by the man I'd admired and loved for years.

"Momma!"

Natalie's voice jars me the rest of the way out of my daydream. "Momma, there's a man staring at you." I jump up and look in the direction she's pointing. I freeze. It's not the same man as last night. His back is turned, and he's rushing off, but the golden sandy brown color of his hair and that frame.

Nathan!

"Wait! Please wait!"

I rush toward him, but then realize I'm scaring Natalie. I pull her close to me.

"Who was that man, Momma?"

Trembling, I force myself to take a breath. "I'm not sure, sweetie. But he's gone. He didn't mean us any harm." I'm not sure how I know he's harmless, but I do. Did he actually look like Nathan, or am I seeing what I want to see?

"I'm tired. Can we go home?"

I pull her into my arms and try to wipe away the tears from my eyes before she sees them.

"We'll go home right after we stop by the inn."

CHAPTER 9

The Stranger

Minutes after encountering my mystery woman on the beach, I pull into Gulfstream Marina. Near the parking lot, boat charter booths line the dock entrance, advertising fishing trips and dive excursions. Still early in the afternoon, the marina is busy. Fishermen clean their catch while some boats launch and others return. The small café beside the pier is filled with lunchgoers, and the neighboring seafood market brags about the *freshest catch in the South.*

I walk up to the booth offering offshore recreational diving.

Carter's Drop, the Experience, takes tourists near the blue hole. You can see the reef and the entrance to the Drop, but you can't go inside. At least you're not supposed to.

Seeing *her* today lit a fire in me. Before I find her again, I have to have more to offer her than a man who has no memories and no stable job. Being part of the film crew is an opportunity to prove what I'm capable of. I know *her*. I've kissed her too many times not to.

"You certified?" The grizzled guy behind the counter asks.

"Yeah."

"Sign the waiver. I need to see your C-card if you're gonna dive." The man grabs my card and pushes a form across the counter. I fill it out, making up the address information.

He flicks his eyes over the form, not giving a damn what's on it, then slides it into a folder. "Got your own equipment?"

"No."

"Rental gear's over there." He jerks his head to the right, where the docks meet a small dive shop beside a larger, recently remodeled building with older warehouses beyond it. "Prices are on the wall. The boat launches in twenty minutes. It doesn't wait."

Inside the shop, the equipment rental counter is covered in souvenir trinkets, postcards, and dive training brochures. I grab a program advertising technical diving certification training. The Maverick Key Dive Club offers contract-based certification programs upon request, subject to availability. I read the instructors' names: Scott and Margaret. Call for appointment. Didn't Sid say she was working with Scott and his team? These might be the people she was referring to.

Shit. I'm going to need to fess up that I don't have the cave certification yet and sell them on my skills.

After I rent the gear, I sit and wait on a bench near the charter docks. The smell of diesel mixes with the ocean's brine. Another place that feels familiar, but I can't reach any memories tied to it. I think of the woman, her little girl, and this potential diving job.

I'll do this dive today and see the Drop up close. If there's a chance to do so, I might sneak in for a glimpse inside the cavern. Only a few minutes, nothing crazy. Being able to describe the cavern interior might make my skills more believable to Scott and Sid.

Laughter rings out from the boat docked in the next slip over from the Charter.

The *Adeline*.

On the boat's deck, a young blonde man is talking to an older man with dark brown hair. The older man is about my age, give or take a few years. "Clint's getting the hang of it, boss. I bet you we'll have him diving with us in the Drop in less than a month."

"I agree." The dark-haired man nods to *Clint*, another young guy standing at the helm, shaking his head.

"Not for me. I'll stay topside. Thank you very much."

"And we appreciate that," a young, unassuming brunette says, waving a thumb between herself and a very large man with dark skin who stands beside her. "Scott always takes Jamie into the caves because he's the skinniest. Now that you're here, Liam and I don't have to take turns."

"Margaret, you know you're my favorite, but I have to keep my eye on him. Make sure he's working and doesn't make excuses to get out of it," *Scott* adds with a straight face.

"That's bogus. You know his sweet talk doesn't work on me," she says.

"I'm right here," *Jamie* says, insulted. But the way everyone jumps in and laughs over him tells me this group is tight. He continues. "Garrett's been telling everyone who'll listen that mapping the Drop restarts this week."

"Yeah, well, I'm not sure about that. But we're ready."

Oh no. This is *the Scott* Sid was talking about.

"I still can't believe you're going to let us swim with a freaking camera crew. Not to mention babysitting them while they work. What happened to your aversion to cameras and showboating celebrities?"

"As long as they're not assholes and keep those things out of my face, I don't give a fuck what they do," Scott says.

Jamie laughs. "Being a family man is really softening you up, boss. When do Maddie and Christopher get home?"

"Tomorrow morning. I'm heading over to the hospital right now to say goodnight." *Scott's* stern face loosens up. "I actually had to convince her to stay there last night, so wish me luck."

"Tell her and the little guy I said hi. Uncle Jamie—I'm claiming the title."

"I'll do that," *Scott* says as he gets ready to get off the boat. "Oh, by the way. I've been meaning to ask you. Who's the girl?"

"What?" *Jamie* freezes, his voice getting stuck in his throat.

"The girl who's been keeping you up at night for weeks."

The blonde man coughs, all his easy humor replaced with a red face.

"We can measure the bags under your eyes with a ruler. Combine that with your above-average work performance and a suspiciously optimistic worldview. It's a dead giveaway. We're making wagers about her identity."

"You don't know her." *Jamie* rushes off and gets busy doing something at the back of the boat.

Scott laughs and steps off the ladder. "Let me know when I get to meet her, Jamie… if I haven't already." The rest of the crew onboard laughs.

Scott heads in my direction, scrolling on his phone, walking past the skipper and dive guide who are preparing the charter boat for customers.

I stand and get ready to head over there for the dive.

When Scott gets right next to me, he glances my way. Then he stops, whirls around, and gapes.

"What the fuck?" he mutters under his breath and continues to stare at me with wide eyes. I'm not sure what he wants, so I stare back in silence.

"Who are you?" he demands.

"Elliot."

"Elliot?" His forehead wrinkles, and he eases closer to me. "You look exactly like…" His face pinches in confusion. "Did you know Nathan Carter?"

"The archaeologist? No, I just moved to Maverick Key. I'm from Miami."

"You look *exactly* like Nathan Carter. But you can't be him because he's dead. Who are you?" he asks again.

Where is he going with this? Now, all the people on his boat are staring at me in shock.

"I don't know who I am." I hate how small my voice sounds, and who the hell does this guy think he is, anyway. "Who the hell are *you*?"

He lets out a short, amused laugh. "Scott Rickter. Sorry. It's just that you… Didn't you just tell me you were Elliot?"

"Elliot's the name I took at the hospital. I have retrograde amnesia."

A flash of recognition crosses his face. He's staring at the leather band around my neck. Or the shell pendant. His breath hitches, and his fixed hazel eyes flicker with a rim of tears in the corners.

"How long have you had amnesia?" he asks in a shaky voice.

"Almost seven years."

Silence.

"The fuck," he mumbles.

I jerk when he puts his hands on my shoulders and he pulls me into a hug. A hard hug. His serious expression softens into a joyful one.

"I don't know how the hell this is possible, but what the fuck!"

"You know me?"

"Yes, man. I know you. I'm your brother-in-law. Damn." He squeezes me again, and all the people from his boat have circled around us, their faces covered with excitement. Unnerved by their attention, I stumble. Scott helps me catch my fall. "Hey, you're good."

I catch my breath. He lifts a hand and motions to the spectators to move back to give us room. "You must have a million questions. But let's start with something simple. Where are you staying?" he asks breathlessly.

I give him the address of the Driftwood Inn and my cell number. He stares at me, puzzled.

"I'm the new housekeeper. I'm supposed to move into the inn tonight. I've been staying at the Cooper Motel."

"Ah, well, is there anywhere you need to be right now?"

I'd forgotten about the charter, and it's already gone. "Nowhere."

"Then let's go see your sister."

In the truck, I try to think while Scott drives.

I'm *Nathan Carter*. Maddie is my sister, and Maverick Key really is my home.

What am I feeling right now?

Happy? I think so. I'm restless in my seat, and there's only so many times I can run my fingers through my hair to keep my hands busy. And as much as I'm trying to control my hammering heart. I can't. My sister's in the hospital because she's had a baby. I'm about to meet her for the first time, along with my little nephew, Christopher. I'm curious and excited, but I know I should feel something more specific and deeper.

Confusion. Definitely confusion. What happened to me? This Mark guy that supposedly confessed to killing me… what did he do to me? Obviously, I'm not dead. Why would he confess to killing me if I weren't dead? Why did he do it?

Can I walk in and ask for my life back? Can I become *Nathan Carter* now that I know that's who I am?

And Fear. Oh yeah. It's strong. But I have an uncomfortable relationship with fear. The stronger it gets, the more I want to fight it.

I think of the diver with a confident smile in the Carter's Drop brochure. How the hell can I be him?

"Anything you want to know right now?" Scott asks, interrupting my thoughts.

"Are you the Scott who's working with Sid to film the Drop?" He jerks his head to the right to look at me.

"Huh?"

"She's going to ask you if I can join her crew. I'd like you to say yes."

I hate hospitals. The harsh odor of bleach and Pine-Sol burns the back of my throat, and the empty halls buzz with mechanical sounds and hushed, clinical chatter.

Scott asked me to wait a few minutes so he could break the news to Maddie. After he told me, *we'll see,* to my question about the dives, he didn't say too much more on the way here.

"We'll need to decide when to tell the cops. Get your identity back officially. You're a legend, man. You're going to get a lot of attention once everyone knows."

We agreed it was best for me to lie low and get my bearings before involving the law.

The door opens and closes, and I hold my breath.

"She's ready," Scott's voice breaks as he swipes his eyes with the back of his hand. He squeezes my arm as he passes. "I'll wait here." He sits on a plastic chair against the corridor wall. "Take your time."

I put my hand on the cold doorknob. My feet feel like boulders, my throat as dry as dust. This is it. I'm going to meet my family.

After spending so long waiting for this moment, it feels surreal to be on the brink of learning more about who I am.

Without thinking about it any longer, I open the door and walk in.

A typical hospital room. But standing next to a small bassinet is my little sister. She's a pretty woman in her late twenties, holding a sleeping baby. I'm stunned by her appearance. She's the female version of me. Light brown hair and eyes. Freckles pepper her nose.

A small, broken sound rushes from my lungs.

She lays Christopher down without waking him and rushes to me, wrapping her arms around my chest. I feel her tears through my shirt.

"How is this possible?" She's shaking. Mirroring her, I wrap my arms around her too. I'm stiff and awkward. And I pull away quicker than I probably should.

"Nathan." Her strangled sob pulls at my heart.

"I'm sorry, I…"

She shakes her head, voice soft. "Scott told me. Should I call you Nathan or Elliot?"

I catch my breath. "I don't know…"

"Did you wake up this morning expecting this?" she asks with a playful voice, widening her eyes.

"No. But I've been looking… for years."

Pain flashes in her eyes.

"We'd given up hope. The police and the Coast Guard closed the case so fast. They were certain you couldn't have survived." She chokes back tears. "I'm so sorry for giving up on you. I should've come back the moment you went missing and never stopped looking."

"Come back? Where were you?"

"Sarasota. That's where we grew up as kids. Where I stayed until… Mom died."

"Is there more family?"

"Dad died when we were still young. You were sixteen. It was the four of us growing up." She takes a breath and tries to lighten the somberness. "There are so many people here who love you."

My mother and father are dead. Even though I don't know who I'm missing, the finality saddens me. I'm never going to get the chance to meet them.

Christopher wakes, and his gurgles fill the room. I think of my friends' babies and the ones at the Miami hospital. I'm good with them. They look at you as if they have all the answers. They're just not ready to share them yet.

"Do you want to hold him?"

Carefully, I lift him from the bassinet and gaze into his eyes. They're blue for now, but will probably change to our brown or Scott's hazel.

"I've been searching for something familiar for so long," I say quietly. "For someone who knows who I am." I swallow. "This is a lot. I want to remember so badly."

I don't want to disappoint her. I do feel something.

But these emotions are strangely detached from my thoughts. It's uncomfortable.

She guides me to a small couch. I sit, cradling Christopher.

"Do you remember anything?" she asks. "Anyone?"

"No." I press my lips together tightly. "Just dreams. I have the same one nearly every night. There's a woman with blonde hair and a beautiful smile. We're… together."

"You're dreaming of Crystal."

Could that be *her* name? "Crystal?"

"She's your wife and…" She squeezes my shoulder and hesitates. "I don't want to overwhelm you. Is this too much?"

"No."

"You and Crystal have a little girl. Natalie."

My wife. My little girl. The girl at the beach. Half expecting to wake up, I focus on something real. Something tangible. I touch the shell on my neck.

"Hey," she whispers.

I look up.

"Take a breath. It's okay to sit and process this," she says. Then whistles and curls her lips. "I know I need to." She lets out a little snort.

I like how she makes cute faces and sounds to dismiss her anxiety. And it's working on me too, at least a little bit. The beating of my heart has finally slowed down.

"Can you tell me about them?" I ask.

She shakes her head excitedly, grabs her phone and pulls up a photo of the beach. Natalie is holding a shovel and a pail in her hands, and Crystal's standing behind her with her arms wrapped around her. Minutes go by as she tells me about my wife. She's a top marine biologist and works for the city. She was recently promoted. A big job, working for the mayor and meeting with officials from the Coast Guard and NOAA. Natalie is in the first grade and is already a gifted student. Maddie claims she's just like her, but she admits that Crystal insists Natalie's just like me.

With every new nugget of information, I feel like something has been added to my soul.

Part of me wants to talk all night, but I know Scott's waiting for me and there's someone else I need to meet.

"I think it's time for me to go." I clear my throat and return Christopher to Maddie.

"All right. Scott can take you to see Crystal next." She smiles softly. "We can talk more when my little guy and I get out of here. Or whenever you're ready. I love you."

"I love you too," I say the words because they're expected, and my mind tells me they must be true. But I want so badly to *feel* that they are true.

At the door, I pause.

Goodbye, Elliot. I don't need you anymore.

"Nathan," I say. "Please call me Nathan."

"I love you, Nathan."

♥

Scott's ending a call when he notices me walk into the hall. "You okay?"

"Can I get a ride to the docks to pick up my car?"

"Sure. And we'll get your things. You can follow me back to the inn. I've got to talk to Crystal about something, too. It's a long story—there's a lot of shit going on."

"I can't just walk up to her and say hello."

He nods. "I'll talk to her first. Wait in your car until I come to get you. I'll make sure she's ready."

"I'm not sure that *I'm* ready."

When we reach the hospital parking lot, my nerves have gotten so bad that I have to sit down on the pavement.

Charging forward, it takes Scott a moment to notice I'm not with him.

"Hey…" He stops and turns back. "Breathe. She's a good woman, and she loves you."

I squeeze my eyes shut.

"There's nothing to prove." He reaches out his hand and pulls me up. "Whatever you need. We're all here for you. No pressure."

"My little girl. Natalie. Will she be there too?"

"No, not right now. She's at Crystal's house. The two of you can decide what's best."

I try to listen to Scott, but I'm not the confident man in the brochure.

“If you’re not sure what to say, just let her know. She’ll take it from there.”

When we get to the truck, he turns.

“You ready to do this?” he asks.

“I am.”

CHAPTER 10

The Widow

"This is outrageous."

Garrett spreads the tips of his fingers on the dining room table and leans in, widening his eyes. His attempt at intimidation just comes off as smug.

When Natalie and I left the beach earlier, I got the call from the office. We have the green light to inform island stakeholders about the reef restrictions. And of course, they begin tomorrow. So now, no one affected has any time to prepare.

Scott's running late.

I called him a little while ago to ask him to join us. Maddie already told him the news, so he's prepared to give me backup. But he sounded a little off on the phone.

Most of the layered communication notices have already started, but I took it upon myself to deliver the news to Garrett and Finn in person. Too much is at stake for the Carter's Drop project. This is the most politically sensitive impact, and if there's any hope of preventing escalation from investors or politicians, I need to reason with them and convince them to have patience while we figure out what's going on. I asked them to meet me at the inn and left Natalie with our next-door neighbor.

After speaking with Garrett and Finn for the last fifteen minutes, it's not going well. Garrett's been doing most of the talking, and Finn has sat quietly listening. *I could really use some help right now, Scott*, I think to myself.

I point to the data in my notes and explain again why we have to take action.

"It's an unfortunate situation. But we've got to implement these temporary measures to protect the reef before it's too late."

"What do you have to say about this?" Garrett shoots a frustrated look at Finn. "This risks the money. You have connections. Something needs to be done about this right now." He looks around the room. "Where is Rickter? They're in-laws. Maybe he can reason with her."

Like it's me who's created a disaster just to annoy him. I guess it's time to stop being nice and tell him he has no choice.

Finn sits up straighter in his chair and clears his throat. "It's important to be responsible." His expression is careful as he looks my way. "All the concerns Crystal has explained to us about the reef are valid…"

Garrett opens his mouth to speak, and Finn raises his palm before he continues. "However, I don't think we can ignore the level of significance those caves hold for us, either."

I shake my head. "No. I'm sorry. The damage could be irreversible," I insist. "This temperature increase isn't benign or static. It's rising. If the rate of increase remains at the pace it's going, the coral may have weeks, not months."

“I agree with you,” he says and pulls out a stapled packet from his portfolio. “We aren’t at cross-purposes.” He hands me the papers. “We can agree we need to find out what’s going on, right?”

“Yes.” I look down. A material analysis report. The first page is a synopsis with a black-and-white image of a rock covered with markings. Beneath it, a bulleted list summarizes the composition and behaviors observed through testing. Several of the listed items show results that remain *undetermined*.

“If we are to find a solution, we have to identify the cause, yes?” Finn asks and then continues. “What we know right now is that the areas showing signs of coral bleaching are near the entrance to the Drop and neighboring locations like Coral Fang. Correct?”

“Correct,” I confirm. I’m not sure where he’s going with this, but he’s not going to get me to agree that they can dive.

“Both Scott and Maddie observed warm water deep in the caves last year. And Nathan’s stone is growing hotter. In fact, it’s so hot now that it’s untouchable. We’re keeping it in a protective cooler.”

I don’t hide the surprise on my face. The self-heating stone Nathan found came from the blue hole. I look at the image again. This is the same stone.

A protective cooler? What in the world could cause a stone to grow so hot on its own?

It’s unnatural.

“I’m certain that something in the blue hole is contributing to the warming water. Something made of the same material as this stone. We have to find out what’s going on in there.”

“What’s it made of?”

“A material unknown to science,” he points to the analysis. “This is the latest series of tests. Right now, we really know nothing.”

“How did you learn about the stone? It’s why you’re here.”

I notice the hesitation, but he's quick to cover it up. His gaze flicks to Garrett, who sits quietly. No doubt pleased that Finn is getting me to listen.

"From Garrett's reports."

At this point in my life, I've learned to pick up on lies and subtle half-truths. What are you hiding, Dr. Clark?

"We'll need to discuss this further with NOAA and the Coast Guard," I say.

"Already done. They've agreed to limited permits. We'll take every precaution to minimize our footprint."

He's already secured their dives, and he let this conversation happen anyway. I feel a jolt of anger and sit up straighter, trying to control my face.

"Why wasn't I included in that discussion?"

"I'm sorry for that. When we got the news earlier, it seemed I needed to act quickly."

His apology, while delivered sincerely, rings a little hollow to me.

"I guess I need to get up to speed on the plans then, since I'm way behind. The mayor's office will expect to stay involved."

"Of course." He covers my hand. "Crystal—we want the same things. Can I ask you to trust me?"

I pull my hand away.

"I'm glad you've brought some sense back from this lunacy, Dr. Clark. It's a constant struggle to deal with these people," Garrett says.

I ignore the insult, and Finn ignores it too.

"Who's going in the water?" I ask.

"Scott and his team. Sid and her team… and me."

"You cave dive?"

"I've done some. I like to see what I'm researching up close." He glances at Garrett. "Get my hands dirty."

"About the dives." Garrett scans the room before he continues. "Sidney can't go."

"I'm afraid she can and is," Finn tells him patiently.

"I insist you reconsider. She has a team, so she can let them do the work. I don't want her in those caves," he says as he raises his voice.

"You don't have the authority to exclude her from this expedition. I do, but I'm not going to." Finn softens the edge in his voice. "I'm sure you love her, and you're worried about her safety. Fair enough. We'll adhere to strict safety protocols. She'll be fine. Besides, it's not her first rodeo, is it? She's already a pro."

Garrett swears and mumbles something to himself. "She's worse than her mother. I'm constantly trying to keep her out of trouble and… keep trouble away from her." He lets out a puff of air. "To no avail."

"I'm on my way to meet with the Coast Guard right now to go over the logistics and pull together those permits," Finn says. "Garrett, I'd like you to come with me. Is that okay, chap?"

Still grumbling about Sid, Garrett follows Finn out.

This meeting didn't go as I intended. Frankly, I'm pissed. But Finn may already be close to narrowing in on what is causing the problem, and he's working as fast as possible to find answers. That's what matters most.

I walk out to the porch and look down the drive.

Where's Scott?

CHAPTER 11

The Stranger

I follow Scott's truck as he pulls into the Driftwood Inn and Cottages' gravel driveway. My home. I park. When I turn off the engine, the loud thrum of my heart pounds in my ears. While I thought the inn was charming earlier this morning when I showed up for work, it feels a little different now. Like I'm intruding. The wide front porch is dotted with swaying flower baskets, and there's a handmade Welcome Home sign hanging from the side of the railing.

Who the hell is Nathan Carter?

The sun has set, and it will be dark soon. I try to push the air out of my lungs. What will I say to *her*? Crystal.

Focusing my thoughts on her, I can't quite make out the details of her face. In my dreams, her image is clear, but when I'm awake, it's blurred and fragmented. Did the day we kissed really happen? Was it our first kiss, or were we already lovers?

I can't even remember what it's like to touch a woman. Hot blood rushes up my neck to my face, and cold sweat pours down my back and out of my palms.

I'm not sure I can do this.

It's dark now. Electric lanterns and the porch light flicker on. Scott told me to wait. He climbs up the stairs and glances over to the area of the porch that's obscured by hedges and walks that way. He's not going in. He's talking to someone on a swing. I can see the metal chains moving.

It has to be *her*. My wife.

Time stops. I stare at a patch of sable palms and wait for something to happen. I'm so excited to meet her. And I already know I want her. Does that make me a freak? To want her and know very little about her and absolutely nothing about us.

I think about my friend Karen in Miami. We'd meet every day in the breakroom to chat. I knew how she liked her coffee and what she liked to eat for lunch. I knew her favorite color to wear was green, and that she had three cats and a dog. All those little things had to stack up before we could call each other friends.

I don't want to wait for all that. I want to give Crystal everything now, and I want my family back.

She jumps up off the bench and looks past Scott. He tries to stop her, but she runs toward me.

I can see her clearly now.

You can do this, Nathan.

I pick up the pink rose I brought with me and swallow the rest of my nerves.

When she's a few feet away, she sees me through the open window. Her eyes lock on mine. A flash of astonishment and disbelief. Then, she throws her hands over her mouth and collapses to her knees before she falls.

I'm out of the car and to her in seconds. The brunt of her fall was softened by the grass, but she passed out cold from the shock. I crouch to her and gently raise her head off the ground. Scott tries to take her from me, but I swipe his hands away.

"Let me help you check her out." Reluctantly, I nod, and he quickly looks her over.

Her eyes flutter open, dazed. I'm startled when I recognize that they're the exact shade of blue I remember from my dream—my memory.

"Nathan…" she says in a raspy whisper. She tries to reach out to me, but lets her arm fall and closes her eyes. I look up at Scott.

"She's okay. Let's get her inside. Do you want me to carry her?"

I shake my head. "I'll do it." Gently, I cradle her and stand. She's light, warm, and soft. Following Scott to the small cottage on the side of the inn, I wait as he unlocks the door. I gaze at her face. Her full lips are slightly open, and I can see a sliver of her teeth and tongue. She's making small, jerky movements with her arms and legs.

When we get into the cottage, I gently lay her on the bed and turn to Scott. "Go."

"Are you sure…"

"Yes." My voice is steadier than I feel. "I want to be alone with her. I know what to watch out for."

He hesitates, searching my face, then nods. "I'll be inside the inn if you need me. I've got some calls to make. A few people need to know. I'm not sure how long we can keep this quiet, but I'll try." He pauses, then presses something into my hand. "You may need this."

The rose.

I put it on the nightstand by the bed, along with a glass of water, and pull up a chair. I watch her, clinging to the proof that she's real, afraid that if I blink, she may disappear.

And then I wait.

♥

My name is Nathan Carter.

I am an archaeologist and a cave diver.

I discovered Carter's Drop.

I live on Maverick Key.

Crystal matters to me.

I repeat them once, twice, three times. Dr. Paulson's five constants exercise. Five things that are true no matter what. Not memories, but facts I can verify and build from. I gently pick up her wrist, rubbing my thumb across the comforting stream of the pulse beneath her skin.

My name is Nathan Carter.

I'm in my old cottage.

Crystal is breathing.

My hand is on her wrist.

I'm not leaving her.

I stare at her face, so peaceful in sleep. Everything about her looks soft and bright.

Will her voice be the same as I remember?

Our day with the dolphins wasn't a dream at all. It's a memory. A real one. It happened. If I can remember our kiss in the ocean, her taste of salt and honey, I might be able to remember more.

More of Dr. Paulson's words come back to me, and I remember another one of our conversations.

"Memories don't usually come back because you *try* to remember them. They come back when your brain feels safe enough."

"I've been reading about shocking the brain," I said, leaning forward. "If that's what it takes to get my memories back, I'll do it, Doc. Wire me up."

He shook his head slowly, concern etched on his face. “That’s not how it works, Elliot. It’s a myth that shock will ‘reset’ the brain. In reality, it almost never works that way.”

Then he leaned forward. “When memories return suddenly, it’s usually because the brain reaches a tipping point. After a steady stream of emotional and physical triggers, things can settle back into place. And recall happens. Not because it was forced.”

He’d paused.

“Or?”

“Or when something deep inside bypasses conscious control,” he said carefully.

“You mean if my mind snaps.”

He didn’t correct me.

“We don’t understand everything,” he said.

When I look back down at Crystal, my pulse quickens. This is just the beginning. You’re my future. I pick up her hand and hold it tightly.

CHAPTER 12

The Widow

I force my eyes open.

Ouch. It feels like I've run a thousand miles, and my head is killing me. My tongue is thick, my throat dry. Slowly, I turn toward the nightstand. A white ceramic lamp sits there, casting soft light across the dark room. Beside it, a long-stemmed pink rose. I can smell its faint sweetness.

Where am I? I recognize this room, but it isn't my bed. Or is it? Then I remember.

This is Nathan's cottage.

All these dreams about Nathan are making me go crazy. He's occupying my thoughts as if I'd just lost him yesterday.

Someone's holding my hand.

I flick my gaze to the person who's sitting beside the bed.

My breath freezes in my throat, and my heart slams against my ribs once, then stops.

Nathan?

I squeeze my eyes shut to stop the sudden tilt of the room as my vision blurs. My stomach rolls, and I force myself to inhale slowly through my nose, trying to fight down the wave of nausea flooding over me.

He can't be real.

But I can still feel his hand.

Afraid I'm seeing things, I force my eyes open. He's staring down at me, his grip on my hand tightening.

Wake up, Crystal. Please wake up. I plead with myself.

"There you are," he says.

It's his voice. I haven't heard it with this clarity in so long.

"I'm dreaming."

He squeezes his eyes shut, his jaw tight.

"Crystal, you're not dreaming. I'm here." He lets go of my hand and cups my face.

His palms are warm and familiar.

A wall inside me crumbles. A dam that has held back the worst of it. The worst of the sadness. The fear. It's kept me alive for more than six years, but it's also been slowly killing me. I used it to turn all my colors to black and white. And I used it to hide from hope as much as from sadness. Everything inside me stills.

Then I shake. A few silent tears run down my face and gather where his fingers hold me. I feel the sting of the air against my skin where they fall.

"Steady there. Stay with me." He slides his hands down my neck to my shoulders. "You're okay."

Now I remember Scott telling me something on the porch. He'd warned me that what he was going to say would be shocking. But before he could get the words out, my heart knew. I knew it was Nathan. When I saw the car in the drive, I ran to him.

It's been over six years. Where could he possibly have been for so long? How can this be real? Am I alive or dead?

"Where were you?" I ask, my voice scraped raw. I'm weirdly detached from my emotions and overwhelmed by them at the same time.

"Miami." His gaze is intense, like he's memorizing me.

For years, I thought if I ever saw him again, it would only be remains. A corpse. Fragments of the man I once held and loved.

But fate has given him back to me. Or I'm still dreaming. Or dead.

"How?" I ask.

He shakes his head, frustrated. "I have no memories…"

I take his hand and pull it to my chest. "Just talk to me. Tell me anything. I just want to hear your voice."

He takes a deep breath. "I woke up in Miami…"

"Wait." I'm afraid to ask him this, but I need to. I sit up against the headboard and rest my palm on the sheet beside me. "Can you hold me?" I ask, my voice trembling.

Fear crosses his face, but he pushes it away and picks up the glass of water, handing it to me. "Here," he whispers.

Grateful, I take it and sip—the cool water soothing my dry throat. He moves to the other side of the bed and eases in beside me. When he slides an arm around my shoulders and pulls me back into his chest, I let out a small sound and finally let myself really cry. Gut cry.

He soothes me with low murmurs. He's crying too.

I clutch his arms, which are wrapped around me tightly, and we sit like that for a while, sharing little things that don't make that much sense. Then he explains his amnesia and how he restarted his life in Miami. He doesn't know that's where we met. Suddenly, I'm filled with an urge to share everything with him. To fix him.

But for now, I listen, desperate for answers, but he has none. He was stolen away from us, and now he's back with no explanation. He tells me as much as he can about Miami, then asks me about our lives and the people here in the Key.

I don't care that this doesn't make sense. He's here. That's the only thing that matters. His body, his warmth, his smell. This is really him.

Continuing, he gets to a story he's reluctant to share.

"What?"

He blushes. "There was one dream I had every night. I really want to know…" He stops and swallows the lump in his throat. "I need to know if it was a memory." He can't look at my eyes as he describes our first kiss. His innocence and the loneliness in his voice break my heart.

"Was it real?" he asks.

I nod. "It was our first kiss. There was no going back after that."

His gaze lingers on my lips, then he refocuses.

I reach out and trace my fingers along his jawline.

My quirky genius. At thirty-five, there are the faintest lines on his forehead and at the edges of his eyes. His face is slightly more lived-in. And if it's possible, he's grown even more handsome. Self-consciously, I put my other hand against my stomach. I've never completely gotten my pre-pregnancy figure back, and I have the same lines he does. I'm only a couple of years younger.

What does he think of me?

I'm still waiting to be ripped out of this fantasy.

Unconsciously he kisses, then holds my hand closer to his jaw, closing his eyes. Then he shifts. "Do you feel like you can get up?" he asks. "Let's get you some fresh air."

With his help, I pull myself out of bed, and I'm not sure if it's the bump on the head or the shock, but my body is numb and I struggle to find my balance. Slipping his arm around my waist, he helps me get up and walk.

Outside, I point to the gated fence. "The garden's that way."

He nods and guides me in that direction.

It's dark, and the path lights illuminate the garden steps. We sit on the bench swing, quiet. Smiling. Swinging. Holding hands. His hands are warm and strong. No one's hands feel like his.

My gaze drifts to the Mutabilis shrubs we planted together years ago. Covered in blooms of pale sulfur, apricot, pink, and dark crimson. Their soft petals, still moist from the afternoon rain, release a delicate scent that drifts through the garden. Butterfly roses—whose colors deepen as they age.

Another swell of tears coats my eyes. I blink to get rid of them, and they spill over, streaming down my face.

"Crystal," he mouths, his voice a whisper. Tentatively, he reaches for me, his fingers brushing my cheek. "Please don't cry. I don't want you to be sad."

His touch steadies me, and I try to stop crying.

"Is someone going to tell me I'm dreaming?" I ask with a sniff.

"I don't know." He lets out a little laugh—one I recognize. This is as crazy for him as it is for me. Not true. This has to be a million times crazier for him.

He closes his fingers around mine more tightly. "I'm not sure what else to say… forgive me."

I squeeze his hand and pull him a little closer to me. "I know you can't remember me yet, but you're home. You'll get everything back with time."

A flash of hope crosses his face before he pushes away a frown. He's silent. I know his doctors must have told him there are no guarantees, but that doesn't matter to me. I'll help him get his memories back.

"We have a daughter," he says, forcing the words out as he stares at the palms across from us. His unfocused gaze meets my eyes. He's lost.

I want to comfort him, to reassure him he's going to be okay. "Her name is Natalie. She looks so much like you."

"She was the girl on the beach today." His eyelashes flutter. "I saw you both." His jaw works as if he's going to say more.

"And we saw you. I knew it was you. I felt it in my gut… but it seemed so impossible."

"Nothing's impossible." This gives him confidence, and he rises to his feet to face me, his eyes shining. "Can I see her?"

I hesitate. I want to introduce them immediately, but then I think of Natalie. We need to do this carefully, in a way that won't scare her. It's late. She'll already be in bed when I get home.

He's staring at me, waiting for my answer, the corners of his eyes squeezing the longer I take.

"Soon. I'll talk to her—"

A tear slides down his cheek.

Nathan, I'm so sorry.

I stand up from the swing and wrap my arms around him. He holds me, his embrace firm and desperate. I can feel his heart racing beneath my cheek.

But then he pulls away. It's jarring. Like he's just realized I'm a stranger.

I need to be careful with him.

"We'll get through this." I clear my throat. "You don't have to say this yet, but I want to… I love you."

He looks at me with uncertain eyes. "I love you, too." His voice is weak and a little pained, like he's upset that he can't really feel it. "I do, believe me, I just need… time to…"

Remember? But he can't say it because he thinks that may never happen. It's already been so long.

"You're sleeping here?" I ask.

He nods. "I'm the housekeeper—for now."

The housekeeper? I hold in my laughter. It's his inn!

"Where do you and Natalie live?" he asks, leaning forward. Getting nearer. Wanting to hold me again. It's in this moment that I know this isn't a dream and that I really have him back. I know him. He doesn't want to wait weeks to get his life back. He wants it now. He may not know who he is, but I do, and I see him.

"Just a few blocks from the inn. It's a nice, quiet neighborhood."

He shifts on his feet. "After tonight, when can I see you again?" He's acting like he's asking a pretty girl on a date for the first time.

"I have to work tomorrow, but I'll be back Tuesday morning. Scott usually holds the dive meetings here at the inn on Mondays, but he's moved it a day since Maddie and Christopher go home tomorrow morning."

His eyes light up.

"Do you remember anything about diving?" I ask.

"Oh, yeah." He perks up. "I learned to dive—again, I guess—in Miami. I'm trying to get on Sid's crew and film the Drop."

What?

"Okay," I say carefully. On one hand, wow. He's jumping right back into his life. On the other… cave diving? No way will Scott say okay to that. But I don't want to shatter his confidence.

"It sounds like you've been busy," I say softly. "And we have a lot to catch up on." I glance at my watch. I really need to get back to Natalie. I press a gentle kiss to his cheek. "I've got to get back home. Tuesday morning? We'll figure out the best way to introduce you to Natalie then."

His face softens.

"Crystal." Still holding my hand, he draws me closer, his other hand settling on my waist. He hesitates. "I… can I kiss you?"

I nod. "Please."

He cups my face and leans down, brushing his lips over mine, the softest, shy wisp of his tongue against my lips. Like he needs to taste me to be certain I'm real.

He lets out a soft sigh. "Thank you."

CHAPTER 13

The Stranger

We're kissing in the ocean.

She tastes the same as she did last night when I brushed my lips over hers. Sun and honey. But this time she doesn't leave. She holds me and pulls me into her arms.

My heart races.

Then we're in the clouds, and everything is bright and soft. I feel like I can fly.

Then thunder. Really loud. Annoying thunder.

I wake to pounding on the cottage door.

"Give me a minute," I call out, sitting up and rubbing the sleep from my eyes.

I still smell her. Her light, citrusy fragrance clings to the bedsheets. My bed. My cottage.

Where is my wife?

I stare at the untouched pillow on the other side of the bed as if it will give me an answer. Then the pounding comes again.

"You almost done in there?" Scott asks.

I groan as I pull myself out of bed and drag myself to the door. I'm exhausted because I had the best night's sleep I can remember—and my body wants even more.

"Hey," I say, opening the door in my boxers. "Why the hell did you wake me up so early?"

Scott smirks. "It's eleven. Come on. Get dressed." He jerks his thumb over his shoulder. "Time to meet everyone."

"Is Crystal here?" I picture her from last night. Thinking of her is like coming home.

He shakes his head. "She's working. And Maddie and Ms. Connor are home with the baby." I must look disappointed, because he adds, "Don't worry, you'll see them tomorrow."

He waits outside while I get dressed.

I put all my things away in the cottage last night. I was supposed to make breakfast for the guests this morning, but was told not to worry about the housekeeping job.

I glance at my diary. Last night's entry was messy but cathartic. Calling yesterday an exercise in *emotional whiplash* feels like the understatement of the century.

I expect to follow Scott into the inn, but instead, he points to his truck. There's a cooler, balls, and other recreational gear in the back.

"Ready to work up a sweat?" he asks.

♥

I help Scott carry the gear to the shore.

Tiki Beach is nothing like Sunset Strand. This one's wild and remote, tucked along the sanctuary side of the island's northwest coast. Dunes rise high behind the narrow shoreline, their slopes thick with sea oats. The sargassum drifts in heavily here with a distinct rotting-eggs and fish odor. Offensive at first, but you get used to it. There are only a few patches of clear sand wide enough for beach play.

The best thing is that there are very few vehicles here.

"A little smelly," Scott says as he waves to the group who've gathered near a volleyball net. "But I thought we could avoid the crowds here."

I recognize everyone from Scott's and Sid's crews. And there are a few more people gathered around that are new to me.

"I'll introduce you to Garrett when we get back to the inn," Scott says. "He's not into outdoor fun."

"He's no fun. Period."

The man speaking steps forward and grins. "Hi, I'm Jamie." He shakes my hand. "And this giant over here is Liam."

Liam has to be close to seven feet tall. "Hi, Nathan. It's an honor to meet you, man."

I brace myself when I shake his hand, expecting a bone-crusher, but his grip is firm and comfortable.

A small brunette approaches, her brown eyes bright. "Can I hug you?"

I nod.

"Margaret," she says as she wraps her arms around me. "I'm going to try not to fangirl, but I've studied all your work. You're a genius."

"Clint." A younger man shakes my hand.

"He's our pollywog," Jamie quips.

Clint gives him a closed-lip smile. "You mean boat captain."

Sid introduces me to everyone on her team. Little by little, I learn I'm something of a legend on the island. I manage to smile and laugh, but every compliment slides off as if it's meant for someone else. It doesn't fit right, like I'm wearing the wrong clothes.

"Finn told us he'd worked with you before," Sid says. "Professionally." She scans the beach. "He's around here somewhere." She points. "There."

I follow her gesture to a blue Prius parked near the dunes.

A tall black man steps away from it, dressed in a white linen button-down and trousers that look pressed. Wireframe glasses. He's polished, but not the kind that belongs on a beach. And he walks like he's late for an academic conference. He's carrying two six-packs that he drops into the cooler. He takes out one can, walks straight to me and extends his hand.

"Dr. Nathan Carter." His smile is broad. Genuine. "It's fantastic to see you. The world's a better place with you in it."

We shake.

"I'd offer you a beer, but you don't drink." He cracks the can open and takes a swig.

"All right," Sid says, clapping her hands. "Time to break out into teams. I'm with Liam."

CHAPTER 14

The Widow

I wake to the shrill bells of the four a.m. alarm after a restless night.

Reaching for my phone, I turn it on. The photo fills the screen, and there's Nathan. Standing by my car window, waving goodbye.

I'm so exhausted I can't feel my body, and I don't care. This is a good kind of tired to be. I feel lighter today. Less burdened. Ready to get to work and make a difference. I feel like myself again.

I glance at the made side of the bed. Is it wrong to want him here? I picture him asleep in the cottage right now, alone in that bed. Our bed.

A darker thought follows. What if he wants different things as he moves forward? What if he doesn't exactly find his way back to me when he finds himself?

No stinking thinking, Crystal. Get up.

Usually, I drop Natalie off at the school's daycare around seven and go straight to City Hall. Today, I move through the house on careful feet, leaving her with my next-door neighbor before sunrise to meet my team at the marina at five.

As the city's lead marine biologist, I'm overseeing the operation to start temporary mitigation efforts at the reef. It's the first day, and I expect it to be long, but if we turn things around, even a little, it will be worth the hard work. After today's setup, I'll split my time between the conservation dives and office days and try to find a balance with what I've got going on at home.

We have all the support we need with NOAA's CERF money and a few wealthy locals who are bridging the gap until those funds are released.

This is the first time we're using these quick-hit methods for coral preservation. Anything is better than nothing, but these techniques are limited in scale and impact. We're only talking about a reduction of one to three degrees Fahrenheit. But it matters. One thing that we have going for us is that we're in the late fall, heading into winter. The dropping ambient temperature helps. This would have been ten times worse had it been summer.

The reality is we may fail. If the conditions can't be reversed and continue to deteriorate, we'll need to consider what to do next. We're discussing the salvage extraction of unique genetic lines if it becomes necessary. We've already identified the coral we'll *save.*

The thought of those choices and of our beautiful coral reef seascapes being reduced to lab specimens sickens me.

God, please don't let it come to that.

After our morning prep and briefing, the six of us meet Fred and a couple of NOAA officials at the *Reefing Around* and begin loading. Shade canopies. Submersible cooling fans, LED lights, and ancillary equipment are packed onto the deck. Somehow, we all fit.

Fred casts off, and we head to Coral Fang.

♥

The dive meeting is in full swing when I walk into the inn's dining room.

Yesterday's reef mitigation dive was productive but emotional. When we got to Coral Fang, even more polyps were showing signs of bleaching. Our efforts seem woefully inadequate based on what we're facing. We didn't have time to get to Carter's Drop. We're going to speak with NOAA officials about next steps.

I scan the crowd for Nathan first. He's sitting quietly by Ms. Connor, who's holding baby Christopher. He glances at me, raising his hand with a smile, then looks back down at his plate. Is he nervous? There have to be more than twenty people here today. He told me about his beach day last night when I called him. He must be shell-shocked by the rapid introductions. All these people are strangers to him. Strangers who expect different things and are here for different reasons.

I want to sit beside him so badly, but I'll wait. I take a croissant and a bottle of water and squeeze into the only spot left—next to Garrett.

"We don't know what's down there," Scott barks. "I'm not sending my team into what could be a death trap on a whim. You're going to have to lay down some hard facts to sell me on why we need to expedite our schedule and change our plans."

"And we haven't even been in the Drop in over six months," Jamie adds and points to the profile map of Carter's Drop on the wall. The map is Scott's latest survey of the Drop. It draws the distances traversed to date and lays out planned exploration routes based on sonar readings.

"Isn't that what cave explorers do? Explore." Garrett's tone is snide and frustrated. Scott raises his hand to caution Jamie not to respond.

"I, for one, am itching to get in there," Sid quips, rubbing her hands together.

Scott shoots her a stern look. "Yeah, well, you're not going anywhere unexplored. Main line travel only, Miss Diva."

"Okey dokey, boss. You've told me that a few times. I've got good ears. My crew will stay on the lines."

"I don't see why you can't wait until the experts map the area before you try to film it. You're only going to get in their way," Garrett says. He's still trying to keep her out of the caves.

"She's okay if she stays on the main lines." Scott smiles at Sid. "One of us will supervise the film crew on each dive. We'll rotate so we don't get bored."

She gives him the OK sign and snickers.

Scott turns back to Finn. "We can re-prioritize traverse however we need. What I don't like is the rush. Rushing gets people killed."

Hearing the danger spoken aloud makes this real. These people are my family. I don't think I'll survive if I lose anyone else.

Finn's calm voice cuts in. "Scott, understandably, you have concerns." He walks over to the map like a professor about to lecture the class. "Let me get us all briefed on the science, then we can jump into logistics and the dive plan. Before I begin…" He turns to me. "Crystal, do you want to summarize the current coastal impacts so we have a reading of what's at stake?"

I pick up my notes. Nathan looks at me intently from across the table. His gaze makes me burn up, and it's hard to think for a moment. I clear my throat. "We're running pH/salinity tests daily now, and the trends are grim. We don't have much time. The water temperature in those areas is already consistently measuring over eighty-six degrees. That's enough to cause bleaching, and if it's sustained or increases, it will cause death. It's already dying."

I stop and take a breath, trying to hold in my tears.

"That's bad." Scott's eyes and voice soften. "But what are we supposed to do about it? Do we even know what we're looking for?"

"All we can do is try to buy the coral time," I continue. "We're focused on those tactics right now. Restricting aquatic activity near the reef, deploying shade cloths, cooling pumps, and feeding lamps. And we'll continue to monitor impacts." I turn to Finn. "What we need is to find out what's actually causing the heating and stop it."

Finn nods and jumps back in. "Back to the question about what we've learned. My team has been running dozens of surveys and tests over the last couple of days." He pushes up his glasses. "We've identified the hot zones in the caves. And Nathan's stone is giving us valuable data about the material in those areas."

Nathan jerks his head toward Finn at the mention of his name.

"I have theories… but let's not get ahead of ourselves."

"How hot is the stone right now?" I ask.

"Two hundred and sixty degrees."

Scott stands. "We can't swim in water that hot."

"Oh no," Finn says quickly. "The main flow won't be that hot. Warmer, yes, but the heat drops off fast once you're away from the source. Think of geothermal vents. The hot water is localized, then it mixes." He rubs the bridge of his nose before continuing. "We'll use temperature probes and, of course, everyone needs to avoid the rocky walls."

"Who else knows about this?" Scott asks.

"I've kept the findings of the stone and the temperatures to a small group of scientists I trust, and now all of you. We haven't notified outsiders yet. But we're in contact with local NOAA and Coast Guard officials." He looks in my direction. "And the mayor's office, of course."

"How long before the Feds show up and this place turns into a shitstorm?" Scott asks.

"Two weeks at most."

Scott shakes his head. "Fuck."

He looks up as Maddie comes back into the room and takes Christopher from Ms. Connor. She looks exhausted.

"Time for his feeding." She walks over to Scott and squeezes his shoulder, then lifts onto her toes to give him a short kiss. Her touch instantly calms him down.

He gives her a kiss, then kisses Christopher on the forehead before they turn to leave.

I look over at Nathan. His eyes are locked on the map. He's been tracking every word, and curiosity is seeping from his pores.

Fear hits me hard. He wants to be a part of this. And when he sets his mind to something…

"All right, thanks for the science lessons. Let's get to the plan," Scott says.

"So do you want to tell us where we're all going, *Mr. Big Brains*?" Jamie asks Finn.

"Yes, well." Finn points at a large section of the map. "The *Megaron.* I want to collect the artifacts Nathan discovered, and it's also where Scott and Maddie observed heat last year."

It's also where Mark died, I think, bitterly.

"It can be frigid in the deeper areas of the cave. At least it was. How do we plan to balance out the swim? Dry suits, wetsuits, no suits?" Scott asks.

"My suggestion is light swimwear under thin wetsuits. Ninety-two degrees is generally the upper limit for low-exertion dives. With medium to high exertion, I recommend a conservative safety maximum of eighty-seven degrees Fahrenheit. Above that, hyperthermia becomes a concern. If we encounter anything warmer, we'll need to consider other options."

"I'd like to come." All heads turn to Nathan. "Looks like you can use another hand."

He's looking at Scott for an answer. Finn sits down, amused.

Oh no.

"Sorry, man, that's not happening," Scott says.

"Why not?" Nathan asks. "You know I'm a cave diver. A damn good one. I'm in."

Scott studies him. "No doubt. But you just got back, and you may not remember..."

"This is bullshit. I have it all in my head." He lets out a frustrated exhale, his words coming out fast. "I can do everything I used to do. I just don't remember doing any of it. Don't treat me like I'm clueless."

Scott pauses, thinking.

Maddie walks back into the room and hands Christopher to Ms. Connor. Then she moves to Nathan and clasps the back of his chair, leaning down to his ear. "Hey… the technical dive we're talking about is happening this week. Why don't you plan to go on the next one? Get your feet wet with something simple first so you can convince this guy you've still got the skills." She points her thumb at Scott.

Nathan's nostrils flare, but his eyes soften when he looks up at Maddie. "Fair enough." He shifts his gaze back to Scott. "Thanks."

"Saturday," Scott says. "We'll check out the water near the Drop. Then we'll figure out what you're ready for next."

"Here." She hands Nathan a stack of folded papers. "*Your* maps of Carter's Drop. You've gone farther than anyone else has." She motions to the others in the room.

"Thank you." He takes the maps from Maddie and flips them open. His eyes light up with excitement.

As I watch him immediately start examining it, I realize this won't be easy. I can already imagine myself losing him again, and once Natalie meets him…

The table conversation shifts back to the dive plan.

"Sid, your team is with Margaret and Finn this time—only as far as the line takes you in the *Megaron*."

"Yippee!" Sid's all exuberant energy, while Scott just huffs.

"When you reach the end of the line…"

"Yeah, yeah, I know, boss…"

Nathan gets up and walks to the back porch. I follow. He rests his elbows on the railing, looking out over the pool and garden. When I step up beside him, he turns toward me.

"Did you get any sleep?" I ask.

"Yeah, actually. I did."

His skin is smooth, and the dark circles under his eyes from Sunday have disappeared.

"Talk about jumping right back into the deep end," I say.

"I want this." He leans into the railing, bearing more of his weight against it. He turns to me. "I feel more alive than I have in six years. I can make a difference."

I believe him, and that's what terrifies me. But I refuse to put up another wall. Time is short, and I won't let fear waste any of it.

"You will." I take his hand. "I wanted to ask you if you'd like to come over tomorrow night. To my place. Let me cook you some dinner, and you can meet Natalie."

A grin breaks free. "Is there anything you need? I can stop by the general store."

"Just you."

CHAPTER 15

The Stranger

Small children and their pets play on the sides of the crunchy shell rock street, running, laughing, and getting into all sorts of trouble in the afternoon sun. On my sixth turn around the small beachside neighborhood filled with modern pastel-colored bungalows, I get up the nerve to park in front of the pale yellow one-story I'm looking for. This is like a first date for me, but for her… She must have expectations. I carry the bouquet and the small gift bag to the door. Pressing the tiny conch-shaped doorbell sets off a tinny chime.

When the door opens, she's standing there in a navy-blue velvet dress and meticulously curled hair. Was she wearing any makeup yesterday? I don't think so—she doesn't need it. But today she's wearing light mascara and liner, and her lips are glossed. Stunning.

"Are those for me?" When she reaches for the bouquet, I catch the diamond on her ring finger. Unconsciously, I look at mine. It's bare. My breath hitches when I realize she wore the same ring around her neck yesterday. "Come in." She puts her arm around me and leads me through the small entryway to the living room. Her fresh, citrusy, floral perfume drifts over me, stirring something familiar.

When I step inside, she turns to me. "Natalie's playing outside. Are you ready to meet her?"

Yes.

I hold my breath.

She opens the glass sliding door and peeks out, curling her fingers inward, calling Natalie to come inside. I feel every hair on my arms stand as I wait. Natalie runs in, a bundle of excitement with white-blonde curls like Crystal's and light brown eyes like mine.

She holds her mother's hand and watches me—her face filled with curiosity.

"Hi, Natalie. I got you something." Opening the bag, I pull out the teddy bear I bought at the general store. I wasn't sure what she'd like, but the white bear with a dark blue nose seemed right. "Here you go." Bending down to her level, I offer it to her.

She squeals and eagerly takes the bear, hugging it. "I'll call him Mr. Blue Nose." She hugs him to her chest and looks directly into my eyes. "Are you my real daddy?"

My heart bursts, and at first, I can't speak. "I am. And I'm so happy to meet you." Slowly, I reach for her, and she throws her arms around me. Squeezing me with all her strength.

"I love you, Natalie."

"I love you too, Daddy. I made a wish to meet you, and it came true." She chatters then, asking me all sorts of things. Then she asks. "Why did you leave us?"

I keep my gaze on her despite the burning behind my eyes. My words catch in my throat when I try to answer.

Crystal takes Natalie's hand and whispers something in her ear. Natalie gives me a cute wave and runs off into the kitchen. A few seconds later, there are sounds of drawers opening and pans clanking. Crystal returns to my side.

Lowering her gaze, she reaches for my hand. I feel the ring. "I haven't told her much. Until Mark died, she thought he was her father. I wanted to tell her so many times… but."

"I understand." There are so many questions I want to ask her about Mark and about our own marriage. But I've picked up on enough to know that her story with Mark isn't a happy one. Scott filled me in on some details of what Mark did—to me and to others. What kind of mess had I gotten my family into? When I think of what she must have been through living with a man like Mark…

"She knows now," she continues. "I told her Mark was her pretend daddy and that her real daddy is you. When I told her, she decided she was going to build a time machine one day so she could go back and find you." She lets out a small laugh with a breath. Frowning, she looks at the floor. "Mark was a distant father…" She swallows, her voice hoarse. "…but he never…hurt *her*."

Her words make my stomach twist. If there is one thing I could have right now, it would be Mark standing in front of me. I'd kill him.

"Whew… maybe we can talk about all the heavy stuff a bit later." She smiles weakly and asks me to let Natalie give me a tour of the beach while she finishes dinner.

"Come on, Daddy, let's go." Natalie takes my hand. Unlike the rest of us adults, she needs no warm-up, no getting to know you period. She's already accepted me and is eager to share her world with me.

"Your momma told me you're going to build a time machine one day?"

"Yes, Mr. Finn will help me do it when I get older. He's almost as smart as Mr. Hawking."

"That's super cool. Tell me more about it?"

"Mr. H.G. Wells wrote the book. A time machine can take you where you want to go in the past or future. Going to the future is no good. But if you go in the past, you can fix things."

"Why is the future no good?"

"It spoils the surprises."

"Can't argue with that logic." Giving her head a ruffle, I laugh when curls land in every direction.

"Daddy, you're messing up my hair. Here." She hands me a piece of paper. "I wrote this for you." The handwriting isn't bad for a six-year-old. There are doodles of turtles, dolphins, and fish in the margins.

I luv the ocean and my momma and daddy.
My daddy is a sayler and he is brave.
He swims in the ocean.
and saw a hole at the bottom.
I think about him a lot.
I wanna find him one day.

"Daddy, don't cry." She raises her little hand to my cheek and brushes it with her fingers.

I concentrate on her touch. This is unconditional love, and I feel it. Some may say you can't without your memories. But that's not true. Because I do.

"Something happened to my brain, and I can't remember anything. There's so much I want to share with you, I just can't remember."

"It's okay, Daddy. We can learn everything together."

How did I make a kid so wise at her age? She must get it from her mother.

"I'd like that."

Holding hands, we walk back inside.

"Ya'll are just in time. Dinner's ready." Crystal has the table set with enormous bowls of pasta, sauce, bread, and salad.

"My favorite! Sketti."

"It's Daddy's favorite too," Crystal says and smiles playfully.

It is my favorite.

We eat and chat about Natalie's schoolwork and what she wants for Christmas. After dinner, I help Crystal with the dishes while Natalie wipes the table.

"Do you want Daddy to put you to bed?"

"YES… read me a story… please, Daddy!"

Dozens of books line the shelves in her room. There are too many to choose from.

"Do you want me to tell you a story I made up?"

She nods eagerly.

"It's called *The Sailor and the Siren*." She's enthralled as I start the story of the beautiful siren who lives on an island far away from the sailor. An island he'd never seen but knew existed.

She scrunches her face. "Daddy, the mistake is sirens aren't pretty. They're mean and have big, sharp teeth."

"Yes. Well, in this story, the siren is a little different. She's the most beautiful girl in the whole wide world, with golden hair and blue eyes. The sailor was searching and searching all alone on the big sea. He was looking for a secret island. The one he saw in his dreams."

"I like this story."

"One night, a big storm comes and breaks up his boat, and he's in the water, drowning." Natalie's eyes widen in fear.

I give her a gentle pat on the knee, and I mouth, "It's going to be okay."

Continuing… "He's about to give up when he hears the most beautiful sound he's ever heard, singing to him."

"Sirens do sing to sailors." She nods in approval.

"So, he swims as hard as he can in the direction of her voice. For hours and hours until his arms get too tired to move anymore."

Natalie moves the blanket over her eyes.

I'd better wrap up.

"He starts to sink when, through the surface of the water, he sees her face. She dives to him, pulling him out. Then she kisses him. They live happily ever after."

She claps, bouncing up and down. "That's a good story. I like nice sirens."

"Me too, Sugar Muffin."

I tuck her in and get ready to turn out the light.

"Daddy?" Her face is all scrunched up. "My tummy feels weird."

I walk back over and sit on the edge of the bed. She's too young to understand her emotions. How they rise, surge, and fall like the sea. I take her hand and smile.

"What's that?" she asks, her eyes wide and curious.

"This?" I glance down and lift the shell pendant. "It's my security blanket."

"It's pretty. Was it the siren's?"

"Yes." I take the band off and put it around her neck.

"And now it's yours."

I tuck her in and watch her fall asleep.

When I rejoin Crystal in the living room, she's fixed us two teas and lit a soft candle. It smells like a morning sea breeze.

"Sit?" she asks.

When I sit down beside her, I'm comforted by her scent again.

She squints. "So. Where are your glasses? I haven't seen you wear them since you've been back."

"I wear contact lenses."

"You used to wear contacts when you dived, but you liked to wear glasses the rest of the time. Your eyes would get tired." She pulls the drawer in the coffee table open, takes out a case, and hands it to me. "In case your eyes need a break."

"Thank you." I shiver when her fingers brush my skin.

"I'm not sure how tired you are, but I've made the extra bed." She takes the fluffy white throw that hangs over the couch and folds it, placing it into my lap. "Get cozy." Her lips curl into a small smile, and I notice the blush deepening on her chest and neck. "Stay tonight?"

I swallow.

"There's an extra room. All yours. I want you here with Natalie and me."

"I don't want to be a burden…"

She puts her finger over my lips. "Never. Your home is here." She gently pokes my chest, over my heart. "With us. You'll find it soon." It's hard to breathe. I want everything. But I have nothing to give her yet. She picks up a large photo album and hands it to me. "Why don't we go through this together? We'll take it one photo at a time."

"Thank you, Crystal." Our fingers touch again when I take the album from her. I want to kiss her, really kiss her this time. But it's too soon.

"Let me show you one more thing." I follow her to a small closet across from her bedroom. "When you… disappeared… I wasn't sure where I should put all your things. They made me so sad. So, I put them in here… there are so many memories of you in here."

She opens the door. Several stacks of journals and boxes line the walls from the floor to the ceiling. Excited to learn more, a part of me wants to go through them now. But I don't want to cut this time together short.

She looks at me sheepishly. "You'll probably be up all night combing through this. Try to get a little rest, yeah?"

"Are you okay with it? That I'm diving," I blurt out. *Real smooth, Nathan.*

Her downcast eyes look up, and she exhales. "It's who you are, Nathan. I'd never change you." She nods toward the couch. "You want to watch some TV?"

We sit down, and she leans against me, resting her head on my shoulder. I put my arm around her and breathe in. We talk about what's happening on the island and Natalie. She doesn't bring up the past or any expectations for the future.

Hours go by. When she dozes off, her head is nestled against my chest, and her fingers are curled around my waist. I sit with her like that for a while, soaking her in, watching her breathe. When she shifts, trying to get comfortable, I lift her into my arms and carry her to her room, trying not to wake her as I lay her on the bed.

She wakes anyway.

"Sweet dreams, sailor." Her lovely face is haloed by her golden hair spread across the bed. She's so beautiful, and she's looking at me like she loves me. I can't stop myself from kissing her. At first, it's a gentle peck, but when she opens her mouth, inviting me, I go deeper. I want her so badly. She puts her arms around my neck, and I know. She'll let me make love to her if I ask.

She has all of her memories.

I pull away. Is she so relieved to have me back that she has blind faith I'm the same man she fell in love with? I need to get my head on straight before I take anything from her.

She gives me a hug before I leave. “Nathan, time’s on our side now.”
Reluctantly, I leave her, closing the door behind me.
Then I head to the closet.

CHAPTER 16

The Widow

"Crystal, any guesses about what the hell that is?" Scott's voice rings out over the marina noise as he points across the water. He's standing beside *Adeline's* slip. The vessel he's pointing to has a simple number painted on the hull, but no name and no NOAA insignia. Anchored about a quarter mile offshore, it's an eyesore against the tranquil setting of the island's coast.

I don't know what it is—but I know who's responsible. He's getting out of his car right now, carrying armloads of stuff and wearing another fancy suit. Even though I'm still a little mad at him about going over my head, I have to laugh. Some people have quirks that tell you more about them than their words.

"No idea," I say.

The salty air now tastes sour.

Nothing screams emergency like a huge vessel planted on your doorstep.

The locals are going to have a field day.

Scott and I are waiting at the docks for Nathan. Today's his first dive to see the blue hole. We're not going in, of course.

The blue hole. Carter's Drop.

Nathan knew it was there long before there was any physical proof. Everyone who's heard of him knows of his genius. But what most people aren't aware of is his faith. Faith in his ideas. In himself. In the truth of something that can be studied and understood before it's ever seen.

He'd spent his entire life poring over scholarly and field material on the myth of Atlantis. Once, I'd asked him what made him latch on to that story at such a young age and then stick with it throughout his academic career.

His answer wasn't what I expected.

"I'm not particularly interested in Atlantis," he'd said.

"Uh?" I looked at him like he'd turned into an elephant.

"Do you remember who's credited for the scientific method?"

I'd thought about it for a moment. "Sir Francis Bacon? I think?"

"Yes." He leaned in and kissed me quickly. "But so much of the groundwork was laid by Aristotle's formalization of logic."

I raised an eyebrow. "Does this have anything to do with your fondness for poetry? I feel like you're about to recite me something."

He'd laughed. "No. When I was a boy, I wanted the legend to be true. Badly. As I learned more, I wanted to understand what the legend was based on. Because it was based on something."

"The hubris of man?" I asked.

Surprise flashed across his face, and he nodded. He was always so proud when I solved one of his puzzles.

"When technological power exceeds moral restraint, collapse follows."

"That's a bit grim. What does this have to do with your research, sailor?" Sometimes he could get lost in his head.

"By sticking to logic and not myth, I'm on the brink of finding the truth that inspired the myth. Right here in Maverick Key."

I didn't doubt him.

A few months after he told me he would, he discovered the blue hole. Then, seven months later, he was gone.

Now here we are, years later, still looking for answers.

"What the hell, Finn?" Scott asks as Finn reaches us.

"It's my research lab," Finn answers as he walks up the pier, carrying a huge metal box and his briefcase. "Want to come on board? I'm heading over there right now."

"Who's paying for that monstrosity?"

"There are private investors."

"Has the Coast Guard cleared it?" Scott asks.

"Not quite yet. It just arrived."

"Good luck hiding that thing. They'll be boarding it within the hour."

"Right." Finn throws his stuff into the RIB vessel, unties it, and boards. "I'm getting these specimens to the lab. Based on the condition of the metals and ceramics, they must be tens of thousands of years old. I'm particularly intrigued by the one with the beautiful patina." Waving goodbye, he sails toward the ship.

Finn got all his goodies from the team's first technical dive. Nathan and I were there for the post-dive debriefing. The team successfully reached the *Megaron* and collected the artifacts they were after. Controlled chaos was the best way to describe what they encountered. Halfway down, temperatures approached the upper limits of what could be safely tolerated. And some rocks soared to over four hundred degrees in small clusters throughout the walls of the room. The water was so hot in those spots that it shimmered. Everyone had to stay meters away from the walls. Presumably, this means that the water in some portions of the caves won't be accessible.

Scott turns back to me. "Where's Nathan?"

"Taking Natalie to school. He'll be here soon."

"How are *you* holding up?"

"Good," I say quickly. As much as I love my brother-in-law, I don't want to get into the mess that is my emotions with him. "I'm excited to see him get back into the water today."

Nathan has moved in with us, and I'm relieved to have him back, but my dread about what will happen in Carter's Drop and the diminishing returns my conservation team is experiencing is disheartening.

Our coral restoration dive activity may be doing more harm than good, and we're about to decide whether to pause our work and instead focus on how we can support Dr. Clark and the dive team.

We see Nathan's car pull into the marina lot. He steps out wearing sunglasses and a yellow rash guard. He looks exactly as he used to on boating days. Grabbing his dive bag, he slams the door and walks down the pier.

"There he is."

"Ready to get wet?" Scott calls out as Nathan approaches.

"Ready to see the blue hole."

"It's waiting for you. Let's go see it."

When we board, Maddie's standing there waiting for us on the deck. None of us knew she was coming.

"Maddie? Where's Christopher?" Scott asks, eyeing her and the pink tanks stashed over in the deck's corner suspiciously.

"Ms. Connor."

"...and why are you here, sweetheart?"

"I couldn't miss this." She walks over to Nathan. "You took me on my first dive. So, I'm going to take you on this one," she beams.

Nathan, looking a little worried, smiles back at her.

"Hell, Maddie. You're not diving. You just gave birth a week ago."

She shoots Scott an annoyed look. "I can handle it. I'm prepared, and I won't go too deep. It'll be fine."

"No, ma'am." Scott walks up to her and gives her a sweet kiss.

Maddie pouts. But she knows she can't dive.

"I'll be his buddy on this dive," I tell her. "You can have him next time."

"Dang it. I wanted to, Nathan. Give me a few more weeks, and we'll go."

"I can't wait, Maddie." He hugs her.

"Mads," she whispers. "You always called me Mads."

"Mads."

Her gaze drops to his belt. She stills, then reaches for something. Pulling out one of his dive knives, she stares at it.

"I found it in the closet last night."

"Dad gave this to you."

"Son, be brave. Be free," Nathan recites the inscription.

"He wanted that for you," Maddie says. "You've always been those things. He wanted you to have a tangible reminder of who you are."

Nathan's a graceful diver. Not a word you'd use for most men, but it fits him. His movements are fluid and controlled, seemingly effortless, and his body is perfectly streamlined for swimming. We're wearing thin wetsuits and carrying slates for communication. Scott is with us but stays at a distance, doing his own thing as Nathan and I swim close together side by side. As we near the blue hole, I wonder what he'll feel when he sees it. I expected to see more fish than there are today. When we approach the coral encroachment, I freeze. It's worse than it was last week. Among the vivid golds, reds, and blues are batches of ghostly snow white. Not dead yet—but dying. Tears run down my face, fogging my mask. Nathan looks in my direction and gently touches my arm.

That's when we see it. The entrance to the blue hole.

Still remarkable, but its oasis of life is drying up. Thinner schools of Chromis, deflated sponge, and milky white particles dancing in the air. Beautiful, but fraying at the edges.

Nathan freezes. His eyes are fixed on the dark mouth of the cavern. I touch his back and watch him. He eases closer to it. And closer. Oh no. I tap my tank to get his attention. When he turns, I point away from the hole. He raises his hand and signals to give him a minute. Then he moves forward.

He's going in. Nathan!

Screaming at him isn't an option, and I can't dive caves. Desperately, I search for Scott and see he's not far away, already seeing what Nathan's up to. Is he smiling? Scott gives me a *wait* signal. Then he follows Nathan into the hole.

Forever seems to pass by before they both reemerge. Scott gives us the thumbs up, ending the dive.

Back on the deck, Scott walks over to Nathan and helps him out of his gear. "Not cool, man. Not cool."

"I needed to see it."

Scott tilts his head in my direction but says nothing.

Nathan presses his lips into a thin line, then looks down. "I was out of line."

Scott smiles faintly. Nathan walks over to me. "That was shitty of me. I'll stick to the plan next time. I'm sorry I scared you, Crystal."

It's impossible to be mad, and I believe him when he says he won't do it again.

As we clean up, there's a sudden shift in the wind.

"Maddie, Crystal. Take cover," Scott calls out. "This is going to be a nasty one."

Dark, near-black clouds have swallowed the sky. Where in the world did they come from? Thunder slams in the distance while flashes of electricity scatter overhead. Scott and Nathan immediately start securing the *Adeline*. While Maddie and I find shelter in the cabin.

Storms have always marked turning points in our lives together. They don't scare me anymore. Nathan told me I was the living personification of storm winds to him. Sudden, strong, impatient…

This one is violent, but oddly familiar. So similar to the one Nathan and I encountered on one of our journeys to Belize. After graduation, Nathan remained affiliated with the University of Miami and often worked on marine heritage programs with NOAA. One of those projects was a joint expedition with the University of Belize. For weeks at a time, he'd travel to complete fieldwork. He took me with him a few times, the first shortly after we became a couple. He'd usually fly to Belize, but for this one, he wanted to take me on the *Natalie Dawn*. A weeklong sail. A week that flew by like a dream.

On the first night of the trip, we found ourselves in the middle of a raging storm. Sailing in the big ocean—no land in sight. Somewhere northeast of the Dry Tortugas, the pressure in the air dropped, and we could sense the storm coming. Eerily calm, we prepped the boat as quickly as we could, taking shelter in the cabin as the rain started coming down in curtains. In seconds, it erupted into violent gusts and choppy seas. I tried to act brave, but I was scared.

"Do you know the best thing to do when the waves are rocking your boat?"

"What?" I eyed him suspiciously. More nervous with each shake of the boat and crash of thunder.

"If you can't beat them… join them."

"That's so lame." I laughed at his silly joke anyway. Then I looked in his eyes, and it wasn't so funny anymore.

He eased past the cramped furniture in the berth and stood in front of me. His short gray cotton shirt was soaked, with every muscle I'd memorized visible through the cloth. The urge to touch him was too strong to ignore, even with the fear that the boat was going to be torn apart around us. I pushed my fingers through the belt loops on his shorts and pulled him closer.

Not touching me at all, he tilted his head slightly without easing the intensity of his gaze. Did I do something wrong? His lips were still. Pressed into a firm, straight line. So serious. I'd never seen him like that. I caught my breath as warmth in my core spread through my body, followed by a pleasant tingle. I really hoped I was in trouble.

"You're gonna make me melt," I whispered. I could barely recognize my voice.

Running his tongue across his bottom lip, still not moving an inch, not touching me. "Well… if you're about to melt." Then his face broke into his signature lopsided grin. "I'd better eat you up fast."

My cheeks flamed. Now my whole body was on fire.

Tossing me onto the bottom bunk, he gently pushed down on my chest until I lay flat on my back. Slowly, he lifted my legs and bent my knees to make room for him to get in. With his gaze still locked on my eyes, he crouched between my legs and slowly slid his fingers over my hips. When he got to the waistband of my shorts, he jerked them down and off, slinging them to the floor.

"There's not an inch of you I don't love. I could spend weeks out here on the water. You. Me. This. If everything else in the whole world fell away—you're all I need." He kissed my belly and started the slow trek down, tasting me as he went. "There's something I've been wanting to ask you," he said breathlessly.

"Yes?" I asked, gasping at his light caresses.

Ignoring my question, he continued to trace his tongue along my skin, stopping only when he got to where I wanted him to go.

Distracted, I begged. "What is it you want to ask me? Tell me."

"Mmm," he murmured, blowing wicked puffs of air against me.

"Tell me right now. Nathan—I don't like waiting," I squirmed.

Lifting his head, he gripped my hips tightly. "Patience, you harpy. Lie still." We stared at each other as he pulled me closer. Gently, he stroked my bottom, then squeezed, lowering his head back down, teasing me with one lick. "I'll tell you when I'm done eating."

I forgot all about the storm.

Later that night, after the rain stopped, and the ocean stilled, we held each other under the covers. When he fell asleep, I shook him awake.

"Are you ever going to tell me what you wanted to ask me?" I reminded him.

"Will you marry me?"

CHAPTER 17

The Stranger

Scott and I were battered and soaked by the time we finally eased the *Adeline* into her slip. The squall hit hard but moved on fast. Scott had most of the gear secured before it could become a problem, and I stayed at the helm. By the time the sky cleared, I'd changed into dry clothes in the cabin, but the chill had settled into my bones.

Crystal and I both headed straight back to her house so we could shower, eat, and get cleaned up before it was time to pick up Natalie. This morning, I asked if I could start dropping her off and picking her up from school. I wasn't sure how Crystal would feel about it, but she agreed right away.

It feels good to take a hot shower.

I step into the kitchen, moisture still clinging to my skin. A sandwich and a glass of water are waiting for me on the table.

She made me food.

I swallow hard and try not to look all flustered. She's done this a few times since I moved in, but my body still reacts. After the hospital, no one ever made me food. I want to do something for her.

"How was your morning with Natalie?" she asks as we eat.

"She told me more about her time machine."

Crystal chuckles. "I thought she had put that behind her since you were back."

"She considered it. But she's decided she still needs one. Just in case someone breaks something. Then she can go back and fix it."

"She gets her imagination from you."

We both laugh about our creative daughter. But Natalie believes it's possible, and the best part is she's doing real research to find answers. It's something we can work on together one day.

"Did you do much sailing in Miami?" she asks as we eat.

"Yeah. On friends' boats, mostly. I didn't own one." I shrug. "Another one of those things I just know how to do."

Her gaze lingers on me, softening as if a forgotten memory has drifted back to the surface. "You do own a boat. Her name is *Natalie Dawn.*"

I've always wanted a boat. Curious, I lean in. "Did I name it after Natalie when I found out you were pregnant?"

"Your father named it after your mother." She gets up and puts our empty plates in the sink. "We'd take it out all the time. An '88 Cape Dory. Sometimes you took me with you to Belize on your work trips. Once we even took a weeklong sail."

My mother. Her name was Natalie. The urge to know everything, all at once, hits me again. Hard.

"I've gone through most of the boxes in the closet," I say. "And I've been studying the map of Carter's Drop."

Other than the dive knife my father gave me, most of what I found in the closet was just generic stuff. Dive equipment, framed certificates, college photos, and other odds and ends. Nothing triggered any memories.

"I haven't started on my journals yet. I'm going to dig into those tonight."

She starts washing the dishes, and I take a closer look at her. In a short white cotton dress, she moves through the kitchen like a light breeze. The soft folds of the fabric skim her toned legs as she moves from side to side. She's barefoot, her hair slightly damp from her own shower.

I step closer, closing my eyes for a moment as her scent reaches me. My muscles tense all at once—wired, restless—like I need to move, to do something. "Here. Let me get these," I say, my voice tight.

She doesn't object, stepping aside to let me take over, watching me from the counter. The memory of kissing her rushes to my head, and I try to push it away. I'm so distracted by how my body reacts to her when all I want is for my mind to catch up.

"It'll take time to go through everything, but you will." Her eyes light up. "You were so comfortable today. Right back in your element."

I laugh at that. "Oh, so did I always do stupid shit like I did today?"

"Well… maybe you have always pushed it a bit. But you were a natural out there. Still a sailor through and through."

And she's my siren.

"Do you think there's time to look at some photos together?" I rinse the last dish and dry my hands. "I know you've got to finish getting ready for City Hall."

"I have time. And I'm about as ready as I'm going to be."

"Did you find out what happened with the Coast Guard and that ship?"

She nods. "They were on the ship by the time Finn got there. He handled them. Apparently, he's got someone powerful in his back pocket.

He won't say who." She rolls her eyes. "We're expecting tonight's meeting to be a spectacle. The meeting should answer the townsfolk's questions about the reef restrictions, but with that huge ass ship parked just offshore, it's becoming sensational—fast."

"What do you think of him?"

"Who? Finn?"

I study her face.

"Honestly, I'm not sure what to think. Do I think he's who he says he is, and that he wants to find answers? Yes. Do I think he's telling us everything? No. He's as much as admitted so."

"Do you trust him?"

"Trust?" She bites down on her lip. "Ask me that again in a few weeks."

Leading me to the leather armchair, she opens the picture album and snuggles in beside me.

I slide an arm around her. Her closeness kicks my heart rate up, and I swallow audibly. Her soft curves press against my side, warming my skin and my blood, and that scent of her…

"Is this good?" she whispers, her weight shifting slightly.

I nod. It takes a moment to find my voice. "That's some album," I say hoarsely. At least eight inches thick, it's crammed full of photographs.

"I only keep the ones that mean the most."

She flips to a page filled with photos of a place I recognize right away. In the middle is a photo of me lying on a towel, eyes closed. I look so young.

"Miami," I say.

She nods. "The day we met."

"Tell me about it…"

An hour goes by as we turn the pages. Crystal tells me each story of my life in such vivid detail, it's like I'm there, experiencing it.

She tells me stories of my college years in Miami, and how Mark and I were friends first, before we met Crystal. Then she rescued Mark and became my mentee. For a moment, I wonder what would have happened if Mark had drowned that day. Fate can be incredibly merciful and cruel.

As we go, she turns back to the pages of the years before we met. Mom. Dad. Maddie—I mean Mads.

And my dreams about Atlantis.

"I'm going to pace out all the big stories—not tell them all at once." She tells me with a playful smile. Her protectiveness of our memories warms my heart. These photos are treasures to her. Her most valuable possessions.

She's bringing me hope. Maybe I can relive my life through her memories, even if I can't reach them myself. Is a distant memory any different from what a great storyteller can create for you?

I'm at war with my mind. She's already won my heart.

She closes the album. "Whew… maybe that's enough for now." Flushed, she looks at me with those eyes of hers. She shifts on my lap, searching for comfort, and instead finds the heat coiled tightly beneath my skin. I'm on fire.

Not thinking about what I'm doing, I pull her toward me and kiss her. Our tongues begin to dance, and she moans my name, which kills me.

"Crystal." My body reacts instantly. Like muscle memory, I know exactly how to hold her. Pushing my hips into hers, she opens to me with her warmth and her trust. When she sighs in my mouth, I no longer think about all the things I don't know. I know I want her.

I carry her to my room, gently laying her on the bed. Flat on her back, she pulls the white dress over her head and tosses it. The sight of her kills me. No bra. No panties. God help me.

She's more gorgeous than I imagined—and I've fantasized. With no shortage of opportunities for sexual encounters in Miami, and no lack of desire, I still felt a primal need to remain faithful. Just because I couldn't remember didn't mean there wasn't someone waiting for me. And it felt important to wait.

But now I don't want us to wait anymore. Rushing to her, I pull her legs around me. God, she's so soft and warm. Desperately, I push forward and stop just at her entrance. I want nothing as badly as I want to be inside her right now.

But I freeze.

I don't know what the hell I'm doing. A wave of guilt washes over me.

This isn't fair to her. It's too soon.

What if I take something I can't give back?

If I could remember one thing. One detail. Her favorite way to be touched, the sounds she makes when I'm inside her, what she looks like when we've finished. Something. I don't just want sex with her. I want to give her all of me.

"Nathan?" Her forehead creases as her gaze searches mine.

"Crystal..." I gently pull the sheet around her and sit, turning my head away.

"I want this. It's okay…" she says. Sitting up, she lifts her hand to my face, turning me back to her. "Let me give this to you." Tears fill her eyes. Her hands trace my neck and slide down until she stops at the dip in my neck.

"I can't do this. Not yet. I'm so sorry." Heat rushes to my face.

She lets go and puts her finger to my lips, taking a deep breath. Then smiles. "I had so much fun today."

"Me too," I say quickly, thankful to push past the awkwardness. My failure.

She glances at the wall. "Oh shoot, I'm almost late for the town hall meeting. Come with me? You can leave when it's time to pick up Natalie. I'll get a ride home."

CHAPTER 18

The Stranger

We've been circling the City Hall parking lot for over twenty minutes. It's slap full, and the lines of cars parked along the roadsides stretch in all directions for over a mile. I grip the steering wheel tighter as a truck coming from the opposite direction cuts me off and stops right in front of us. The passenger jumps out and attempts to direct the driver into a narrow opening. Then the tailgater behind me taps my bumper, waving his arm out the window as he slams on his horn.

Damn it. Dropping Crystal off at the entrance may be the only option at this point.

"What the hell are we about to walk into?"

She raises a finger, still talking animatedly with someone on the phone.

I notice the news vans and cameras parked right at the entrance. Shit. What are they here for?

Finally, she hangs up and turns to me. "Scott wants us to park at Spock's Ice and meet Sid and her team. There's still some parking there, and they've got bikes."

The truck in front of us has squeezed a couple more feet over to the right, enough for me to edge around it. After a few more near collisions, I get us back on the road and fall back three blocks to the ice cream parlor.

Spock's Ice. With bright pink walls, light green trim, and a striped awning, the building looks good enough to eat.

"You want some ice cream while we're here?" I ask her, only half joking.

"Maybe later." She laughs as she gathers her notes and puts them into her tan satchel. "Or you can stop by with Natalie. She loves it. Her favorite is wild watermelon with lychee popping boba."

"Over there." I point to Sid and the bikes. She's standing with a few of her crew at the curb.

As we walk up, Sid hands me a helmet while another guy hands one to Crystal. "Hop on. Nathan, you're with me. Crystal, Heath's got you."

I buckle the chin strap of my helmet and get behind Sid.

"We're going to get y'all right to the entrance," she says. "When we do, head straight for the door. Don't stop for anyone. Scott and Liam are already waiting and ready to fight them back."

"Fight them back?" Crystal asks. Her voice is hoarse.

"Looks like the word's out that Nathan's alive. This is all about him."

What the hell? I'm already creating chaos for the people I love.

Crystal looks my way and mouths, "It'll be okay."

We take off.

It's even worse now. There's not an inch of space left, and anyone who arrived early is blocked in. It's going to take hours for this mess to clear out later.

"I've got to pick up Natalie in about an hour," I tell Sid as we move at a slow crawl into the parking lot.

"No worries. I'll get you back to your car when you need to go."

Is she sure about that? The bikes can squeeze through for now, but it's a challenge even for them.

"K, Nathan. Listen up. You've already got eyes on you, and they're about to charge. I'll get us right on the steps and will try to hold them back. Run for Scott."

I glance over my shoulder, looking for Crystal.

"Hold on tight, here we go."

Sid presses hard on the gas, and we whirl around the sharp corner into the building's porte-cochère. She jerks the bike, and it bounces up several steps of the staircase.

"Run," she commands.

Jumping off, I run. Instantly, a crowd of reporters swarms around me. Calls and shouted questions from dozens of voices ring in my ears.

"Nathan, where have you been all these years?"

"What are you hiding?"

"Can you do an interview? We'll pay you."

Sid throws her arms out, blocking a handful of the mob behind me. "Hey guys, I'm his rep. You want to ask him something, you go through me."

Liam and Scott are by my side now and begin shoving those who have followed me. The guard at the front door opens it and closes it as soon as I'm through. Scott and Liam stay outside. Scanning the room, there's no sign of Crystal.

I consider going back when Sid rushes through the door, Crystal by her side.

Then her crew comes in, walking their bikes.

"Who did this?" Crystal's shaken up and angry. "Scott told everyone to keep their mouths shut. Nathan deserves some peace."

Pulling Crystal to my chest, I try to calm her.

"Daddy Dearest." Sid glares at the stage. Garrett and Finn are already there. "Sorry, guys. This was a rotten thing to do. Even for him."

"Thank you for your help," I say.

"I'll be in the back. Let me know when it's time to pick up Natalie."

Holding her hand tightly, I escort Crystal toward the stage. "Are you sure you want to do this? You could call in sick."

"It's a little too late for that." She laughs half-heartedly and brushes down the creases in her dress and squeezes my arm.

Finn notices Crystal and walks over.

"You okay?" Finn asks her, "This is a mob."

"We're good," she says.

Then he looks at me and grins. "You're famous. Seems like everyone in this town wants your autograph."

He rests a hand on her shoulders. "Mind if I steal her?"

What I want to do is punch his arm away, but I nod, and he guides her the rest of the way to the dais.

I find a seat a few rows away from the stage. Thankfully, no reporters were allowed inside, but I can feel the heat of hundreds of curious eyes burning my skin. As soon as I meet anyone's gaze, they dart their eyes away.

And the whispers—I try to ignore them.

One set of eyes grabs my attention—because they are hidden behind dark glasses and seem to be fixed on me.

And the man they belong to is smiling. At me?

Immediately, I'm on guard. But then a woman walks up to him and whispers something in his ear. They laugh and walk off.

Something's off. I get the sense that I know him. I look for him again in the crowd, but he's gone.

The audience is getting restless, the chatter louder, and less of the crowd's attention is on me as they become focused on the stage.

A heavyset man finally walks in from the back of the curtain to the microphone. Tapping it, he clears his throat and begins speaking with a warm, easygoing drawl.

"Welcome, folks." He smiles and calmly waits for most of the chatter to stop. "Most of you know me, but for those I haven't met, I'm Mayor Bent." There's still some light murmuring in the crowd. But most have quieted down and are waiting to hear what's going on.

"You want answers. I do too. That's why we've got these smart folks here with me." He gestures to the speakers behind him. "Dr. Harlow—you may know him from the Carter's Drop dives, Dr. Phineas Clark from West Virginia, and Mrs. Crystal Glassier, our very own marine biologist." He gives a curt nod. "They'll bring us up to speed. Hold your questions till the end, and we'll get to 'em."

He steps aside and motions for Finn to come forward.

Finn takes the podium and politely bows his head to the crowd. His tall, elegant stature and science-nerd style of dress signal trustworthiness. He gives a brief introduction and then jumps into the facts.

"The truth is, we don't yet know what's warming the waters." Fearful gasps fill the room. He continues to explain the current situation and what he and the team of cave divers and scientists are doing to find answers.

"But we *will* find out what's going on, and we *will* find a solution. You have my word."

I roll my eyes. I don't care who the hell you are. You can't make guarantees like that. Failure is always a possibility.

He wraps up his presentation and then opens the floor for questions. Most people raise their hands to speak, but a few shout out rudely, canceling each other out. He ignores them until everyone behaves.

"You, yes, you. Lady in the green dress."

The woman speaks fast, tripping over her words. "My friend's son got a rash a few days ago. After swimming at the beach. And some of my neighbors aren't feeling well. Hundreds of dead jellyfish cover the beach every morning until they're cleaned up." Her voice rises, strained. "Is it dangerous?"

"No. It's not dangerous, but we are concerned. Ms. Glassier will go over the environmental impacts. And I'm afraid those impacts have brought us to a difficult decision that I'll let Mayor Bent speak to."

Loud chatter erupts from the crowd. The woman sitting to my left twists her closed hands tighter, her face a wall of worry. I get her attention and whisper, "It's going to be okay." Some of the tension leaves her face.

Mayor Bent walks back up to the microphone, relieving Finn.

"Friends. When I was told this news, I swore like a sailor and demanded we find another way. But NOAA and Coast Guard officials have made the call, and I'm on board. We're closing all the beaches and suspending recreational aquatic activity from Maverick Key's shoreline to the waters surrounding the reef."

An explosion of loud conversation takes over the room as some people surge to their feet as if they plan to storm the stage. Police officers who have been idle until now move quickly, corralling agitated citizens back to their seats.

"Why is that big military ship anchored less than a mile offshore? What aren't you telling us!" one man yells over the commotion.

"Folks, I need you to quiet down a little so I can speak." A flurry of shushes rolls through the audience. Mayor Bent continues. "We've called in all the big guns. That ship is where they're doing their fancy lab work."

The man eyes the mayor skeptically and asks another question.

My alarm vibrates. It's time to leave so I can pick up Natalie.

Standing to leave, I try to wave goodbye to Crystal, but she doesn't see me. I hate leaving her here in this mess.

When I find Sid, she waves me down the hallway and out to a narrow alley where she's moved her bike. The passage is squeezed between two sections of the concrete block building.

A quiet hiding place tucked away from the curious mob who's waiting for a glimpse of Nathan Carter.

"You and Crystal are going to get a lot of attention you didn't ask for now. And your little girl." She frowns. "Take her somewhere else until all this settles down."

"Won't your dad just tell them anything we do?"

"Yeah, well." She swallows. Fighting *tears*? "He and I are going to have a little chat. I'm fucking tired of him messing around with everyone's lives." For a moment, her tough exterior slips, and she's just a little girl. One who loves her father. And still knows he's a world-class asshole.

"For what it's worth. You're not him. Thanks again for today."

She drops me off at Spock's Ice, and I drive to the school.

I'm on the parent pickup list and have all the instructions for following the school's safety protocols. Sweat pools at my hairline. I'm late. School was dismissed twenty minutes ago.

When I pull into the parking lot and scan the sidewalk for Natalie, I spot her sitting alone on a bench. Thank God. No other kids are left, but there's an older man standing beside her. He must be a chaperone.

Closer, I notice he's not wearing a volunteer safety belt. A jolt of fear shoots through me. Picking up the pace, I rush over to her. His eyes widen in shock when he sees me, and he turns and bolts.

What the hell?

"Hey!" I shout, getting a nearby police officer's attention. "He was talking to my little girl."

The officer darts off after the man.

Crouching down, I catch my breath and put my hands on her shoulders. "You okay, Sugar Muffin?"

Her little face crunches up in concern. "He's a nice man, Daddy. I know I'm not supposed to talk to strangers, but I'm at school with the policeman." She points to the policeman who's returning empty-handed.

I hug her.

After the officer confirms he lost the guy and takes my information, we go home.

♥

I look at the clock for the five-hundredth time. Crystal's still not back. I hate that she's still in the middle of that chaos, and I'm worried that anything could have happened to her. Car accident, mugging. I should have stormed the stage and taken her with me. I check my cell again—no response to my text. Even though Natalie's just finished a jumbo watermelon gelato with bursting boba, I cook her some mac and cheese.

She finishes her plate and asks for more.

I shake my head. "Where are you putting all the food?"

She laughs and rubs her tummy. "In here, silly." I poke the tip of her nose, which earns me a squeal.

After we finish eating, I ask her to tell me what the man said to her, and then brace myself for her answer.

"He said he knew you, Daddy, and he was sorry you died." What? My muscles tense, every protective instinct flaring. "He told me I needed to tell my momma to stay away from the scientists. That they are all dangerous. And he said a *Big, Mean Man* is in Maverick Key."

What the hell?

How am I going to protect them when I can't remember what I got myself into as Nathan Carter? I think of the guy with the sunglasses and the man who scared Crystal. I'm the root cause of all this. I know it. I've got to get through my journals and find some answers fast.

"I'm scared, Daddy. The scientists and the *Big, Mean Man* won't hurt Momma, will they?"

"No. I won't let that happen. I promise I'll always keep you and Momma safe." Thousands of possibilities race through my mind. "Did he say anything else?"

"He said his name was Walter."

CHAPTER 19

The Widow

The lock turns with a click. Careful not to make a sound, I inch the door open. It's ten thirty, so I know Natalie's asleep, and Nathan might be too. I'd texted him back earlier to let him know not to wait up for me.

The town knows Nathan Carter's alive, and it won't be long before they know where he lives. At least no one followed him home tonight, but we both know those crazy reporters will show up eventually.

What a long day.

A soft glow spills from the living room. Nathan's up. He's on the floor flipping through his journals with a plate of Natalie's chocolate chip cookies beside him—half eaten. Another favorite food they share. When he sees me, he gets up and crosses the room, reaching for me. His walk is relaxed and confident. There's my Nathan.

"Missed you," he says.

He brushes his lips against mine.

I gesture toward the books and papers scattered across the floor. "Find anything interesting?"

"A lot, actually." He sits back down and pats the floor next to him. "Join me?"

Sliding out of my heels, I cross my legs and settle in beside him.

"When I'm reading through my text, it feels like I'm writing the words down for the first time."

He moves through a stack of journals until he finds the one he's looking for. Flipping through its pages, he shows me his college dissertation. The one that earned him a ProQuest award and put him on the academic map. A thesis about the descendants of Atlantis.

"Did you learn you're a genius today?" I wiggle his chin.

He lets out a short laugh. "Hah, right?" He shifts and riffles through another stack of papers and notebooks, pulling out a newer leather-bound one.

"What's that?"

"Elliot's diary." My heart skips. He kept a diary as Elliot.

He flips through the pages and turns them to face me. He has the same handwriting, and the sketch he's pointing at was drawn in the same style as the other work he drew years ago.

Am I looking at...?

"It's the stone," I whisper.

"This was a hobby of mine in Miami." He laughs. "This, along with watching Discovery Channel, National Geographic, Expedition Unknown—all of them."

"See... you've never been that far away from yourself."

"This drawing. It's the stone Finn is talking about, right?"

"Yes."

"I thought I drew it for fun. But it had to be something I remembered." He shakes his head. "Anyway, there's something that's bothering me."

Curious, I wait for him to continue.

He turns back to one of the older journals. “My theories changed—evolved—into something more complicated than archaeology. Especially toward the end... I started consulting with others on...” he stops.

Oh no. Not this again. “Nathan, what? Tell me.”

“I’m not sure where I’m going with this. I don’t want to scare you with any half-baked assumptions right now. Let me dig into it a little more.” He picks up another journal.

I put my hand over his.

“No more secrets. You’ve tried to keep danger from me in the past—look what happened.”

A red flush flares across his cheeks. “I’m so sorry I left you with him.” He lowers his head, defeated. Immediately, I regret my words and feel my own face heat.

“I shouldn’t have said that.” I have to make him understand that I can’t do this again. “I’m your ally. You’re my best friend. Don’t keep secrets from me this time. I can help you.”

He lifts his gaze, opens his mouth, then closes it. He’s a man at war with himself.

Finally, he nods.

“Okay,” he says as he clutches my hand. “I’ll share what I know. After I found Carter’s Drop and the warm stone, I started questioning how a civilization as advanced as Atlantis could even exist more than a myriad years ago.” He takes a deep breath. “The isolation of technology to a single location with one destruction event didn’t make sense, even though my research was leading me to evidence that an advanced society did indeed exist.” He shakes his head in frustration. “I consulted with other scientists in rapid succession. But in typical-*me* fashion, I never spell out exactly what I was looking for anywhere in these journals.”

He frowns and runs his fingers through his hair.

"Keep looking. You'll figure it out. I know you will," I say, gently pulling his hands away from his head. "And I'll be right beside you this time."

I pick up an old book lying on the side of the pile of notebooks. A bookmark taken from the ones I keep on the end table holds his place at about 30 percent.

Has he read this from the beginning?

"Look at this one yet?" I ask innocently.

He glances at the book of poetry by Lord Byron. "Yeah." Heat rushes across the skin on his chest to his neck. He tugs on the collar of his shirt and sits straighter.

"You used to read these to me sometimes… and works from other poets… and even your own poems." He can't quite make eye contact. Might as well make him blush some more. "Especially when you were horny."

He coughs and tries to stop smiling.

I laugh at him. "Reciting beautiful poems and bad jokes. Those were your tells."

"Maybe I'm not all that different now." His voice is low and husky. I feel the heat rising on my neck now. It felt so good to be in his arms earlier today. I want him so much. All of him.

"You're just the same, Nathan. There's no difference."

It's true. It's strange, but there's absolutely nothing different about him. How is that possible with no memory? More than ever, I want him back. I'm crawling out of my skin.

His eyes soften and glisten. Tiny tears bead at the edges. I gently remove a few with my thumb.

"Show me some more of your research," I say.

He jumps back into his journals until he flicks his eyes back up to meet mine, remembering something. "I can't believe I didn't lead with this." Hesitating, he continues. "Something happened when I picked up Natalie."

A cold rush of fear sweeps over me. "Is she okay?"

"Yes. When I drove up, a man was speaking to her alone. He was about sixty, with a trim beard."

As he tells me about the encounter with the man Natalie called *Walter*, my heart drops to my stomach. Could it be the same man who was watching me that night with the dogs?

"He didn't touch her, but the things he said to her..." he tells me what Walter said, and I share what happened the night I watched the dogs.

"God, Nathan. What in the world is going on? Who is he?" I stand and start moving in circles. I need to do something. Get her out of here.

He puts his arms around me and takes a breath. "Ssh… I'll keep both of you safe…"

"She can't stay here right now."

"No. Where can we take her?"

I could take her to a motel out of town, but then I'm abandoning all my responsibilities and the town's folk during a crisis. And where would we go? Some random place far away from all the people in our lives and from the answers we need to find. Neither of us has family living outside of Maverick Key.

"Maddie," I say. "Natalie's comfortable sleeping over at the beach house, and she'll be nearby with family."

He nods, agreeing.

After we call Maddie and triple-check the doors and windows to be sure the house is all locked up, we sit back on the couch.

When will this day end? I'm so exhausted. Inside and out. But when I look at Nathan, he's still wide awake. The photo album in his hand.

He turns back to the photos of our first beach day in Miami. "Can you tell me the story of how we met again? Please."

Should I tell him I admired him in silence for months before we met? And that I asked for that exact lifeguard duty when I heard his friends talking about their plans for the beach. Not only did I want to learn from him—that was true—but I also had a huge crush on him. A crush that grew into friendship and into love at the same time.

"When I saw you on the beach, I decided to shoot my shot and ask you to be my mentor. I was all coolness and confidence. Drew you right into saying yes."

"I'm sure you did." His golden-brown eyes sparkle.

"You had one task for me—explain diel vertical migration. I aced it. And the rest was history."

"Do it again…" he whispers. His voice is low and deep. "Describe it all to me, every detail. Go slow."

"All right." As I retell the lesson that I gave him beat for beat, he holds me to his chest, massaging my neck with an occasional murmur and chuckle. The faint scent of salt from the ocean clings to his skin. It never completely washes away. And he's warm. His heart is beating a million beats a minute. And he's… My voice grows breathier as I soak him in.

When I get to the end, he gazes into my eyes.

Then a switch flips, and that quiet fire of his flares.

He clears his throat. "She…"

Kissing my hand, he lets his lips linger against my skin. "*She walks in beauty like the night… and all that's best of dark and bright… meet in her aspect and in her eyes…*" I hold my breath and wait for him to kiss me.

He doesn't make me wait long.

Warm, soft lips cover mine, and he eagerly explores my mouth. Murmuring appreciation, he pulls me onto his lap, moving his hands from my waist to my breasts. Firmly but gently squeezing them.

I moan and deepen the kiss.

Moving on, he caresses my back—then lower. A shiver jolts down my spine when he bites down on my bottom lip at the same time. I pull his shirt out of his pants and slide my hands up his chest.

Letting myself breathe him in and breathe him out, I take in his oxygen and let go of all my doubts.

When he finally breaks the kiss, his words are choppy—rushed.

"I want you so much, Crystal. But."

Please don't stop this time. I need you, Nathan.

"I need to be sure that I'm the man you want. I know you think I will right now, but I may never get my memories back… In fact, it's more likely that I won't."

I hate that for him. That he may never regain the beautiful memories of his life. But I wasn't lying. All our interaction, and how I've seen him act around others.

He's the same man.

"I love you, Nathan. You. Just as you are right now. I don't want anyone else."

He lets out a small sound and pulls me closer, kissing my neck, working his way back to my lips.

Before I let him take me to bed, I get the one thing I've been holding on to off my chest. I don't want to do it. But I have to. I gently break our kiss.

"Do you have questions about Mark and our… *relationship*? I'll never mention him again if you don't want to know anything, but if you want to know—I'll tell you everything."

"I don't care a damn thing about Mark." He glances away, pure hate etched across his features, then returns his softer gaze to mine. "But I do want to know everything. To know what he put you through."

Taking my mouth with more urgency, he adds on a breath. "Just not tonight. If that's okay."

"What are you waiting for, sailor?"

He carries me to my bedroom and sets me on my feet while he locks the door and turns on the fan and radio. Fiddling with the knobs until he gets to a station playing something passably romantic. That makes me giggle. He doesn't want Natalie to hear anything. He's forgotten that he's a quiet lover.

Then he turns to face me.

Taking the air in quick gasps, I search his face, wondering what he'll do next. Will he pull me close and lose himself in me like he did during the storm at sea? Or ask me to undress slowly, the way he did on his birthday after I told him I was pregnant. Or maybe it will be like our honeymoon in Belize, when he promised to make love to me all night and kept his word... and then did it all over again the next morning...

His hands tremble as he reaches for me, fumbling with the buttons on my dress. I gently still his fingers and kneel in front of him instead. When I look up, his desert eyes have darkened. Full of desire and something else.

Slowly, I unbuckle his pants and study his face as he watches them fall. His heart is beating so loudly.

Or maybe that's *my* heart.

Pushing his hips toward me, he gives me his answer, and I take him.

He slips his fingers into my hair, holding me there as he draws me closer. I follow his lead, hands tight on his hips, glancing up now and then to catch the storm in his eyes.

"Please. Just like that." His grip tightens.

His moans build until he takes over, shifting the pace with confidence. When I take a breath, he scoops me up and tumbles with me onto the bed.

He slides his fingers under my panties. Impatient, he grunts and quickly pulls his own pants down, positioning himself at my center. But then he stops.

He looks up with desperation in his eyes. “Can I?”

“Please, I’m on birth control.”

He rolls his hips once, watching me closely. “Like this?”

“Yes, but more. Make love to me, Nathan.”

He moans and squeezes his eyes shut tightly, and I gasp when he pushes into me and lets himself go, muttering words I’d never heard him use in bed. He rarely said anything. He didn’t have to. I join him, running my fingers through his hair, down his back, further.

Still a quiet lover, he’s overcome with so much pent-up desire that he lets out his baser thoughts in undertones. I urge him on and let him know everything he’s doing right. Even though it’s like the first time for him, he instinctively remembers all the right ways to touch me, and he takes his time.

After, we hold each other under the covers. Saying little things. Sweet things. When we’re on the verge of sleep, he gently rolls me over to face him. “Crystal?” he asks, brushing hair from my eyes.

Yes, I mouth silently. I’m too tired to speak.

“I’m ready for this. For us.”

CHAPTER 20

The Stranger

The weather's perfect today. Clear blue waters for miles and a white-hot sun. The mid-December air smells fresh, alive, bursting with energy.

Just like I feel.

Crystal's working, Natalie's safe with Mads and Ms. Connor, and I'm about to take my first dive into the tunnels of the blue hole—Carter's Drop.

I still haven't gotten used to the name.

During the deck briefing, we confirmed today's assignments and buddy pairings. I'm a part of something.

And now *I know who I am*—Dr. Nathan Carter. Albeit with a terrible memory, but still.

The more I read through my journals and spend time with my family and friends, the more connections I'm making with my past. It all fits. Crystal says I'm the same man she fell in love with. Being together feels easy and natural. And I dream of her. Not the one lonely dream anymore. But memories. Each one building on the last.

After the last few nights, I should be exhausted. Instead, I'm exhilarated. I can take on the world.

Scott walks over.

"You're in a good mood," he says. He's trying not to smirk, but it's not working.

I shrug.

"One of those nights, huh?"

"Maybe."

He smiles and squeezes my shoulder. "I'm happy for both of you. Ready to do this today?"

"Absofuckinglutely."

I've memorized the maps. I know the layout of everything charted so far. On the map I drew years ago, it's just numbers and notes. Nothing's labeled. The newer surveys show the names the team has been giving to the rooms and passages as they chart the system. The *Megaron* is the biggest chamber. It's the one I discovered the day I went missing. *Hecate* is the longest run of tunnels, and that's where I'll be going with Finn and Margaret today.

"I envy you. Jamie and I are stuck with Sid's camera team. She wants to complete the footage of the *Megaron* for her documentary trailers." Frowning, he mutters, "Fucking cameras."

Yeah. I don't envy him.

"You good on the *Hecate* route and the jumps?"

I nod and tap my temple. "Are we focusing on *Hecate* because of Finn's heat scopes?"

"No," he says. "Other than the branches off the *Megaron*, *Hecate* runs the deepest on sonar. Finn wants to go deep. He thinks the heat's the most intense at the ends."

"So what? Are we going to scrape the heat from the walls?" I'm still waiting for someone to clarify the plan. Oh, that's right. There isn't one. "What do you think *this* is?" I ask.

"I've got no idea. That's why we're here. Explorers." He grins and picks up his gear. "Today's about data and assessment. All that science shit you nerds go crazy for."

"Do you trust Finn?"

"No," he says without hesitation. "But I'm not the best judge. Either way, watch your back. Margaret's in charge today. Don't go any farther than the lines, Nathan. Not today."

"Got it."

He walks toward the platform. "All right, let's gear up," he calls out.

Beneath the surface at the drop line, we equalize and check each other for leaks and trim. Scott and Finn decided we were going to use full-face masks with comms to make team communication easier.

We begin our descent, equalizing every few feet as we swim toward the blue hole.

My heart rate picks up as we get closer.

When I dove with Crystal and Scott the other day, it was an out-of-body experience. I felt like I was going to die. Or that I already had. As we neared the entrance to Carter's Drop, I saw myself from a distance. I watched as I swam into the mouth, and then as it closed around me.

Then I followed myself in.

Scott gave me shit as soon as he reached me, but I'd gotten a glimpse of the thing that had killed me. Not my body, but my mind.

Now here I am again.

It looms in front of me. The same. But slightly different.

As if it's alive.

And waiting.

Our lights illuminate the cavern's limestone walls as we swim into the main chamber. We level off at twenty-five feet. Stalactites hang from the ceiling like crystal chandeliers, while wide stalagmites rise from the floor in columns of varying height and diameter, like ancient pillars. It's a large, open, well-lit cavern, with seven main tunnel openings. A jagged entrance to the right leads to the *Megaron*. The unassuming, nearly flat opening to the left marks the start of the *Hecate* tunnels.

Scott calls Clint on comms. "Clint, we've reached the cavern, and we're about to split."

"Copy boss. Everything's good topside. We're ready to check in at the sixty-minute mark."

Scott ends his communication with Clint and turns to us.

"We regroup here in two hours max. Safety check at sixty. Stay alert." We make eye contact, and he gives me a Shaka signal.

Then our teams split and head in opposite directions.

STOP! Prevent your death...

Our team passes the Grim Reaper cave-diving warning sign and enters *Hecate*.

It's gorgeous.

Most of the limestone is sculpted smooth, and the water is so clear that the passageway takes on a velvety midnight-blue hue under our lights. Per the surveys, the *Hecate* passages are much wider and easier to navigate than the tunnels leading to the *Megaron.* With a large area and limited mineral formations due to the stronger channel flow, there's plenty of space to move around in here and avoid the walls. At least as far as it's been explored. Sonar suggests a main flow crossroads about a third of the way down, where the routes start to pinch tight, and the traverse options become gnarly. But we'll be going nowhere near that today.

I didn't notice it in the cavern, but the water is getting uncomfortably warm in here already. I check my dive computer.

We're only thirty meters in.

Margaret and Finn also notice the heat.

"If we run into any of your shimmering patches, what's the protocol?" Margaret asks Finn.

"If we see them, we'll turn back at once. But we're unlikely to run into a sudden shift in temperature that we won't detect in time to survive."

"That's reassuring," Margaret says sarcastically.

For a scientist, Finn acts on gut and intuition more than I'd expect. But I guess that's why we're in the caves right now, actually doing something instead of in a room talking in circles.

Finn curses. "Eighty-four degrees. Bloody hell."

We've got summer open water temperatures in here, in a cave. I'm going to be just as pissed as him if we have to end the dive before we've even started it.

"Bollocks. We just jumped to eighty-six degrees."

"One more degree of buffer," Margaret says.

Finn pauses and studies the data on his computer. A small nod, as if a decision has been made. "We can push to ninety-two for a short period. Watch your exertion. Fifteen minutes tops once we get there."

The hell? What's he doing? He's the one who suggested the safety maximum of eighty-seven degrees.

"We're not doing that. We dive the plan," Margaret states, staring at Finn with disdain.

"Right. Well, for now we're still holding at eighty-six degrees."

We continue. Pointing my flashlight at the line for Margaret so she can inspect it, she checks it quickly and then moves to the next tie-off. After a few minutes, I notice our breathing is elevated, and my cheeks are burning. I pull away the neck collar to flush my suit. It does very little to relieve the heat. We'll get heatstroke if we don't get out of here soon. Margaret snaps her head toward me.

"It's too hot." She swivels around. "Where's Finn?" I look around and don't see him either.

She presses on her PTT. "Finn, where the hell are you?"

Margaret raises her voice. "Finn?"

She switches channels. "Scott, we have a problem. Finn's pushing limits. Suggested we could go hotter. Now he's out of sight."

"When?"

"Six minutes. My temperature reading is ninety."

"The fuck—" Scott says something to Jamie. "I'm calling the dive. Jamie and Liam will guide Sid's team out. You and Nathan leave now. I'm heading to the *Hecate* for Finn."

"Copy." Margaret anxiously scans the passages, still looking for Finn. Then she turns to me. "You heard him. We're ending the dive."

I stare at the tunnel offshoot where I last saw Finn and point.

"I'm going to check that tunnel. He was there. He couldn't have gone anywhere else."

"Scott said…"

"I know. But there's no time. It's too hot."

Reluctantly, Margaret nods. "Ten minutes tops."

Quickly, I enter the tunnel. My God. It's like a hot tub in here. I was sweating in my suit a few minutes ago, but now I'm too hot to sweat. I'm cooking. Checking the temperature, I'm shocked to see ninety-six degrees. No wonder my heart is pounding in my chest and ears. I'm already way past the danger zone for hyperthermia. I swipe my light from left to right, top-down, searching for any sign of him. This will take longer than ten minutes.

"Finn, where are you, man?"

Silence.

Then I spot him. His head is tilted to the side, and his body has drifted toward the ceiling. His fins are still. The light in his hand points aimlessly as his arms move in slow, erratic reaching motions. His leg is wrapped around a line, the only thing keeping him from crashing into the limestone.

He's completely disoriented, but he's alive. We've got to get out of here, or we're going to die.

Approaching him with caution, I catch his harness and yank him back into position. After I flush his suit, I try to talk to him. His eyes are still open, but he's listless. Adjusting his torso to move his body parallel to the guideline, I push his light to point ahead and adjust his wing inflation and position.

Keeping my grip on his harness strap, I haul him back through the offshoot into the tunnel where Margaret is waiting.

My head is pounding, my fingers growing weaker, and it takes everything I have to keep my hold on Finn. Margaret grabs onto him, and together we drag him into the main tunnel. As we swim toward the exit, the water cools fast with the fresh flow. My breathing finally evens out. Margaret's does too. Finn is conscious, but he's out of it, mumbling incoherently.

He's lucky to be here. We all are, I think darkly.

We cross paths with Scott a few meters from reaching the main cavern.

"Is he?" Scott asks.

“He’s alive,” I say.

“Great. Because I’m killing him when we reach the surface.”

CHAPTER 21

The Widow

Parking behind Scott's truck, I turn off the engine and sit with my thoughts.

As an orphan, I learned early on not to let my emotions control me. Anger. Fear. Sadness. Controlling them has been my key to survival. Nothing good ever comes from committing to an action while you're emotional. Expectations are also dangerous.

People will always disappoint you.

Hyperthermia.

As soon as I'd gotten the call from Maddie, I'd rushed to the inn.

Finn almost got everyone killed.

I'd given him the benefit of the doubt and trusted his initial kindness. The arrogant piece of shit nearly got the man I love killed—again.

Natalie has her father back. And Nathan and I have spent some of the best nights of our lives together. Not only are our nightly photo sessions bringing his memories back, piece by piece, but we're also discovering a connection that's even deeper.

There's nothing like knowing—really knowing—what you have to lose and how quickly you can lose it to put things in perspective.

If there's anything left of Finn when I get inside…

My phone rings. My boss.

He's pausing our daily sample captures and all other diving activity. Fourteen more residents were admitted to the hospital for toxin exposure and jellyfish stings. He's handing the reins over to the Feds. Consultation and analysis for us only.

NOAA has escalated this as an environmental emergency.

A cold fear brushes over my skin. The Navy and DARPA are involved now. It's that serious. I respect authority, but I'm worried.

"Do you have any idea where Finn is?" my boss asks. "The mayor's team has been trying to get him on the phone all day."

They don't know that Finn's been at the hospital all afternoon, along with Nathan and Margaret, being treated for hyperthermia.

"He's here at the Driftwood," I say and leave it at that. I'll let Finn explain his own shit to them.

I take a breath and try to calm down, then I walk to the inn.

It's silent inside. I smell the remnants of dinner—fried chicken and mashed potatoes. Takeout boxes are stacked in the kitchen trash can.

Where is everyone?

I know Maddie and Ms. Connor are at the beach house with the kids, but Scott has been staying over here every night along with his crew so they can work around the clock and consult with Garrett and Finn. They're using it as an operational base camp.

The back door is open. I step out onto the porch.

There they are. Gathered around the pool, talking in low voices.

Finn is wrung out on a chair, eyes half-closed, with a towel around his neck. I don't care that he looks half dead. He's going to get a piece of my mind. I walk straight to him. Startled, his shoulders pull back.

"You could have killed them."

He looks at the ground. "I know," he says, his voice a rasp. "At the time, I thought we could manage it. It was the wrong call. I'm sorry."

I stare at him, my blood hot.

Nathan walks up to me and gently puts his hand on my back as he leans in. "Crystal, he knows it was a mistake. We're okay now."

I look at him. My Nathan. His face is washed out with large, puffy eyes and dry lips. The skin on his neck is still patchy with large, sickening blotches. Finn and Margaret look similarly ragged.

I'm so pissed.

They all need to rest. Not be out here planning to put themselves in danger all over again.

"Can we talk?" I ask Nathan, pointing to the back door.

Back in the kitchen, I face him.

"Nathan, I thought I could do this." I can't keep still, shifting my feet. "Accept who you are, but…" I swallow tears that are already in my voice. "I can't lose you again." I let the tears flow. I hate myself for this. I know I'm adding another burden to his shoulders, but this is self-preservation, and I have to protect Natalie's heart just as much as mine.

"I know this is bad," he says.

He holds the back of his neck and squeezes his brows. I can't let him do this. Not again.

"Please. Just don't go back. Don't do this right now. Think of Natalie."

"Crystal—"

"I wanted to be strong. But I'm not."

He stares at the floor.

Guilt and anger consume me at the same time. Why can't he just choose us?

"They need all the help they can get, and this is important." He gently cups my shoulders. "I can help." He closes his eyes, as if it hurts him to ask me this. "Please don't ask me to abandon them."

Damn him for being honorable. Damn him for thinking he can do anything.

"Nathan, please." I hate myself for begging.

He says nothing. His body rigid, his eyes fixed to the floor. He's not going to listen to me. He's going to dive no matter what. What did I expect? He's the same man.

Jamie walks in and stops when he sees us. His smile is tight, apologetic.

"Sorry to interrupt you guys. We're about to start the debrief."

Nathan looks up at me, his eyes a question.

"We'll be right out," I say. Not sure what else to do right now, I hold Nathan's hand and we walk back outside. The briefing's already underway.

I've got a decision to make, but I'll sit on it.

"The water is getting too hot for standard methods of cave diving," Finn says.

He's drawing shallow, uneven breaths as he lies back on the lounge chair, his fingers tightly gripping the notes in his hand.

"You think?" Jamie mutters under his breath.

"Do you need some water?" I ask Finn.

He shakes his head no.

"To continue exploring the system, we're going to need alternatives. Unfortunately, exposure suits and atmospheric diving suits won't work in this situation," Finn says.

"What about ROVs and AUVs?" Margaret asks. "Those are used to explore hydrothermal vents. The small ones can fit in the caves."

"Remotely operated vehicles are a logical first choice, but those will only get us so far. Their lack of dexterity is less than ideal in a constricted environment like caves. They'll be clumsy, and with their tethers, we'll probably lose more of them than we'll gain distance. Autonomous vehicles aren't any better."

"So, what's your solution?" I snap. I'm not sure what the others are thinking, but the last thing I want to hear about is all the things he already knows won't work.

"To reach the heat source at the speed we'll need, we need a different suit. Fortunately, one already exists."

Everyone looks at each other. Confused but curious.

"I just had a quick word with Navy and DARPA officials a few minutes ago. There's no holding them off now—they're already on their way. The good news is they have exactly what we need, and I've worked with them before."

"As a JASON," I blurt. He looks my way, amused.

"What's a JASON?" Jamie asks what everyone else is thinking.

"Ask him." I snap my shoulder toward Finn.

"JASON is a scientific advisory group of which I'm a part. I know you won't believe me, Crystal. You've been wary of me since you met me. But they've got nothing to do with why I'm here. And until now, neither did the government. I swear it."

"Right." I stare.

"The Navy. DARPA. They trust my judgment, and they're involved now. My history with them gives us a measure of influence over decisions. We need that. Because now that this is being treated as a potential national security matter, there will be no shortage of ideas on how to handle it. Some of them will do more harm than good."

"Since when does the military care about coral reefs?" I ask.

"What they care about is there's something heating the water that they don't understand." He breaks off, coughing uncontrollably.

I glare at him.

But then I can't help but feel sorry for him. He's sick, and I do believe he's sincerely sorry. It doesn't make him any less dangerous, though.

Jamie throws him a water bottle. He takes a few rapid swallows.

"Tell us more about the suits," Nathan says, putting his arm around me. He's trying to dampen down his excitement, but it's not working. He's like a kid in a toy store.

Clearing his throat, Finn continues. "For years, DARPA engineers have been developing specialized dive equipment built for thermal-gradient protection in underwater environments where a diver has to operate in confined spaces and extreme heat."

Another round of coughing and a swig of water.

"The suit's unofficial name is *Dante's Shield*. The prototype has completed testing, and additional units have been produced. These shields provide divers protection in thermal extremes."

Diving with heat shields. Everyone looks around at one another. Some with excitement. Me with dread.

"Damn. It's *seaQuest*!" Jamie shouts, grinning ear to ear. Most of the guys join in. Even Margaret and Sid geek out.

Finn continues. "In theory, the Shield can withstand temperatures of up to eight hundred degrees Fahrenheit."

Silence.

"Sounds like a solution to me," Nathan says.

There's going to be no stopping him now.

"Wait… did you miss the *in theory* part?" Jamie asks Nathan.

"Right," Finn continues. "Let's discuss the limitations. Once activated, the heat protection lasts roughly fifty-five minutes. Give or take. When the coolant's gone, it's gone. Failure is virtually immediate. There's little warning."

"How much time?" Nathan asks.

Finn shrugs. "Maybe a few seconds?"

"Enough time to know you're gonna die," Jamie says grimly.

Oh God. Someone's got to stop this. There's got to be some other way.

Scott, who's been quietly listening, asks. "Where are these magic suits, and who's going to be using them?" His face is stoic and calm. The way he usually looks before he loses it.

"The Navy SEALs are bringing them. They're all trained on the suits—but I've confirmed—none have cave diving experience."

"So, you're going to have untrained men down there navigating an unexplored cave environment in deadly conditions?" Scott raises his brows, still calm for now.

"That's the question, isn't it? Do we train them to cave dive, or do they train us on how to use the suit? The suit's the simpler option. It'll take a day for us—if that. Getting the commander on board will be our challenge."

"Finn, let's be clear about something. I will not experiment with my team's lives. Only when we have clear facts in front of us and come up with a sound dive plan that assures everyone makes it out safely will I consider it… Or we don't dive."

"That's reasonable. I'll ensure…"

"Stand up," Scott says.

Finn looks confused but stands.

Scott steps directly in front of him and fixes him with a hard stare. "I don't like you. And I don't trust you."

"I'll own that. But we don't have any other options—at least none we're prepared to entertain."

Staring for a few beats more, Scott walks back to Margaret. Finn stumbles back down to the lounge.

"Okay, I have one more question for now," Scott says.

"What the fuck is anyone who gets down there supposed to do? You've got no clue what the hell this even is. And you expect we're going to figure that out on the fly when we're down there. With a ticking clock? Make this make sense."

"You're quite right. This will require a series of incremental dives for discovery and analysis, all within a tight timeframe. I recognize the risk and the uncertainty. But again… what alternative do we have?"

"Finn, when do they get here?" Nathan asks.

"The suits? Two days. But Commander Nicolaus is already here. I'll introduce you in the morning. On my ship."

After the dive meeting wraps up and Nathan and I gather our things, Finn walks up to me.

"May I have a moment?"

I glance at Nathan, then back at Finn. "Make it short. I need to get Nathan home." I follow him to a quiet corner in the garden.

"I'm sincerely sorry for putting Nathan's and Margaret's lives at risk today," he says, his voice still hoarse and raspy. "You must hate me, and I don't blame you. But your opinion actually matters to me."

I meet his eyes. "I thought you were smart."

"I am smart." He exhales slowly. "But sometimes that's the problem, isn't it? When you know so much, you start to think you know best. That's a fallacy." His jaw tightens. "This is the second time I've made that mistake, and the last time—"

He removes his glasses and squeezes his eyes shut. A couple of tears silently streak down his face.

"It didn't end well."

"What happened?" I ask softly.

"I was overseeing an LTF," he says. "A thermal mechanical stress test on a new composite material. We were pushing it to failure." His gaze drifts past me, unfocused. "We were almost finished. Very close to the upper limits. I only needed a couple more minutes to finish collecting the data we were after."

His fingers close harder around his glasses. "Alfred detected a minor fluctuation in the readings. Nothing immediately alarming. Most likely an anomaly." His mouth twists. "I decided it was noise and made the call to finish."

He returns his gaze to mine. "Less than a minute later, a containment unit failed. It released the stored pressure and heat. Not an explosion," he says quietly. "But fatal to anyone standing nearby."

"Alfred was the closest," Finn says. "His death was instant."

I study his face. Grief etched into the corners. And his hands are trembling. There's a hollow wound inside this man—an empty space. From his failure or his loss, I'm not entirely sure.

"It's one thing to take risks with your own life," he continues. "It's another to make the call for others. They deserve a say in what risks they're willing to take."

"I'm sorry for your loss. But it doesn't seem like you've really learned anything from it."

"Today reminded me."

"So then, what are you going to do about it now?"

"I can't promise it won't be dangerous. But I promise to dive the plan."

CHAPTER 22

The Stranger

Miso soup and saltines with a side of fruit. More food.

Crystal sits across from me, watching me eat. In the dim lighting, her blue eyes catch and hold the light, like a shimmer.

We've got to talk about this. I'm not too bothered by what Finn did. Though I'm in the minority. He made a call. It was a mistake. We've all made mistakes.

But when I think of Crystal's face the moment she saw me at the inn… the way it dropped… It was like I struck her.

I don't want to ever feel that way again.

"What did Finn want?" I ask.

"He apologized. I believe that he's sorry." She frowns and brushes her fingers across the collar of her blouse. "But that doesn't change much, does it?"

"No."

We haven't spoken about it yet. She wanted me to rest during the car ride, but my mind has been busy. Turning over every argument, searching for something that might convince her to say yes. In the end, I'm prepared to do whatever she asks. After what she's been through, I owe her that much.

She puts her hand over mine.

"Nathan, I trust you to do what's right." She takes a deep breath. I hate that she looks so sad. "Whatever you decide… I'm here for you."

I've promised to keep her and Natalie safe, and part of being safe is not worrying about me. But can I do that and also do what's right?

"They need me," I croak. "I can help." I hate myself.

"Okay." A tear falls down her cheek. She sniffs.

She clears the table and takes my hand, guiding me to the bedroom. A clean pair of boxers lies on the quilt. I fumble with my shirt, struggling to pull it over my head. Giving up, I lean toward my side of the bed.

"Here," she whispers. She steadies me and pulls the shirt over my head. Then she helps me with my pants and boxers and tucks me in. Sliding in beside me, she buries her face into the crook of my neck and starts combing her fingers through my hair.

She talks about random things, her tender voice coaxing me to sleep.

"I love you," I whisper.

Her voice hitches, then she sings to me.

"Time to rise and shine." Her sweet voice.

"Hmmm," I mumble, prying open my eyes and glancing at the clock.

No alarm. Shit. She must have turned it off last night. If I don't get to the docks on time, they're going to leave my ass.

I jump out of bed. I consider skipping the shower, but instead I set the timer on my phone and haul butt.

Five minutes later, I'm ready to go. On my way to the door, I see the bacon and eggs and a steaming cup of coffee waiting for me on the table.

"You're an angel." I pick up the coffee and give her a quick kiss. "Eat fast, sailor. You've got less than three minutes."

When I put the empty dish in the sink, she presses the back of her hand against my forehead. "You look much better."

"I have an excellent nurse."

"But you're still a little peaked. Take it easy today—nurse's orders." She wraps her arms around me and rests her head on my shoulder.

"I can't wait to come home." I lean down and kiss her goodbye, then grab my gear. *I hope I have my keys,* I think to myself as I storm out.

"Good luck," she says with a laugh and closes the door behind me.

I take the RIB to the research ship and greet Scott and the rest of the crew on the deck. Why does everyone look like they're in a bad mood?

"Still waiting," Jamie grumbles. "Twenty minutes and counting."

Margaret and Liam stand beside him, pissed.

And Sid's scowling. She's been keeping her distance from Scott since last night. He told her she might have to sit out on the thermal dives, and it hasn't gone over well. She's alone today, without her team.

I survey the vessel. It's about two hundred and fifty feet long and resembles a naval ship. There's a low hum of engines, and everything's painted in stark whites and grays. The deck is covered with the functional features you'd expect on a research vessel, including ROV storage racks, an A-frame crane, and dive stations. Watertight doors line the bulkheads, sealing off the interior.

Margaret walks up to me, smiling, then she motions for me to bend down so she can whisper something in my ear.

"Your shirt's inside out," she says, then giggles and points to a door on the side of the interior.

Damn. This isn't the impression I want to make in front of a Navy commander.

"What's up with him?" I hear Jamie ask as I rush to the head.

After I change and return to the group, the main interior doors open.

Finn walks out and greets a glaring Scott.

"Sorry," Finn says. "I've been in the middle of a rather heated debate with our guests for the last half hour. My attempts to smooth things over before this meeting may not have yielded the outcome I was hoping for. And Dr. Harlow's enthusiasm about the prospect of the SEALs taking over the diving didn't help our case."

He glances at Sid.

"Well, he can back off. It looks like he's going to get his way, regardless," she huffs and gives Scott a lethal look.

Finn turns his attention back to Scott. "This may be a hard sell."

We follow him through two laboratory rooms and a galley, entering a conference room aft of the wardroom.

After he introduces us to the commander and his officers, we all gather around the rectangular table, where Garrett's already sitting. There aren't enough chairs for everyone, so the officers remain standing, and Sid perches on the corner of the table. Scott and I stand next to her. The body heat in the room is palpable.

The commander nods for Finn to begin.

"Commander Nicolaus's SEALs arrive tomorrow," Finn says. "We've agreed to run a few reconnaissance dives with ROVs to collect as much data as we can, as deep as we can, while we wait. We'll also start staging supplies at the cave locations we can still reach in wetsuits. There are eight Dante's Shields, so we need to decide who's diving and where. Thin wetsuits are still usable in sections below ninety-five degrees, but only for limited exposure times."

"That's a lot of information, Dr. Clark," the commander says. His face is weathered, and he doesn't frown or smile.

He inhales sharply and continues. "It makes the most sense for my men to wear the Shields. They're trained, and they can use cave maps and anything else you can give them to get familiar with Carter's Drop's architecture."

Finn clears his throat and glances toward us.

"Very good, sir. But if I may," Finn says, trying to ignore the commander's hard stare. "Scott and Nathan are two of the most skilled cave divers in the world." Finn clears his throat again. "It's taken them hundreds of hours of dive time to get that good. Their teammates are also experts. Please understand that Carter's Drop is one of the most complicated systems we know of, and with this heating anomaly, it increases the risk tenfold."

He pauses, gauging the commander's reaction. There is none.

"You mentioned that none of your men have experience in caves yet. As skilled as they may be as divers, that doesn't mean their skill will automatically transfer to cave diving, at least not in the time we're talking about."

"Do I look dense, Dr. Clark?" he asks. Finn shakes his head. "We already discussed this twice. My men do the diving in the Shields." He looks at Scott and me. "What I *will* agree to is allowing your team to train with the suits, and Scott and Nathan can go on the missions. We'll consider rotating more of your people in as we progress."

"Fair enough," Finn quickly agrees.

"Good. We'll start the training tomorrow, when my men get here." He gets up and makes a curt goodbye gesture to the room. "Appreciate it." He walks off briskly, his officers in tow.

"Did we do something wrong?" Jamie asks.

The Dante's Shield schematic lies flat across the table. I'm going to get to dive in that suit. How awesome is that?

After we leave the room, I look at Scott. "You were quiet in there."

"No point fighting it right now. I can't tell him what to do with his men. But none of us are getting in the water if I think it's unsafe." He stops walking. "You don't have to do this. You've just got home. It's all right to focus on Crystal and Natalie. I know you don't think so, but we can do this without you. You don't have to prove anything."

"I'm in."

♥

On the drive back home, I stop at the general store to pick up some groceries that Crystal asked me to get.

We're having fish tacos.

With Natalie at Mads's and Scott's place, we have the house all to ourselves, and I feel much better than I did last night. I smile at the thought of dinner.

"There he is," a woman's shout and a scattering of footfalls.

Turning, I see half a dozen people coming my way with cameras and a microphone.

"Nathan, I just have a few questions for you. Is now a good time?"

"No." I stare at the woman, dumbfounded.

One cameraman shoves his camera in my face, accidentally slashing my cheek as I try to turn away. "Is it true you're living with Crystal Glassier, the widow of the man who tried to kill you?" the woman asks.

Fuck this. We can eat takeout tonight. I try to squeeze past them, and another man sticks out his leg, blocking me.

The hell?

"Did you have an affair with her? Is that why he wanted you dead? Is his little girl really yours?" she drones on and on.

I shove the cameraman aside. He trips and mutters something about me assaulting him under his breath.

"Do you have an anger problem, Nathan? Is that why you fled?" the reporter asks.

They continue to follow me as I rush to my car. Faster than they are, I whip out of the parking lot before they get into their van. If they've already connected me to Crystal, how long will it be before they show up at our front door?

I flinch when the cold cloth touches my cheek. Crystal gingerly cleans and dries my wound, then slathers a liberal amount of antibiotic ointment over it. Finishing with butterfly closures.

"You were this close to stitches." She pinches her fingers together. "You're not even done healing from the hyperthermia, and now you're getting all beaten up." She frowns.

"They were asking about you and Natalie. They know we're together."

"Oh."

"I'm sorry for dragging you into this."

"How? By existing?"

"I'm putting my family in danger again."

"Natalie is safe because of you. And we'll handle those jerks if they show up."

"I didn't get the fish."

She laughs. "How do you feel about Totino's Pizza?"

♥

After we finish eating pizza, Crystal asks me to join her on the back porch to look at the stars. We sit for a little while picking out the ones we can name, and she pulls out another picture from her purse.

These little story times have become my favorite part of the day. I take it eagerly. The picture is one of her, me and… Mark.

I feel sick.

In the picture, she's face down on a lounge chair crying, and Mark is laughing. I'm looking at him with a death stare.

In the picture. And right now.

"We were all snorkeling, and I accidentally surfaced in a patch of sea lice. A little while later, I felt some itchy spots on my face that got more intense as the hours went by, then these horrible pimples popped out all along where I had been wearing my mask. I looked like a rabid raccoon."

She shakes her head.

"Mark laughed at me when he saw my bumpy face, and do you know what you did?"

"Tell me."

"You held my hair back and gently rubbed my face with hydrocortisone. You stayed with me all night to make sure I didn't scratch, and you reapplied the cream every few hours. We played board games and watched TV." She laughs and squints her eyes. "Would you believe me if I told you that it was one of the most fun nights of my life?"

She takes another look at the photo. "Sometimes we just don't see what's right in front of us."

She meets my gaze, waiting.

"Please tell me everything," I whisper and brace myself. "If you're ready."

She sits down beside me, holds my hand, and tells me everything.

Everything.

And I'm destroyed.

My choices put her in the clutches of a monster.

"You didn't do it, Nathan. Mark did. I didn't know what he was, and neither did you."

"I should have known," I spit out, unable to catch my breath—unable to reconcile my emotions. I've been feeling sorry for myself for all these years, when she… she…

"Look at me." She puts her hands on the sides of my face and lifts my gaze to meet hers. "Evil can be very good at disguising itself. But you know what?" She caresses my jawline. "We're here, and he's not."

She leans in and kisses me. Her soft lips open, and I taste her sweetness.

I want her so badly, but I need to stop.

"Crystal, do you need time? What happened… I don't want to hurt you."

"What I need is the man I married, the man I love. It's true I'm still healing. Every day. But he didn't change me." She takes my hand. "You're not him. And I'm still the same woman who loves *you* and wants *you*."

"But…"

She puts a finger across my lips and slides my hand, which has been resting on her leg, under her dress. "Badly."

She's so soft and lovely.

But it's been a long day and I'm filthy. I can't touch her like this.

I look at her sheepishly. "I think I need a shower."

"Okay," she whispers. "But don't make me wait too long." I watch her trail her fingers across her neckline to her chest. Slow. Inviting.

I rush to the bathroom. I'm a mess. What she just shared with me is heavy. I feel guilty for wanting something from her. But she wants it too.

We both deserve this, and we deserve to bury the past and never think of that asshole again.

Getting under the stream, I close my eyes and give myself a moment to soak in the hot water. It feels so damn good. Then I think of Crystal's body and what it felt like to be inside her. I grasp the handle to turn off the water.

The curtain moves, and she steps inside. Naked.

"Oh?" I choke on the word, eyes locked on hers. And then I let my gaze drift.

She motions with her index finger for me to turn around and takes a washcloth and soap from the shower caddy. The spicy fragrance of ginger mixed with sweet vanilla wakes up my senses.

I hold my breath as she works up the cloth until it's filled with suds. I can hear her, but I can't see her, and it's driving me crazy.

She puts the cloth on my back and begins washing, moving in slow circles. I let my shoulders relax and lean back into her touch.

She moves on.

When she reaches the place between my legs, I jerk as intense pleasure surges up my spine.

Unable to stand still, I turn around to see her, her soaked white-blonde hair a darker shade of gold and her blue eyes staring at me.

"Come here," I rasp. Catching the back of her waist with one palm, I pull her to me and breathe in the pleasure of her soft curves pressed against my body. Taking some soap into my hands, I cup her breasts and knead them, rolling over her nipples with my thumbs. Watching them harden, I push myself against her belly.

She bends her neck back, letting out a sexy moan.

"Are we clean enough now?" I husk, breathing heavily against her neck. She nods, and I spin her around to face the wall. Her hands fly up against the tile to brace herself.

“I love you so much,” I call out. She gasps as I push into her. Her warm softness surrounds me as I roll my hips.

Yes. My thrusts at first slow, grow desperate, and in minutes, we’re clawing at each other, begging each other for release.

When she tightens around me, I shout as the orgasm rips through me.

Trembling, I will myself to keep standing and hold on to her, softly caressing the curves of her back and stomach.

She’s still catching her breath. Knowing I’m the reason sends a slow, primal satisfaction through me.

“Wow.” She laughs out loud, uninhibited, still facing the wall. “I’m a satisfied woman, sailor. You have my permission to be proud of yourself.”

I laugh and kiss her back, just beneath her shoulder blade, while I tickle that spot I’ve found beneath her ribs. She jumps. “Ready to go again?” I sigh, completely serious about a round two until cold water pours over us.

“Out,” she says. Giggling and freezing, we stumble onto the rug.

It takes us a minute, but we eventually dry off and make our way into bed.

Resting for a little while, I think about going to sleep, but the memories of what we just did and how good it felt overtake the fatigue. I roll to my side and pull her toward me, nestling my face into her sweet hair—already needing her again. And ready.

“Tomorrow, I dive in the space suit,” I murmur into her ear, trying to sound pitiful and not laugh.

She laughs and doesn’t try to hold back. “And?”

I graze the lobe of her ear and whisper. “Any chance of an encore before I go?”

CHAPTER 23

The Widow

Dashing through the snow
In a one-horse open sleigh
Over the hills we go
Laughing all the way
Ha, ha, ha...

We pass the carolers—Natalie waving and cheering them on—and turn right, walking through the gates of Lazy Shores Park.

Determined to get everyone out of the house this morning, Maddie and I corralled the kids and dogs, loaded the stroller and a bag, and headed out. We've been admiring all the decorations along our walk. Multicolored string lights wrap around the palm trunks, turning them into living candy canes. Hanging from the light posts are holiday wreaths in various patterns, each featuring a popular Christmas character.

The mild South Florida December is still warm enough for sundresses and shorts.

We walk along the crushed shell path toward a small cluster of live oaks planted beside a wooden bench. Their wide branches form a circle of shade over us.

Natalie and the dogs jog nearby, weaving in and out of the brighter patches of grass, occasionally disappearing behind the low hedges that edge the path before reemerging again. Restrooms are close by, tucked behind a large cluster of sea grape trees. The park has plenty of shade and quiet corners. A great place for families on a sunny day.

Maddie settles in to get Christopher ready for his feeding, carefully lifting him from his stroller, and I sit beside her, watching Natalie.

The air smells green, but there are dark undercurrents. Our little town is threatened by the heating waters, and an unknown danger is drifting closer to those I love. As grateful as I am for what I have, the little girl in me just wishes her family could sit here and enjoy the holidays without worry.

Nathan is training in his heat-resistant diving suit today. His *space suit*. I laugh at the memory of last night. I feel like we're back to us, who we were. Almost. He still doesn't have any recall. But I'm loading him up with so many memories—from the past and new ones—that soon it won't matter. What matters is our little girl and us. Natalie giggles as Ding jumps on her in the grass.

Reminding myself that Nathan's dive today is only training, I try to keep my thoughts from spiraling and focus on the fun we're having right now.

"He'll be fine," Maddie says.

"Hmm?"

"You don't have to say anything. The worry is etched on your face."

"That obvious?"

"Yes. But it's understandable. You just got him home, and he's right back to his cave-diving bravado before you've even been able to reconnect as spouses."

"Um, well, we've been doing quite a bit of reconnecting…" I try not to laugh when Maddie scrunches her face. She can't help it. It is her brother we're talking about. "Is Hannah still joining us today?"

"No, she bailed. She's been dodging everything lately. I think the picnic the other day was the first time we've hung out in weeks."

"She's probably really busy at the gift shop."

Maddie shakes her head. "Oh no. That girl is up to something. It's got to be a man."

"Doesn't she tell you everything?"

"She does. And since she's not, he must be a potential keeper. Of course, she's not fooling anyone—we all know who he is."

We do. Aside from Wes being alive and well, it's the worst-kept secret on the island.

"You'd think they'd realize that Scott and I are going to talk."

Her eyes widen. "And neither one of them is any good at sneaking around."

"Especially when they're in the same room," I add.

"Did you see them at the picnic?"

I nod and give her a naughty smile. "I saw them behind the lighthouse."

We howl with laughter. A young couple walking by quickly glances over at us, then picks up speed like we're contagious.

Good for Hannah, she's the sweetest… and so is Jamie.

"Aunt Maddie, can I play catch with Ding and Denver?"

"Did you bring their ball?"

"It's right here." She proudly lifts the pink jingle ball toy.

"You guys ready to play?" Maddie asks the dogs. They bark and wag their tails playfully.

Maddie hands me Christopher and takes Natalie a few yards away, where the grass is unobstructed. She shows her how to toss the ball and play fetch with the dogs. After a quick lesson, Natalie starts to treat it seriously.

Run and toss. Run and toss. The dogs are going to get a good workout.

Denver and Ding circle around her each time she raises her arms, eagerly jumping up and down. They love it. It's good for all of them to get the exercise and the fresh air.

At two weeks old, Christopher is already a curious and alert baby. Gently lowering him onto the blanket I'd spread over the grass earlier, I tuck his stuffie worm next to him and watch. He needs his exercise too. Right away, he tries to roll onto his side and reach the stuffie. With a tiny grunt of effort, he manages a partial turn, lifting his head for a second or two before wobbling back down. His eyes dart everywhere, not wanting to miss a thing.

After his third attempt, he grows frustrated and cries. I pick him up.

Natalie always did the same thing. I miss it. The weight of Natalie as a baby in my arms. Should I let myself even think of that right now? To imagine what it may be like to have another. It's what I want. Brothers and sisters for Natalie. Lots of them. But it seems selfish to dream about that right now.

"Ah, there you go." I slowly bounce him up and down, careful to secure his neck. He crunches his face and cries harder. "Auntie Crystal's not doing a good job, is she? Is she?" I coo as I gently cradle him in my arms and rock. "She's out of practice, you see."

Listening to my voice, he quiets, but his face makes it clear he wants his momma. He's hungry.

When Maddie returns, she discreetly positions Christopher at her breast for his feeding. I pick up the blanket and inspect it to be sure no bugs have crawled onto it before putting it away.

That feeling again. Like a cold, still wind. I glance toward Natalie. Denver's circling her, waiting for the throw.

"Nathan needs to get a restraining order. What those reporters are doing is harassment. Maybe even stalking."

"They haven't shown up at the house. Not yet. They know exactly what they're doing and how far they can go before crossing the line legally. They don't care whether it's ethical."

"They're scumbags. Have you heard anything else from that weirdo Natalie talked to, Walter?"

"Not yet."

"Natalie's safe with us. I just wish she didn't have to be separated from her mom and dad or miss school."

I think about what he told Natalie about the *Big, Mean Man*. A jolt of fear shoots up my spine. How much danger could we actually be in?

I glance up to check on Natalie. I breathe out. She's close by and still with the dogs. They won't let anything get near her.

"Don't go any farther than that, Natalie. K, sweetie?" I call out.

She nods and smiles at me, then turns back to the dogs.

"What about the ocean impacts?" Maddie asks.

"It's bad. There have been more reports of toxin exposure and… Mrs. Clara died last night."

"Oh no. From the rash?"

"Well, she was already really weak from the flu, and her body just couldn't fight the toxins she picked up from the water. We may have closed the beaches too late. And not everyone is even listening to the restrictions."

"Do you think it will spread further than our waters?"

It might. Who knows what the heck this is?

"This is only going to get worse," I say.

Maddie reaches out and holds my hand. "They'll figure it out. They're smart and determined. I wish I could get into those caves and help." She looks down at Christopher. "But this little guy needs me."

I rub her back. "He's the most important job you'll ever have."

Natalie runs to us, puts the ball back, and grabs a huge plastic bone. "Denver wants the bone," she says, running off, shouting for Denver.

"I've been doing some research of my own," I say.

"Into the heating rocks?"

"No, into Finn." She looks at me, curious.

"He's hiding something."

"I'm as furious as you are. But do you think he's up to something really nefarious?"

I think of Finn's confession of the death he caused by pushing too far and how he nearly got Nathan and Margaret killed. But he seems to want to do something—to fix this problem. I want to believe he'll do what's right when it comes down to it.

"What I know is he's got an agenda, and he's not transparent until pushed. Walter told Natalie not to trust the scientists."

"That explains everything," she says as she slaps her knee. "Walter said so." She shoots me an apologetic glance. "Sorry. Okay. What have you found?"

"Finn took a six-month leave of absence about four years ago. Highly unusual for a man in his position."

I'd found an article about Alfred's death. It matched what Finn had described, but the timeline didn't match his leave of absence. Alfred died over eight years ago, but from our chat it seemed they were close friends. Or more. There's nothing public about his personal life.

"There's no information I can find that explains why he took the time off. Only that he went to Alaska. When he came back, he was promoted."

"… that does make you wonder what he was up to. But Crystal, there could be a million…"

I glance up and don't immediately see Natalie. I look toward the bathrooms. Did she go there? I scan the ground in all directions.

Maddie's still talking, but I can't register Maddie's words as my breath is squeezed out of my lungs when I realize I can't find Natalie anywhere.

I jolt up.

"Crystal?"

Denver's growl rings out loud and is immediately followed by a series of frantic barks of alarm. Ding's running at full speed toward us from the left. Why is he so far away?

Oh God.

Denver's still nowhere in sight. Neither is Natalie.

"Natalie! Natalie!" I scream. Racing along the path of shrubs and fences to where I can still hear Denver's barks. "Help me! Please help me!" I yell so loud my throat tears.

As I run, I hear little Christopher's cries and Maddie's terrified voice behind me. "We need help. My niece is gone…"

When I pass Ding, he circles back around and runs with me. Park patrons look on with concern as we rush by, a few of them joining us to help. I keep yelling at the top of my lungs for help as I run as fast as my legs will go. In the distance, the sound of a police alarm grows louder.

Finally, I spot Denver chasing a sleek silver Land Rover.

Seconds later, a police officer runs toward me, and I point to the vehicle as it speeds off out of sight. He calls into his radio, and I see other lights flash down the road. Stopping to catch my breath, which is coming out in harsh rasps, I begin to sob and ask them to tell me where she is. The officer holds my shoulders.

“Ma’am, stop. Take a breath. We’ve got someone tailing the Rover.”

Maddie’s holding Christopher and walking at a quick pace toward me, her face crumpled in worry. “Natalie?”

I shake my head and collapse.

CHAPTER 24

The Stranger

I know I shouldn't be loving this, but hell, it's freaking cool.

Appearance-wise, the Dante's Shield isn't much different from a standard suit, aside from the metallic sheen of its protective materials and a hardened torso that protects the integrated rebreather and backup gas systems. But the outer insulation layer alone only ensures survival for seconds once extreme heat begins to cook whatever's inside the suit.

The second layer contains a thermal protection barrier gel and coolant tubes. Once activated, it begins to deteriorate immediately and loses all effectiveness when the gel melts completely.

Fifty-five minutes, give or take, to get back into survivable temperatures.

The third and final layer of the Shield is a comfortable, moisture-wicking fabric that keeps the skin cool and promotes air circulation.

Entering the Shield from the back, I'm sealed inside from neck to feet with a pressure-sealing, titanium-coated zipper. The helmet is bulkier than a typical mask, but sleeker and more compact than those used in commercial diving. Once locked into the neck of the suit, there's no skin exposed to the outside elements.

Airtight.

It's a remarkable feat of engineering, but with all its complex parts, the failure mode is incredible. But none of us mentions failure again after it's explained once during training.

There's no point. We're doing this.

My biggest challenge with the Shield is losing all micro-control of movement. Its sensors and computers adjust my buoyancy and trim, forcing me to unlearn the skills and instincts I normally follow without thinking. The suit's top-heavy balance and a complete lack of water flow against my skin are disorienting, making me feel as if I'm inside a remote-controlled bubble. But my legs can still do the driving, assisted by thrusters, while my arms and hands handle what remote and autonomous vehicles still can't do with human precision.

After receiving the Dante's Shield overview this morning, we immediately prepped to train in shifts of four assigned to two SEAL instructors at a time. I'm with Sid, Jamie, and Finn.

It's been… entertaining.

Jamie makes another attempt at using the thruster. Bursting forward, he overshoots about two yards this time. Then slowly drifts to the side. "Damn. I thought I had it that time."

At least he's improving.

Sid owns it. She deliberately pushes hard on the thrust to whip around in wild circles. The SEAL she's assigned to reprimands her and threatens to pull her out of the water completely.

"It's my learning style," she says. "I need to get a feel for how to steer everything with my fingers. Like a video game."

She whips around to hover closer to the SEAL. "Maybe you can give me some more one-on-one instruction topside."

He mumbles a curse under his breath but lets her keep playing.

Finn and I have already got the hang of our suits and are just swimming around, enjoying our new toys.

"It's time to run through the emergency features. Who's first?" The SEAL asks.

"Me!" Sid and Jamie say at the same time.

The emergency features concern me the most. While I appreciate the redundancy they've built into the suits—pure genius—the emergency steps are much more complex than they are with standard gear. There's virtually no room for failure. But in hazardous environments like the one we're going into, there rarely is.

It's going to be extremely dangerous in the caves.

I think of Crystal, of what I'm asking her to accept. And then Natalie. She's already lost one father. If I die, I'm signing them up for more pain.

"Did I pass?" Sid asks the SEAL after switching to the backup rebreather loop.

"You're still breathing, aren't you?" The SEAL chuckles.

Sid frowns at him, then asks if she can do the next drill.

"Hey—it's my turn, Sid," Jamie complains.

She shrugs when Jamie frowns after the SEAL lets her do it.

Finn and I have already completed our drills.

We're ready to go.

Finn swims up to me. "Reminds me of the *Action Man* scuba diver I had as a kid. Our very own version of *G.I. Joe*. You have one of those?"

"Not sure." I gesture to my head. "Amnesia, remember?"

"Right."

We've scared away most of the fish, but a huge cluster of Crevalle jack swims by, and all of a sudden it looks like we're in one of those arcade shooter games.

"I found a shitload of PlayStation games in the closet. Looks like I was a fan of *Treasures of the Deep,*" I say.

"Oh, that was a good one—Jack Runyan all the way. When you play it, let me know if you get to Atlantis."

"Yeah. I'll do that."

Even though I'm not sure I should, I like Finn. But it also feels like he's playing a game. The question is, why?

"How did we know each other?" I ask him.

"Hmmm?" His pause almost seems natural, but I notice it for what it is. He's thinking about his answer. "Not that well. We ran into each other… as colleagues."

"Where?"

Before he can answer, the SEAL assigned to the two of us signals to us that we need to end the dive. That's odd. We were scheduled for two hours, and Jamie is still going through his emergency drills. Why is he calling it early?

Confused, we begin our ascent to the surface.

As soon as we're back on deck, Scott darts to me, phone in hand. "Nathan, get dressed now."

When we leave the marina, he's still on the phone. He glances up every few seconds to update me on everything going on.

Kidnapped.

Two hours ago, while I was playing around in the Shield instead of protecting my family.

The whirlpool of fear and confusion I'm feeling right now is like nothing I've ever known. I picture her big brown eyes and large white-blonde curls. With her sweet face looking at me. Calling me *Daddy*.

I can't let anything happen to her.

Scott whips the truck into the police station and parks at the entrance.

"We'll find her," he says, squeezing my shoulder.

Numb, I follow him through the double doors.

The officer at the front desk takes us into a quiet room where Crystal and Mads wait. I rush to Crystal.

Her pretty blue sundress is wrinkled and dirty, and her hair is tangled. She doesn't wear much makeup, but remnants of the light strokes of mascara she wore this morning when she playfully said goodbye shade her cheeks, and her lips are dry.

"Baby." I pull her into my arms, and we cry together.

After staying with us a few minutes, Mads and Scott get up to take Christopher home.

"Give me your keys. We'll bring back your car," Maddie says. I give her the keys to my Corolla, and she hugs me goodbye.

"Nathan, they asked so many questions," Crystal says. "I couldn't think of everything. What if I didn't tell them something they need to know?" Crystal and Mads were interviewed as soon as they got here.

"This isn't your fault." I squeeze her tighter. We're sitting in cold, uncomfortable seats, like the ones little kids use at school.

"I told them about you. That you're Natalie's father."

Another officer comes in to speak with us.

"We've issued a *be on the lookout* and have been pulling video from home and business cameras in the area." He hands over a packet of information including the case number and contact numbers for victim services. "We've already issued the AMBER Alert. We'll find your daughter."

He gently touches Crystal's arm and steps out to speak with his sergeant.

We sit in silence, letting our thoughts run free for a few minutes.

Crystal pulls out her wallet and takes out a photo. Natalie as a baby. She has a few patches of fuzzy white hair and the biggest smile, showing off her two tiny bottom teeth.

"She'd just said her first word and was so proud of herself."

"What was it?"

"Momma." Bursting into another round of tears, she puts the photo away. "Where is she, Nathan? Where is our baby girl?"

Crystal's desperate, terrified words crush the courage I'd been trying to muster. "I don't know, but we'll find her. We have to." I pull her into my arms again, and we wait.

The officer returns with another man in a business suit who's carrying a clipboard.

"Mrs. Glassier, Dr. Carter, I'm Detective Daniels." After he shakes our hands, he pulls up a chair and sits close to us. "We've set up triage and have eyes all over this town. I know the only thing you want to hear is that we've found your little girl and we're working on that."

He flips through some stapled pages and looks at Crystal. "Thank you for answering all our questions. I know some of them are intrusive. But I promise we're only asking so we can get things moving fast."

He pulls out a grainy black-and-white photograph and shows it to us. I take it.

There's a close-up shot of a man wearing sunglasses and a hat. He's near a parked Land Rover and walking toward the park.

"We got this from a street camera near the park. Do either of you recognize this man?"

I do. It's the same freak that was staring at me at the town hall.

"There was a guy who looked like that at the town hall last week. I don't know him."

The detective takes notes and asks a few more questions about the scene and about the people I've encountered since my return.

"I know this is going to be hard to hear," he says. "But you need to go home and get some rest." He pulls out a card and hands it to me. "I'll be in touch, and you can call me any time of day. I'm sincerely sorry this is happening." He pats me on the back as I hold a sobbing Crystal. "We'll find her."

After he leaves, Crystal cries harder. She may not be able to calm down.

The hell? I can't go home and rest. Natalie's in danger, and anything could be happening to her right now.

Scott and Mads are waiting for us in the front office.

It's sunset when we get outside. I turn to Scott. "Can you take them home? I have to look for her."

He pauses a moment before he speaks. "Yeah. Keep your phone charged." He hands me my keys.

I watch as Scott pulls out of the station with Crystal and Mads, then I get into my car.

My first instinct is to take off, but instead I breathe.

Breathe in deeply—then a second sniff of air—exhale slowly. Again. Again.

I tense the muscles in my feet, hold, and release. Then my legs, my stomach, my chest, my shoulders, my neck, and my head.

Tense up. Then let go.

Karen, my friend from Miami, taught me this relaxation technique that she picked up from her Wednesday drama classes.

It takes the edge off my panic—opening the clogged channels of my head so I can think and do this.

I'm going to comb this entire island until I find that Rover.

Most streets in Maverick Key are empty after dark. The only nightlife is the bars and restaurants on Beach Drive, leaving the rest of the island's roads quiet and still.

Sweat pours down my back in cold streams as I move street to street. In my head, I've divided the island into a grid, and I'm combing each neighborhood methodically, one block at a time.

Am I looking for Walter, the *Big, Mean Man* or someone else entirely? There's been no ransom contact. And I have no clue what this person wants. Only that time isn't on our side.

My vision tunnels, causing me to miss a street. I make a U-turn to circle back. I can't afford to skip anything.

Still nothing.

I keep driving. The island thins out. Fewer homes, more empty lots, and residential neighborhoods are replaced by commercial buildings. Sodium lights buzz ahead, harsh and bright, cutting through the dark.

Loud barks.

To my right, a wooden fence shudders as several dogs behind it jump and bark. It looks like a discount car parts lot.

When I turn my attention back to the road, it's too late to see the red light. Slamming on the brakes, I stop right in the middle of the intersection. Lucky for me, there aren't any other cars nearby.

I just sit resting my head on the steering wheel. She's out there somewhere, and there's nothing I can do to protect her.

What is happening to her right now?

Unconsciously, I ease my foot off the brake. That's when I see it—parked at the gas station.

A silver Land Rover.

CHAPTER 25

The Widow

It's dark by the time we pull into the driveway. Scott turns off the engine, gets out, and looks back at Maddie and me.

"Wait by the door," he says. "I'm going to check it out." He sprints to the front door, slipping inside and leaving it open behind him.

Before I can stop it, another horrific vision rips through my mind. Natalie's screaming, her face twisted in fear, followed by another terrible image. These have been replaying in my head on and off since the kidnapping.

Nathan and the police are out there looking for her, and I cling to the small kernel of hope flickering in my chest.

Please find our little girl, Nathan.

Maddie hooks an arm under mine. "Come on," she says gently. "I've got you."

I can't even keep myself upright on my own.

Momma, please, help me, please… Momma!

I lose my footing and drop to the ground beside the front porch. Then I bend and vomit over the roots of the hibiscus bush.

Maddie crouches beside me, holding my hair back. She doesn't offer empty reassurances. Her eyes are as swollen as mine. She's sharing the pain with me.

I can barely breathe through the congestion packed in my nose and throat, and my head is pounding. There are no more tears left, but I'm still crying. Silent sobs that hurt like punches.

Maddie wipes my mouth with a napkin and slips both arms around my waist, helping me toward the front door.

"We'll get you cleaned up inside." She pauses on the porch, keeping me close to her side while we wait for Scott's voice to tell us it's okay.

There are no stars in the sky tonight, but I can see the moon. A waning crescent moon. What is happening to my little girl? The picture of her in terror returns mercilessly, strangling my mind.

"You're going to be sick again," Maddie says with her face pinched with worry. She glances at the door. "Sorry, Scott," she mumbles, and pulls the screen door open.

The moment we step through, there's a volley of loud shouts and furniture being tossed around, followed by a loud crash and male grunts. It's coming from the living room.

"Scott?" Maddie's voice lifts, edged with fear.

She lowers me to the floor and pulls her phone from her pocket as she rushes to the end of the entryway.

"Let me tell you. I know it! I know!" a man shouts. His voice is scratchy and muffled, like he's yelling through clenched teeth.

More scuffling.

A heavy thump.

I force myself up and see him sprawled across the living room floor—it's Walter.

The man Natalie told Nathan about, and the one who was watching me the night I babysat the dogs. Scott's holding him down with one hand at the chest, the other wrapped around his wrists.

Finding a burst of energy I didn't have before, I lurch toward him.

I drop to my knees beside him and grab his collar, yanking his face toward me. "Where is she?" I scream. "Where is Natalie?"

He blinks up at me, his face frozen with fear and wide, unfocused eyes. He's confused.

Noticing Maddie with her phone, he stretches out his arms.

"Wait! Please. The little one's in her room. I'll tell you all of it. All of it," Walter rasps.

I don't wait for anything else and spin and bolt down the hall, stumbling on the rug a few times as I push into Natalie's room.

"Natalie!"

She's sitting up in bed, startled by the noise.

"She's safe," I call out to Maddie and Scott and cross the room in two strides.

My legs tremble like a snapped rubber band. Relief crashes over me so hard I almost faint.

Throwing my arms around her, I squeeze her to my chest and kiss the top of her head over and over.

Our little girl is safe.

"Momma, what's that noise outside?" she whispers into my shoulder. "It scared me."

She's in her blue pajamas, and her hair is damp. It looks like she's had a shower before bed. Other than being frightened, she looks okay.

"It's nothing, sweetie, you're safe now." I pull her closer. "Can you tell me what happened?"

"Mr. Walter grabbed me away from the *Big, Mean Man* and took me in his car."

"Did he hurt you?"

"No," she says as she shakes her head. "He said the *Big, Mean Man* was trying to get me. Mr. Walter saved me."

A cold lump falls into my stomach.

"I'm sorry for scaring you, Momma."

I hug her tighter. "You've got no reason to be sorry, sweetie. None."

"I threw the bone too far, and then we went farther than you told me to. Denver didn't want to do it, but I thought it would be fun to go closer to the street. There was a horse carriage." Her brow furrows. "Momma, I saw him. The *Big, Mean Man*."

I force myself to stay calm.

"He was big like you and Daddy, and he had sunglasses and a hat. He didn't talk. He was just there. Denver bit him. That's when Mr. Walter ran out of the trees and got me." She sniffles. "Denver chased the *Big, Mean Man,* but he got away in a car."

I can hear raised voices coming from the hall.

"What color was his car?"

"Silver."

"You're safe now." I brush her hair back and kiss her cheek. "Let's get you tucked in. Momma's going to talk to Mr. Walter."

"I love you, Momma."

Why is my heart still racing? "I love you too, sweetie."

Back in the living room, Walter sits on the couch while Scott stands in front of him, arms crossed, watching.

Dizzy, I take a moment to lean against the hallway wall.

Maddie comes to me. “I peeked in while you were talking to her.” She blows out a long breath and sniffs. “I tried to reach Nathan, but it went to voicemail.”

“What’s wrong with him?” I ask, remembering Walter’s skittishness and his lost eyes.

“I think he’s delusional,” she whispers. “He seems to be telling the truth about trying to help Natalie, but nothing he’s saying is coherent.”

“Natalie said another man tried to grab her first. She said Walter was waiting in the trees and came to her rescue.”

“The guy in the Rover has to be the one Natalie’s talking about. There’s no good excuse for what he did. He’s dangerous. And Nathan’s out there looking for him.”

“God, Maddie, I thought I’d lost her.”

She lifts my face. “Should we call the police?”

“Not yet. I want to talk to him first. Then we’ll try Nathan again.”

Back in the living room, I take a closer look at Walter.

He’s dressed in nice clothes, but it looks like he’s been wearing them for a few days. His trim beard has grown out, and I’m not sure if he’s brushed his teeth. I place my hand on his shoulder.

“Hello, Walter.”

His eyes are kind and a little more focused than before.

“I want to keep her safe. He will hurt her.”

I inhale sharply.

“Nathan is alive again?” he asks. He fidgets, tapping his knees with his hands.

I pull a throw off the couch and put it around him.

“Yes, Nathan has amnesia, but he’s back home.”

“Amnesia?” Standing, he wobbles around the room, jerking his arms up and down. “Oh no! Go. He’s coming!” he shouts, wild-eyed.

"Who's coming? Nathan?"

He shakes his head rapidly from side to side while twisting his hands.

I grip his shoulders. "Walter. What's his name? Who is the *Big, Mean Man*?"

He shoves me away and I have to catch myself from falling. Scott moves toward him. When I lift a hand to stop Scott, both Scott's and Maddie's phones ring out at the same time. We all look at each other. Maddie answers hers while Scott steps into the corner to answer his.

"Hannah? Hannah?" Maddie's worried voice sharpens. "Hannah, are you okay?"

I watch as all I hear on the other end are incoherent sobs—until Scott swears and storms out the front door. Oh no.

"No…" Maddie's voice breaks as she chokes down sobs of her own. The adrenaline that had finally mostly left my system surges back with a vengeance. Tears are pouring down her cheeks.

I'm too afraid to ask her what's going on.

"Stay there. I'm coming right now. Love you," she says in a raw, throaty voice. I wait for her to tell me what's going on, but I don't want to know.

"It's Jamie."

CHAPTER 26

The Stranger

The Land Rover.

He's leaving. I didn't get a good look at the driver, but I saw his door closing.

I slam on the gas, making an illegal U-turn in the middle of the intersection to circle back into the convenience store parking lot. In an instant, he pulls out and floors it.

"No. No. No. Don't even think about it," I call out, whipping through the parking lot without stopping. Oncoming traffic be damned. I press harder, trying to catch up with him.

My little girl could be in there.

Eighty miles per hour.

Without warning, he cuts hard to the right, his taillights vanishing down a side street. When I jerk the wheel to follow him, my '90 Corolla lurches so violently it nearly rips out the axle.

I'm close enough to see his tag. Holding the steering wheel with my left hand, I fumble for my cell phone with the other. The car drifts onto the shoulder, tires chewing against the gravel. I jerk my right arm up and snap the button, hoping I caught something usable. The phone lands in the passenger seat when I toss it and wrestle the wheel, pulling the car back under control. I stick with him through two more turns.

Then we're back on the main road.

Bright lights cover the street ahead, and I know where he's going now—the Castle Light Bridge.

Naples. And then, anywhere.

We sprint for three more miles, ratcheting up the speed until it's reckless. I'm terrified that we'll wreck. What if Natalie's in there?

But the alternative's worse. I can't lose him.

The engine screams as I press the gas harder. Now the steering wheel is trembling, and the car's frame rattles as I push over a hundred miles per hour, trying to keep pace. The car is about to shake apart, but I don't let up. I can't. Her life is at stake.

But it doesn't matter. I'm outmatched. And my car won't give anymore. Darting off at what must be over a hundred and thirty miles per hour, he soars across the causeway entrance.

Defeated, I ease off the gas and take the shoulder pull-off. I dial Detective Daniels and describe the Rover and where it was heading. I try to think of anything that could be useful. While I have him on the phone, I zoom in on the image I captured during the chase.

Hope surges when I see a clear shot of the license tag.

Washington, D.C.

After I hang up, I start my way to the house. What am I going to tell her? I was right there, but I couldn't bring our little girl home.

The phone rings.

It's Crystal.

Natalie's home, and she's safe.

♥

I watch her sleep. I had to see for myself that she was safe. The quilt rises and falls with her steady breathing. I smile when I see her little hand resting on the leather band around her neck. For the first time in hours, my heart finally settles down.

Back in the living room, Crystal is waiting for me with some tea. I fill her in on the Land Rover, and she explains the incident with Walter and the call from Hannah.

"All I know is Jamie's missing. Maddie called me back to give me an update, but she's got her hands full with Hannah. They're all out there now, looking for him."

I didn't know that Jamie and Hannah were an item.

"Are Hannah and Jamie?"

"They haven't told anyone yet—but yes. We all know."

I wonder what could have happened. Jamie was fine when Scott and I left the ship today. He was assigned to do some gas staging work with the SEALs at the Drop in the afternoon. They were going to lay tanks and other equipment in the tunnels. But they weren't going in too far and were going to wear standard gear, not the Shields. Something that Jamie could do blindfolded.

"I should go help," I say before thinking. I shake my head.

No. I can't leave Natalie and Crystal alone.

Crystal nods. "You should. The police are sending someone over here right now. To stay the night." She holds my hand. "Tomorrow, we'll figure out what to do."

♥

As soon as I pull into the marina parking lot, I see the ambulances and three covered gurneys.

Shit.

Getting out, I walk to Finn and Sid, who are gathered with a group of others on the pier. Scott's nowhere in sight, and neither is the *Adeline*.

"Nathan." Sid motions me over to join her and Finn.

"What happened?" I ask.

Finn exhales slowly. "One SEAL made it out and explained how they got turned around in the tunnels," Finn says. "It was a silt-out. Looks like they lost the line and got separated." He lowers his gaze to the planks. "They've recovered three bodies so far."

"Jamie?" I ask.

"Looks like he was caught in the middle of it. They're still looking for him and one other SEAL," he says.

"How long have they been searching?"

"Nearly two hours now. Scott and the rest of his team took the *Adeline* out to search. Maddie and Hannah are with them."

"I should be out there."

"I expect they've got all the help they need right now," he says.

But I'm already walking toward Finn's RIB with my dive bag. "Give me a lift."

CHAPTER 27

The Widow

The doorbell rings.

A stiff wind of fear brushes over my skin. What if it isn't the police? Nathan and I don't own guns. I grab a butcher's knife and move to the door.

When I peer through the side window, I see Detective Daniels and his partner.

Strange. I thought they were assigning a junior officer to us tonight.

I open the door. "Detective."

Daniels's eyebrows lift at the knife in my hand.

"Sorry." I set it on the foyer table. "I'm still a little jittery."

"Completely understandable." His voice is gentle. "Can we come in?"

"Of course." I gesture toward the kitchen. "Have a seat. I'll fix us something to drink. Water? Tea? Cola?"

Tea it is. I pull out the pitcher of sweet tea and pour three glasses as I talk. "I wasn't expecting you, Detective. They told me it would be someone else."

When I sit down, I uncover a plate of cookies and set down a stack of napkins. "Thank you for coming. I'll sleep easier. Has there been any news about the Rover?"

"We have some news about Walter," he says, taking a sip. "We found him."

All of the tension in my muscles releases at once. Thank goodness. Walter might be able to tell us more about the *Big, Mean Man*. We need to find him.

Daniels sets his glass down, his mouth tightening into a frown.

"We found him just a little while ago. Behind the old Cooper Motel." He pauses. "Shot through the head."

For a heartbeat, my brain goes numb.

What?

"I know you want more answers, Mrs. Glassier, but to be honest… I think Walter acted alone."

I'm trying to listen. But I can't. Walter was in this house a few hours ago, and now he's dead. Murdered. Which means the man who tried to take Natalie is a murderer.

Daniels continues. "We don't have any evidence that this other man is dangerous. The park video didn't show him taking Natalie, and we know for a fact Walter did. I think this *Big, Mean Man* is just some poor guy who became involved in this because he was there at the same time."

"But Natalie said—"

"A child has a big imagination," he says. "Especially in a scary situation. Do you think it's possible she thinks he exists because Walter told her so? A protective mechanism her mind built to help her manage her fear while Walter had her?"

No. I don't. I know my daughter, and she knows what she saw.

"But Nathan… he found the Land Rover."

"Yeah, we ran the tag. It's not in the system. Maybe Nathan was off by a few digits? Whoever he was chasing may have gotten spooked by being followed by a stranger."

That's not possible. None of this makes any sense.

"Mrs. Glassier?"

"I'm sorry. It's just…" I glance toward the hallway, afraid Natalie may be listening. "You're still going to stay with us tonight, right?" I force myself to push aside my rising panic.

"Yes." He tips his head toward his partner. "Bill will be right outside all night. But try not to worry." He gets up and rests his hand on my shoulder. "I really think it's over."

I know that's not true.

CHAPTER 28

The Stranger

Jamie is alive.

By the time Finn and I reached the Adeline, they had Jamie, and the SEAL pulled out. The SEAL was trapped in a pinch point in one of the offshoot tunnels, and Jamie couldn't get him out by himself. They'd used a couple of the staging bottles to breathe while they waited to be found. They're physically fine, just shaken up.

Instead of going home, we're on our way to an emergency briefing on Finn's ship.

After a grim-faced Commander Nicolaus enters the ship's conference room, he gives Finn a short nod to begin.

"Today's tragedy underscores the danger of the Drop," Finn says. "We must use trained cave divers."

The DARPA liaison seated to the side of the commander asks to speak. Nicolaus inclines his head once.

The liaison looks around the table, making eye contact with each person before he speaks. "First, I want to acknowledge the work this team has done. Seeing the DS100 prototype operate in real conditions is exactly why we're here. The people on this mission are the best at what they do."

He waits for his compliments to land, then goes in for the kill.

"That said, I think we all recognize the dominant risk factor isn't mechanical. It's human."

Scott shifts in his chair. I don't care for this guy either.

"Before we make any decisions on the dives, and potentially risk more human life, I want to ensure we have a full set of options on the table. We've got tools and contingencies we can employ to triage this. Right now."

Finn's face drops, and he swallows. We all know what that means. Plan B.

"I think it's too soon to—" Finn starts.

The liaison snaps his gaze to Nicolaus.

"Dr. Clark. Let him finish."

The DARPA liaison continues. Sure enough, he lays out alternatives. Freezing agents and a targeted seal of the caves. Methods that would be disastrous to the reef and the blue hole.

I'm grateful Crystal's not with us. Hearing the liaison's cold, clinical tone as he explains how he could make our problems go away with a click of a button would crush her. And piss her off.

When he finishes, he turns back to Commander Nicolaus and waits.

"Thank you," the commander says at last. "Those are all valid alternatives. If they become necessary." He pauses. "But I don't believe we're there yet. My men can properly train for cave diving. They'll do it fast. That's the next step."

"Respectfully, that's not going to work," Scott jumps in. "Your men can learn fast, but our priority is execution. We're already trained on the Shields. Let's get this done."

The commander studies Scott for a moment, then leans toward the DARPA liaison. They exchange some words privately. Commander Nicolaus gives a small shake of his head. "Fine. If you're confident in your readiness, we'll put your team in the Shields—with our oversight. Are you confident, Rickter?"

"Yes."

"Very well." The commander straightens. "Given how quickly this is escalating, I agree we need to move. I don't want our next conversation to be about those alternatives we just discussed." He gives the liaison a hard look. "And I, for one, would consider it a tragedy to lose a geographical treasure like Carter's Drop." His attention returns to Finn. "Let's brief after each thermal dive."

The DARPA liaison, commander, and his staff leave.

As soon as the door shuts, Scott turns to Garrett, dropping his fist on the table. "We need every skilled cave diver who has experience in the Drop."

"Isn't that what we have?" Garret asks sarcastically.

"Garrett, we need Wes. Get over whatever grudge you have with him—NOW."

"Wes Harrington isn't an option," Garrett says.

"Why not?"

"I have my reasons. Anyway, he's off the table."

Scott looks like he's about to tear into him until Sid stands up.

"Daddy Dearest." She smiles sweetly at Garrett.

He looks at the table, unable to meet her eyes.

"Scott's right. You need to let this go and *stop* meddling in people's lives. This is too important, and it's not about you."

He gives her a long stare.

What is going on with those two? Why doesn't he just chill? She's his daughter, for God's sake.

Natalie's little face pops into my head. I promise you I'll always be on your side, Sugar Muffin. You'll never feel less than around me.

"What exactly are you expecting me to change, Sidney?" his voice goes dark. "I can't take back what Harrington has done. Or fix the lives he's ruined." His expression is pure venom.

She doesn't break her stare.

"The tape," Scott says. "You need to give us the tape, and we'll destroy it."

"No—"

"Dad…"

Completely flustered, he relents. "Ah, very well. I have conditions. Conditions I'll go over with Harrington himself. In private."

"I want to talk to him first," Scott says.

"Fine," Garrett says. Turning his angry eyes away from Sid, he stares at the wall.

♥

"He's going to be so thrilled to see you." Mads, Scott, and I are back at the Inn in the dining room. Scott has his laptop on the table getting it ready for the Zoom call. Crystal told me about Wes and our shared adventures in Belize. Apparently, we became close friends during our time exploring the Great Blue Hole. Last year, after he learned about Crystal and Natalie, he stepped up and maintained contact with Crystal to help her with bills and to be someone she could rely on.

For that alone, I owe him more than I can repay. Not to mention what he did for Mads.

I've seen a few of his videos since I've been back, and as with everything else in my life. Nothing. No recollection of the relationship he and I had.

Scott starts the call and squeezes in beside Mads, who stares at the screen, beaming. The image of a blonde man with intense green-gray eyes flashes on the screen. I'm standing off to the side, out of the camera's range.

"Harrington." Scott gives him a stern look.

"Rickter." He tilts his head, looking past Scott's shoulder. "Hi there, Maddie. Always a pleasure to see you, rookie."

"Apprentice, remember?" She laughs.

"That's right. Where's the little guy?"

"He's at the house with Ms. Connor. You'll meet him when you get here."

"When hell freezes over or when Garrett finds a soul, right?"

"All right, you two, enough of the banter." Scott tries to hide his smile and look serious. "Harrington, not sure if anyone's told you yet, but Maverick Key's in a situation."

"Surprising."

"There's something in the Drop that's heating the rocks, and it's created an environmental nightmare. Coral and marine life are dying. People exposed are getting sick, and worst of all, we've got DARPA and the Navy down here calling the shots."

"How hot are the rocks?"

"Changes every day, but some have been measured at over four hundred plus."

"Fuck."

"Yeah. We need every skilled cave diver familiar with the Drop down here, and we've finally convinced Garrett to use some common sense. He's agreed to drop the blackmail."

"Well, I didn't expect it would take an environmental crisis to get me out of hiding, but I guess I'll take it. When do you need me?"

"As soon as you can get here. Where are you anyway?"

"I could tell you, but I'd have to…" He uses the gun hand gesture. "I should be able to get there in four days."

"Try to get here sooner if you can," Scott says. Mads pulls on his shoulder and raises her brows. "Oh yeah. As you'd expect, Garrett has terms and conditions before he hands over the tape. Says he wants to speak to you about it privately."

Wes's face freezes for a moment. He knows exactly what Garrett's conditions are. "I'll call him. And I'll see you guys in a few days. Can't wait."

"Before you hang up, we've got another surprise for you," Maddie teases him. She's so excited she's bouncing.

Wes's eyes light up with Mads's attention. "Two surprises in one day, and it's not even Christmas yet."

Mads takes her hand and motions me over. I swallow. When I step into view, Wes's eyes open wide, and his jaw drops.

"What in the…" He grins.

"He came home, Wes. He's been alive this whole time with amnesia."

"Hi, Wes," I say.

"Nathan Carter."

Mads and Scott excuse themselves, leaving Wes and me to chat.

He laughs. "We're hard to kill."

"Crystal and Mads have told me stories about you."

"I bet they have. It's good to see you, brother. Any memories?"

"None. Except for a few dreams. I've been warned I may never get them back."

"You've got no idea how you made it out?"

"None."

"I wonder…When we were exploring The Great Blue Hole in Belize, you essentially took it upon yourself to train me in cave diving. I was one of those jerks who thought they could teach themselves. So, you stepped in. A good thing since I got into some major trouble the first time down. One thing you said always stuck with me."

Wes is an interesting guy. He's on show, even with his friends.

"As long as you're still breathing, don't quit." He gives me a long look. "You're diving?"

"With Scott's crew. I can remember how to do everything, but I have no context. Crystal has about a million photos of our lives. We've been getting through them one by one."

"Hmmm. By the time you're through, you'll probably remember more about your life than I do about mine. There's so much in our lives we forget anyway. What we remember are the chapter summaries and maybe a few drop quotes… It's the present and the people in it that matter the most."

"What about the future?"

"That's always a gift. You never expect it but appreciate it when it comes."

"But then it's…"

"The present." He winks.

I clear my throat. "I want to thank you personally for saving my sister. I owe you my life."

"She saved herself. I was just there to help… and return the favor."

CHAPTER 29

The Widow

When I answer the door, there's a broody, broad-shouldered man who must be at least seven feet tall looking straight at me. Silver hair. Sharp gray eyes. He looks like he flew in straight from Siberia.

For a moment, I wonder if he's the *Big, Mean Man*.

Oddly, the thought brings relief. Natalie is at the beach house, and Nathan's at the Inn with the dive team. They're both safe.

"Can I help you?" My voice is a squeak.

"Crystal Carter?"

"Yes."

Wait. Did he call me Crystal *Carter*?

"Ziddo. I'm protective detail for Natalie."

"Did the police send you?" I thought they were considering the case closed.

"Wes Harrington."

Uh, okay. That's unexpected.

I text Wes, and sure enough, he's hired a bodyguard for Natalie. I smile. With everything that has been happening all at once, I'd forgotten about Wes.

I wonder if he knows Nathan's alive.

Another text.

Yep. He knows, and he'll be coming to Maverick Key soon. I'll finally get to meet him.

I've tried not to take advantage of his kindness. But right now, we need his help.

I give Ziddo the address, then call Maddie to warn her he's on his way.

♥

The moment I arrive at City Hall, I'm summoned to the mayor's office.

I'm sure this has something to do with the daily press conference. With anxiety rising across the island and the media circling nonstop, the mayor has been on the hook to face the people and the cameras every day.

He's usually calm, immaculately dressed, steady. But the last few days have taken their toll. A shadow of stubble darkens his usually clean-shaved jaw, and his shirt and pants are slightly wrinkled.

Citizens are getting restless, and we've given them very little. No answers. Minimal progress to report. And now, with the arrival of the Navy and the death of the SEALs, Maverick Key is making national news.

"Crystal, we need your help with them today," Mayor Bent says, loosening his tie. "Dr. Clark is busy with the dives, and we need someone who can answer basic questions about the science."

He lets out a long breath and sinks back into his chair. “We can’t afford another bad briefing. Especially with the big networks breathing down our necks.”

I swallow my nerves. I’m used to making presentations to City Leadership, the Coast Guard, and NOAA officials, but the public and the media are another story.

“Mayor Bent, I’m a scientist. I can’t be a spokesperson.”

“Sure, you can,” he says. “Approachable. Pretty. You’ll make them feel comfortable, and they’ll trust you.”

“I don’t know. When does it start?”

“Now.”

I only have a few minutes to freshen up before walking on stage. Standing behind the mayor, I look out at the crowd. I’m not sure how it’s possible, but there are even more people crammed in the auditorium, and now that the press has been allowed in, large clusters of cameras line the aisles.

I can feel streams of sweat sliding down my back, and worry it might be noticeable.

This is not my wheelhouse.

After the mayor delivers his usual introductory remarks to warm up the crowd, he hands the microphone to me.

Don’t say anything stupid, Crystal, I tell myself.

As I approach the podium, a man at the back of the room catches my attention. He’s wearing dark glasses and a hat pulled low over his hair. Mid-thirties? There’s an eerie stillness about him. He doesn’t move. Doesn’t react to the noise around him. His face is blank.

I’m so frightened, I can’t move.

I open my mouth to speak, and nothing comes out.

Instinctively, I know he has to be the *Big, Mean Man*. He looks like the guy in the security camera photo.

What do I do? If I call for help, it'll cause a scene, and he'll get away anyway.

I step to the microphone and try to tear my gaze from his.

"I'm Crystal Car—Glassier." I swallow and continue, speeding through my presentation. I open the floor to questions.

"What killed the SEALs? Was it toxic gas?"

Oh no.

I glance at Mayor Bent. "I can't speak for the military operation," I say carefully, "but I can confirm that no toxic gas has been discovered in the area to date."

"What's in there? What's killing the sea life?" Overlapping, scared, and frustrated voices rise.

"We haven't identified the root cause yet," I say, "but we have the best minds and the bravest divers working on it." I think of Nathan. It calms me down and helps me push forward.

A red-headed woman I recognize stands up. She's a local reporter. Without waiting to be called on, she blurts out, "Mrs. Glassier, are you having an affair with Dr. Nathan Carter?"

The blood drains from my face.

All the energy in the room shifts instantly. No longer focused on the environmental crisis, eager faces turn toward me, hungry now for gossip. For answers about the town's beloved hero and what happened to him during all those years he was missing. Some expressions are curious. Others are openly hostile.

Whispers rise from the floor to the podium.

My throat closes. I'm done here.

"She turned Mark into a murderer. He was a nice man."

"Gold digger."

"Slut."

"Heartless."

"Someone should call Child Services. She doesn't deserve her daughter."

Mayor Bent jumps up to the microphone. "Ms. Kasler, that's highly inappropriate. One more question like that, and you and your team will be removed and banned from future gatherings."

She ignores him and fires off another rude question, but I can't hear it. All I see is the *Big, Mean Man's* face as the corners of his mouth twitch, then slowly curve into a smile.

CHAPTER 30

The Stranger

Walter's dead. He was ill and helpless. Why would someone kill him?

"Tomorrow's dive is thermal," Scott announces. "We focus on testing the Shields in the hotspots we can reach without going too far. Safety is the priority." He nods to Finn. "Finn."

"Right. Data collection is still the best tool for determining what we're dealing with. This is a first step. On each subsequent dive, we'll push a bit farther."

Scott gives him a side-eye.

Finn clears his throat and continues. "We'll dive as far as we can to ninety-five degrees Fahrenheit and then turn on the cooling."

"We discussed ninety-three. We can't shed body heat when it gets much warmer," Scott says.

Finn nods. "The thermal layer cools things down rather quickly when activated."

“Have you thought about sudden temperature increases?” Jamie asks. “I don’t remember that coming up in the training.”

“The suit’s outer shell provides a brief buffer against acute temperature spikes. Should the water reach ninety-nine degrees Fahrenheit, the barrier gel and coolant veins will activate automatically, regardless of operator engagement. Short of a sudden rise over five hundred degrees, this remains survivable. With the gradient factored in once the gel activates, eight hundred degrees is considered the upper bound. Much beyond that, the suit’s exterior fails. Almost instantly.”

“This is insane,” Jamie says. “I don’t want to go out like a boiled egg.”

“More like a marshmallow, J,” Liam says and chuckles.

“You’re gonna ruin s’mores for me, man.”

“Team, any way we look at this, it’s going to be extremely dangerous.” Scott grimaces. “I can’t guarantee your safety. If anyone wants to step out—you have my blessing.”

No one takes him up on his offer.

“Well said, Scott. Everyone needs to make their own call,” says Finn.

Scott ignores him and continues. “We’ll have three divers on a team. Two in the hot zone and one at the cutoff for safety. On the next dive, we’ll have two dive teams. But only one this time. It’s Finn on data. Nathan is on the line, and I’ll be the safety. We’re taking the *Hecate.*”

“What time are we meeting at the docks?” I ask.

“Three p.m.,” Scott says. He looks around the room as if he’s memorizing everyone’s face. “Get some rest.”

After eating a light dinner, Crystal and I compared notes on our days. She spent the afternoon at the police station after encountering that same creep who was trying to grab Natalie.

When we discussed the Land Rover's Washington, D.C. plates, she panicked and told me she'd seen it before—at the dive club. Even before I came back to Maverick Key. This guy has had eyes on my family.

I'm grateful to Wes for hiring protection for Natalie, but I'm still worried about Crystal.

"Maybe you should stay at Mads's. Take the couch or snuggle in with Natalie?"

She thinks for a moment and frowns. "No. My place is with you, Nathan. I'd rather keep Natalie safe while we figure all this out."

"Maybe we can convince Wes to hire a second bodyguard?" I'm only half joking.

She smirks, wrinkling her nose. "Uh, that's a hard no. I'm not sleeping under the same roof with another Ziddo." She shivers. "Besides…" She smiles coyly, snuggling in closer. "I have you to protect me."

That should be flattering, but I feel a twinge of uncertainty. Can I protect her? I'm not around her 24/7.

"How long are the *Hecate* tunnels?"

"We're not certain, but on sonar it appears to be the longest and deepest passage in Carter's Drop. Approximately fourteen hundred meters in total length with a depth of over a hundred fifty meters in the deepest branches."

Our dive plan takes us as far as five hundred meters and to a depth of as much as eighty meters tomorrow.

"Please dive the plan, Nathan. If anything's off, don't push it. And watch out for Finn. Leave his ass if he goes rogue again."

I give her a kiss. "I'll put safety first, I promise."

"*Your* safety."

"Has there been anything new from the police?"

"They were useless today. They've got nothing on who killed Walter or who the *Big, Mean Man may* be. They pretty much laughed off what happened to me at the press conference. But they said they'd look into it."

A flash of anger jolts through me as I think about those damn reporters and their ambush at the meeting. To their credit, the national news focused on the hard news and didn't air it. But those assholes at the local station did. She doesn't deserve any of this. At some point soon, I'm going to have to agree to a press conference and set the record straight.

"Crystal, I know who Walter is." She doesn't hide the shock on her face. "It's in my journals. He was a colleague of mine, a quantum physicist professor I'd been consulting with not long after I discovered Carter's Drop."

"What happened to him? He didn't seem like he could still be practicing."

"I'm not sure what happened to him to make him ill. He wasn't like that when I knew him. From my notes, we were collaborating on a theory I was working on about the descendants of Atlantis. Apparently, I'd recently changed my hypothesis, and I didn't believe that what I was looking for was based on the myth of Atlantis at all."

At least not how the stories tell it.

"That's what most people think, right? That it's only a myth made up by Plato."

"My journals don't say. I just listed the academics I was consulting. My research brought me to Dr. Walter Stanley. And that's not all."

She waits for me to continue, her face lined with worry.

"Dr. Stanley and I both knew Finn…"

"And?"

"We didn't trust him… or his colleagues."

"Nathan—" She jumps in surprise. "When Maddie found your things, she found coded notes. Mark stole them, and they were taken into police custody for the investigation. But when they returned your belongings, they didn't have the notes. They claimed they never did. Someone had to take it."

"Finn."

"He's hiding something."

"He is. And those notes are probably where I documented the details I didn't want to keep in my journals."

"We've got to confront him and find out what he knows. All this ties together, and it's a threat to Natalie."

"I'll talk to him about this after tomorrow's dive. We'll figure out where he stands in all this." I glance at my watch. "But, right now, you and I have a date with the sunrise."

CHAPTER 31

The Widow

The coast is deceptively beautiful. Waves crash along the shoreline, and at high tide the ocean keeps its secrets—for now. Later this morning, when the waters recede, low tide will reveal the sickness and death hiding beneath.

Nathan and I aren't supposed to be here on the beach, but there's no one else around. No one to tell us not to. It's still dark, though the lights from nearby houses, including ours, are enough to see the sand and water.

As I gaze outward across the sea, I let myself cry. I know some of the coral is dead now. And most of the reef at the zones closest to Carter's Drop and Coral Fang—already sickly white—will soon follow. If water temperatures in those areas remain the same, it will happen before Christmas. My boss has gotten approval to begin salvage triage operations, focusing on genetically distinct lines. We'll begin *ex situ* conservation immediately.

A crushing wall of sadness falls onto my heart. In my teenage years, I wandered lost and lonely, finding solace in the ethereal promise of the sea. It's unimaginable to me that the ocean itself may not be eternal, that, like all of us, it will die one day.

But here we are, facing just that.

In my gut, I know this will expand beyond our shores.

I glance at Nathan. He's spread out the beach blanket and is working on arranging our picnic.

"This may not be here for Natalie's children," I whisper sadly.

Nathan stops what he's doing and moves next to me, pulling me onto his lap and folding his arms around me, closing me in a protective embrace. He shakes his head, adamant. "I don't believe that." He rests his chin on my shoulder and whispers into my ear. "Nature is mysterious and resilient. If we don't get in its way, it'll overcome."

"I once told you that everything has a purpose, that nothing's accidental or random. I'm not sure I believe that anymore." Although I've felt this way for a while, saying it out loud leaves me feeling lost, as though the core of my identity has been an illusion. When Nathan returned, I allowed myself to hope that wasn't true. But maybe it is, and maybe he'll be gone soon, too.

"Don't. Please don't." He lifts my chin and looks into my eyes. "You were right. We may not know why this is happening. And it seems grim right now… but it won't stay that way." He squeezes me tighter. "You and Natalie make this world worth fighting for. We'll figure this out."

I want to believe him. But there are so many unanswered questions, and seemingly little to no time left to figure this out. I wish I had Nathan's faith.

I move to face him. "Nathan, please come home to us tomorrow."

"I promise."

"Can you… can you promise that?" Silently, he bites down on his lip.

"I believe you," I tell him.

He takes a sharp inhale. "Did you believe me that day?"

"Yes. I did."

He clutches my hand and pulls it to his chest, over his heart. "I promise to do my best. There's nothing in this world that means as much to me as you and Natalie. That's why I'm doing it—for us and for what we love." He motions to the shoreline. "I promise I won't take unnecessary risks this time."

"Make me believe it, Nathan."

"Every night, I dreamed of you, Crystal. And then I found you. Never lose hope." His hands slip beneath the straps of my sundress, easing them down as he breathes me in. He brushes his lips, warm and reverent, across my collarbone. His mouth opens, teasing me with little wisps of his tongue.

He leans forward, pushing me back onto the blanket. I feel the sand crunch beneath it and the chill of the wind. He cradles me in his arms and kisses me. Wrapping my arms around his neck, I give in to him. All my trust, all my love.

He looks deep into my eyes.

A cool, gentle breeze stirs his golden-brown hair, and his eyelids flutter from the sensation. His bright eyes darken.

"I love the way you look at me," he murmurs.

He shifts his weight, diving into me, surprising me with his assertiveness. Lightly brushing his lips across my skin, he pauses at my navel and blows butterfly kisses that make me shiver. I gasp, feeling a rush of warmth in my core. Then, I curl my fingers through his hair and lead him down further.

"Greedy little thing."

I smile.

After we love each other as if we'll never get another chance, we finish our picnic.

Spreading some cheese and jam on a cracker, I offer it to him. He takes it in one bite.

"It's not overrated," I say.

"What?"

"Sex on the beach."

He laughs. "Who told you it was overrated?"

"You."

"Well, obviously I lied." He leans in for another kiss and another cracker.

"I love your surprises." He picks up the bottle of jam and squints his eyes, unable to read the label in the dark.

"Fig." I take the bottle and fix him another. "Fig jam and brie are the best."

"Fancy."

We laugh, and I fix us more crackers and something to drink. Champagne for me, water for him. "I'm planning something special for you tomorrow when you come home. A memory," I say.

His eyes light up. "Another surprise?"

"Kind of, but I'm going to tell you what it is. I'm recreating our honeymoon."

I take the photo out of my purse and hand it to him. A local took the picture right after we arrived in Belize. We're standing in front of a small garden cabana, covered by a thatched roof and surrounded by lush vegetation. We're wearing matching linen shorts. I'm in a black tank, and he's in a white button-down. We're both smiling from ear to ear.

He takes the photo and laughs. "I didn't know you had so many teeth." He kisses me. "I can't wait." Then he lies back down on the blanket, and I join him, taking the obligatory selfie with us lying on the sand.

We stare at the sky, waiting for the sun to rise.

His eyes are restless.

“What are you thinking?” I ask.

“When are you going to show me the picture of the day I asked you to marry me?” he whispers.

He’s asked about that a few times. “Soon. That one’s very special. But it’s going to take more planning for me to tell it right.” I rest my head on his heart. “Come home to me, Nathan.”

He wraps his arms around me tightly as the first rays of the sun fill the sky.

CHAPTER 32

The Stranger

After sunrise, we don't stay to watch low tide peel back and reveal the hundreds of dead jellyfish washed ashore—a daily occurrence now. I don't have the stomach for it, and I don't want to see what it does to Crystal. It's too sad. I don't want her to be sad anymore. Local volunteers will comb the sand, as they do each morning, with buckets and tongs, hauling away the dead creatures. An hour later, no one will ever know they were even there. Maverick Key's beaches still look beautiful.

I carry Crystal home, and we collapse into bed. We plan to sleep for just a couple of hours, but we end up sleeping straight through the rest of the morning until the alarm shrills at noon. Crystal set it as a backup, and sure enough, we needed it.

Trying to stop it before it wakes her, I slam my arm towards the snooze button and accidentally knock the alarm off the nightstand. The repetitive, high-pitched beeps go on for several minutes as I fumble for it on the floor and finally find the right buttons to turn it off.

Sheepishly, I turn back to the bed. Crystal is looking at me and what I'm not wearing.

"Thirty minutes, sailor."

She laughs when I run bare-assed to the shower, grabbing my toothbrush and toothpaste on the way.

"I only need ten," I shout. I can't help smiling when I hear her laughter. I *really* want her to join me, but there isn't time. I brush my teeth and wash up as fast as I can.

When I get to the kitchen, I smell breakfast.

"I made you toast and eggs."

My mouth waters at the sight of a steaming pile of fluffy scrambled eggs and buttered toast. How the hell did she cook this so fast?

"Tomorrow, I make you breakfast," I say. I kiss her, then scarf everything down with a cup of coffee, already thinking ahead to our honeymoon. I can't wait.

"Don't forget your surprise tonight. It'll be waiting for you when you get home." She stands on her toes and kisses me goodbye.

Whatever happens today, I'm sure as hell coming home.

The sky is gray and somewhat cool for a December day in Maverick Key. I speed through the red lights, careful to keep my eye out for anything coming. I still have time for one more stop before the marina if I hurry.

I need to see them.

I know I should be at least a little nervous about today's dive. Some healthy tension. But I'm not. I'm excited. The reason I'm confident today is that I know my limits. And I've already thought of all the things that could go wrong. I'm prepared for them. Whatever happens, I'll put my family first, and I'm coming home tonight.

I turn onto the private side road that leads to my sister's place. A narrow, quiet stretch of beach. The beachfront is small, but the property runs deep, unusual for the island. Scott and Mads have been talking about renovations so they can stay here as their family grows. Two more bedrooms and an office. Scott's a good man, good enough to deserve my sister. I'm happy for them.

I park and start up the sandy path in the front yard. Outside by the fire pit, a huge man sits on one of the Adirondack chairs. He's carving something with his pocketknife.

His hands still when he sees me, and he watches with narrowed eyes as I ease past him to the door. It takes him a moment before a flash of recognition crosses his face. This must be Ziddo, the bodyguard.

I point to the door. "I'm visiting." He shrugs and waves his knife at the door, then goes back to carving.

I knock.

"Coming," Mads calls. She pulls back the sheer curtain over the side window. Excitement brightens her face. Right behind her, I hear little feet running over to us.

"Daddy!"

I open my arms. "Hey, Sugar Muffin."

I look over at Mads. "I can only stay a minute, but I wanted to see you both."

She tries to smile, but I can tell it's hard for her. She has dark circles under her eyes.

"I'm such a nervous wreck, Nathan. Why did I have to have such a brave brother and then marry a man just as brave?"

I put an arm around her in a side hug.

"Can you sit for just a minute?" She motions to the couch.

I shake my head. "I wish I could, but there's not enough time."

"Maybe we can make some," she says. "Where is that time machine of yours?" she calls out to Natalie. "You can show your Daddy what you've been up to."

Natalie runs off down the hallway. "I'll go get it."

"She's been working on it every day since she's been here. She has the design all drafted out and wanted to show you."

"I promised her we'll work on it together."

Natalie runs back and shows me the notebook paper. Sure enough, it's a time machine. One that looks very similar to H.G. Wells's time machine. A gold-framed sled with a seat in the center and a large circular rotating disc in the back.

"Nice! You did a very good job. I can't wait to ride it with you one day."

"I have all the parts we need in my room. I just need the battery. One that will make it go."

I laugh. "We'll find one."

"Now I'm scared," Maddie says. "With both of you working on it, that means we're going to have a time machine around here soon." She gives me a serious look. "You know you're not allowed to go anywhere else ever again, right?"

"I promise I'm here for good." I glance at my watch. "Two forty-five. I've got to go."

Before we say goodbye, I remember the reason I wanted to see her today.

"Remember how I told you about the dream I had with Crystal and how it turned out to be a true memory?" I ask.

She nods.

"I wanted to tell you about my other recurring dream," I say.

Curious, she raises her brows.

"I'm with this little girl with freckles. A tiny little thing with a sassy mouth who's as stubborn as nails."

"That sounds like me." She laughs.

"And this was the dream… She was taking her first dive into the ocean. *Pete's Dragon* was stamped on her swimsuit. Her favorite movie."

Her eyes widen. "The dragon's name is Elliott."

I give her a knowing smile. "I was so worried about her before we went under. It was her first time diving in the open water." Mads's eyes water. "I remember her stepping off the boat, splashing into the water, and taking my hand. She was fearless."

Tears stream down Mads's cheeks. "You *really* remember?"

I nod. "And I can't wait until we do it again."

We hug, and Natalie runs in between and throws her arms around us. "Family hug!"

CHAPTER 33

The Widow

Unpacking the last candle, I toss all the loose cardboard and plastic from my shopping trip into the recycle bin and sit down with a hot cup of tea. The flower arrangements arrived a few minutes ago, and the package I ordered from the boutique got here last night. I've already tried on the nightie, and it fits perfectly.

I'd forgotten how much fun getting ready for little celebrations can be—especially the romantic kind.

I glance at the clock. 4:40 p.m.

I pick up my cell phone. After a few rings, Margaret answers.

"They're in the cavern now. Everything's on track." She promises to update me as they progress.

Relieved, at least for now, I decide to do some research before I get back to the honeymoon plans. I grab my laptop from my desk and sink into the couch.

Big, Mean Man. I type it into the search bar and laugh.

Wow. There are actually quite a lot of pages with results. All of them hilarious, but none helpful, of course. If only it could be that easy.

Dr. Walter Stanley. Enter.

More promising.

I scroll through the long list of photo search results. There are multiple pictures of more than a dozen people of all colors, sizes, and ages. Moving through them one by one, I'm discouraged by the time I reach page eight.

I can't find him.

I type *quantum physics* into the search bar and press enter.

The screen blinks, and there he is. The Walter I'm looking for.

Several academic online magazine articles appear, and I scan them. They're mostly filled with boring science stuff. But when I get to one with a black-and-white photo, I stop and freeze.

Oh my God.

Reflexively, I clutch my chest and try to calm myself down.

The photo was taken at a cross-disciplinary geophysical science conference, and Walter stands among a panel of other academics.

It's him—the *Big, Mean Man*—and he's standing beside Dr. Phineas Clark and…

Nathan.

What in the world is going on?

The Big, Mean Man isn't wearing the glasses or hat, but it's definitely him. Clean-cut, he looks like an average science professor. He's the only one not even trying to smile.

I scan the photo caption and article. There's no reference to any of their names, but I know who they are.

JASONs. All of them.

CHAPTER 34

The Stranger

Finn is watching the water.

He's standing far enough away from the rest of us to signal it's intentional. He wants to be alone.

We're all on the research vessel, now anchored at the Carter's Drop descent point. Finn made the call to move it closer to the Drop so that we could hold a post-dive meeting as soon as we get back.

Today's important. We're making history.

As I gear up, I watch Finn. While I don't believe he wants harm to come to the coral or the caves, I also don't think they're a priority for him. He fought back against the suggestion of easier, more destructive measures, but I don't think he did so for any ethical reason or out of love for the ocean. It's something else.

It's always been about the stone for Finn. That's why he's here.

What is that stone made of? It can't possibly be what I'm thinking, can it?

Where does Dr. Nathan Carter fit into this? I'm a piece of this puzzle. My journals paint a picture. Finn knows I don't have my memories, yet he's done nothing to help me fill in any gaps. Any hints he's given about the past have been more of a test. So, he can be sure of what I know. My records show I shared information freely with Walter, meeting with him casually, like friends. But with Finn, every interaction was formal. Cautious. After I found the stone, I wanted access to his materials expertise, specifically on exotic matter theory. But I was careful not to share anything I knew with him, including the stone. It was Garrett's loose lips that opened Pandora's box when he started talking about the stone Mads found with his colleagues.

I need to confront Finn. But can I trust him enough to even ask him to explain? Or am I going to need backup?

I glance at Scott. I don't want to bring Mads's family into this if I don't have to.

Finn turns from the railing and walks to his Shield.

It's time to go.

My helmet seal locks into place with a final hiss, and I head to the dive station.

Scott, Finn, and I descend toward Carter's Drop. As we approach the entrance, we slow down. Most of the coral is ghostly white. With a few small patches of blue and pink scattered amongst them. With the cavern's water temperatures now over ninety degrees, the coral closest to the Drop's entrance and its vents won't survive much longer. We hope to find a solution that won't cause further damage before the heated water spreads. If it spreads. We don't know how hot it will get.

We enter the cavern, and I can't believe what I'm seeing. Several patches of stone are shimmering. I make eye contact with Scott, who's just as unnerved as I am. We're in over our heads. Finn approaches one patch to collect data, then swims toward the *Hecate*.

He's in a hurry.

After Scott gives me another wary look, we follow Finn into the *Hecate* tunnel.

We're only fifteen yards in this time when we hit ninety-three degrees.

"My stop," Scott says through the helmet comms. He turns to Finn. "No exceptions in there, Finn. I swear to God, I'll make you regret it if you go off plan."

Finn's unaffected by Scott's threat, but nods once anyway. "Got it. We're here for the same reason."

"I doubt that." Scott turns to me, grasping my shoulders. "Be careful in there, brother. Call me on the comms if anything goes sideways."

"If anything happens. Tell all my girls I love them," I say and think of the picture Mads showed me of Crystal holding Natalie on the beach.

Scott's eyes pinch, and he nods his head once.

Finn and I move on, leaving Scott behind.

I focus on the guidelines. My job on this dive is to lay a new line where the existing one ends and, where needed, replace the nylon with heat-resistant co-polymer aramid rope. The existing line should hold until temperatures climb above one hundred twenty degrees Fahrenheit. Anything hotter than one-forty can cause the nylon to weaken and break. Hot water or not, we still need a guideline.

Finn glides through the channel flow as if he's been practicing for this moment his whole life. He darts ahead with childlike vigor, delighting in pulling readings and watching data stream across his screens. Monitoring our dive temperature appears to be the last thing on his mind. It wouldn't surprise me if he plans to let the suits trigger the coolant automatically.

Very well.

I'll handle the responsibility part myself.

Fortunately, *Hecate* hasn't warmed much since our previous dive, so we make quick progress to the spot where Finn ran into trouble the last time. That puts us roughly a hundred and forty meters into the tunnel, about a tenth of the entire trek. The temperature has held steady at ninety-four degrees over the last few meters.

While less suffocating than the wetsuit due to the air circulation layer and wicking fabric, it's still really hot, and I'm pouring sweat.

It's showtime.

I wave to get Finn's attention and tap on my monitor. "It's getting hot."

"Ready?" Finn asks.

"Ready."

I pull back the covered lever on my right forearm and press the yellow button. A rush of cold air sweeps through the suit, as if someone turned on the air conditioning. I check my dive computer monitor.

Green. Seventy-nine degrees.

"Shit," I mutter. "That's cool."

"Brilliant," Finn says.

The clock starts now. We've got about fifty-five minutes until the suit's coolant runs out and, we start to cook if we're still over one-twenty. Much hotter than that, we're just done.

That gives us roughly twenty minutes in before we have to turn back. Less if we were sticking to a true rule-of-thirds plan, as we do with gas. We agreed to stretch it. We have to. What Finn hasn't mentioned, but damn sure knows, is that these numbers aren't adding up if we actually need to reach the end of the tunnels. Even at a breakneck thrust, there won't be enough time to reach the end.

And then get back.

That's a huge problem we'll need to solve on future dives.

"Very good," Finn says, pressing buttons on his computer. "The tunnels are still wide here, so we can afford to increase thruster speed. Thirty-eight meters per minute should be reasonable."

I'm not convinced he's applied any actual scientific thought to that number. But I can navigate easily, so I'll let it go.

We move another three hundred meters through the tunnel, reaching a larger room and the end of the line, which is tied off on a rock protrusion. This is as far as anyone has gotten before. My water temperature reading says one hundred fifteen degrees. Wow. That's scary.

I secure a new tie-off and begin laying the rope, securing it every ten meters for our new traverse.

"Will you look at that," Finn says, awe in his voice.

I stop and turn toward him, then move into the larger chamber he's just entered.

The Torches.

We're in a large chamber, not as big as the Megaron, but close. It's circular in form with low-lying stalagmites scattered throughout the floor. We'll need more time to explore further, but it appears there are only two tunnels branching from the chamber, aside from the one we came from. Near the top of the eastern wall, two nearly identical circular openings gape above like twins.

When the team discovered these passages on sonar, Mads referred to them as The Torches, after the goddess *Hecate*'s twin torches. The crossroads. Seeing them up close, the name is fitting. They seem too perfect in their symmetry to be natural. And they both have tight entrances. This is where the tunnels in the *Hecate* get narrow, and it's going to be a challenge to squeeze into them.

But that's not going to happen on this dive. We're already at eighteen minutes.

Finn adds some thrust and moves closer to The Torches.

"We need to go back," I say.

"Just a peek."

Shit, Finn, do you really want to do this again?

Resisting the urge to go after him, I raise my voice. "Finn, now."

I make a decision. If he doesn't listen, I'll leave his ass like Crystal asked me to.

Still meters away, he stops and hovers there for a moment. Then he shrugs and turns around, only to freeze when he looks my way.

His mouth opens wide with shock, and he lets out a surprised sound of alarm.

Seeing him react like that makes my heart stop. What the hell does he see? I start to turn around to look, but before I can, I'm slammed from behind with a force so hard I spin across the room, clouds of silt and limestone exploding around me. The terrifying thought that I might be ripped from my suit passes through my head. I'm dead if that happens.

Disoriented, I catch a foggy glimpse of something moving—swimming—toward the tunnel where we came. What the hell?

There's someone in here with us. Before I even try to process that, I look down at my arms and realize I'm stuck. My arms are snagged in the damn aramid rope I was tying down when that thing hit me, and I can't reach my line cutter.

This is how divers die.

"Hold on. I'm almost there," Finn shouts as he approaches through the silt. When he reaches me, he takes his dive knife and attempts to cut me out. It barely scratches the rope. He spots the titanium knife secured to my belt and tries it. It's cutting a little better, but not much. At this rate, I'm not getting out of here.

"The steel line cutter. My right leg." I kick my leg up for him to see.

Finn nods and moves to put my knife back. His eyes grow large behind his helmet, locked on the knife's blade. "Christ," he whispers.

He's just staring.

"You good, man?" I ask him, trying to snap him out of his daze.

"Right." He puts back my knife, then finds the cutters and slices me out of the rope with ease.

"Good?" he asks.

"What the hell was that, Finn?"

"We're running a bit short on time."

I give him a long look. I, for one, am shitting in my pants over what I just saw. Finn, while shocked at first, seems to have already gotten over it.

"Yeah, let's get out of here."

The coolant has been running for about thirty minutes. We put on the thrusters at forty meters per minute and go. We're still in survivable temperatures that are dropping as we exit. So, we'll be fine. But who was that? It had to be another diver.

When we get to the spot we left Scott, we see him waiting. He exhales when he sees us.

"Did you see anyone come by while we were in there?" I ask him.

He jerks his head toward me. "What do you mean? Did I see anyone?"

Finn jumps in. "Nathan ran into some silt and got hung up in the lines near The Torches. We resolved it quickly, so we didn't call for help."

The hell? He just fucking lied to Scott.

"You got to The Torches? What did you see?" Scott asks. Ignoring Finn, he's looking directly at me.

"Whatever it was, I didn't see it, but Finn did." I turn to Finn, waiting for him to explain. He doesn't.

"What I saw was you struggling in silt," Finn says firmly.

Scott gives him a death stare but doesn't say anything else. "Let's get out of here," he mutters. We follow him to the main cavern.

♥

Mission successful.

When the briefing ends, Finn pulls me aside. "Nathan, may I speak with you in private?"

"Sure." I'm pissed. Finn completely whitewashed the briefing, giving a sanitized version of events. Focusing on the copious amounts of data retrieved, the distance covered, and the discovery of The Torches. What he conveniently forgot to mention was the unidentified diver who nearly knocked me out of my suit. It *had* to be a diver. But who? And where the hell did he exit the caves?

"You're angry, but please understand. I'm using discretion. We must be careful about whom we share this encounter. Don't tell anyone. I'm going to ask you to trust me—I'll share more when I can."

"If you want trust, why don't you start by being trustworthy? You could hand over my coded notes for starters."

Surprised, he gives me a hard look. "You're right, of course."

We step into the dry lab. Finn moves to the shelves of steel boxes secured against the bulkhead. "*With my crossbow, I shot the Albatross…*" he mutters under his breath.

Pulling one of the boxes off the shelf, he carries it to the table where I stand.

His eyes flick to the wall behind me, and he swallows. Then he gives me another long look and straightens his glasses.

"Dr. Nathan Carter." His voice has changed. He's on show. "It's taken decades for us to get here."

What the hell is he talking about? I feel a prickly sensation crawl up my back.

"It was kismet."

"Finn, can you cut to it? I'd like to go home."

"Like I was saying… kismet… You came back—right when you did. And even more fortuitous, you had no memory. Almost too perfect to be random." He looks behind me again, toward the hatch.

I turn and see a man about my age. He stands where he entered, waiting to be introduced.

Finn doesn't acknowledge him and continues. "As you know, I've been running analysis on the stone you found years ago. It's impossible to formalize conclusions." He pauses. "But when you know, you know."

He nods to the waiting man. "Let me introduce you to a colleague of ours. Dr. Stavon Green."

Green walks over to stand beside Finn.

Both men look at the box, then back at me.

Every instinct I have is screaming that something is wrong. Green locks his gaze on mine. His eyes are black. They're so dark that I can't tell where the pupils and irises meet. Or if he even has both. His skin is smooth and pale. If he's our age, he should have some lines around his eyes or forehead, but he doesn't. It's impossible to draw any hint as to what he's thinking or feeling.

"Hello, Nathan," Green says. His voice is pleasantly pitched with the clarity of a bell.

Saying nothing, I wait for him to continue.

"Dr. Clark and I have a mutual interest. One we've spent years working on independently. Until recently, our work has been theoretical and relatively private." He pauses and grins. It's the most unnatural smile I think I've ever seen. I'm tempted to find a piece of glass and put it under his nostrils to verify he's a human being. But I don't have to—I can see the pulse hammering in his neck. "You have no idea how many powerful people have their eyes on this. It was you who came to us. Seeking. But we didn't know what you found, not until later. That wasn't very courteous of you to keep it secret… as a fellow scientist."

"I have no idea what you're talking about."

"Our work proved it was possible, but we didn't know if it actually existed. You found the *where*. You found what we were looking for. And today. You showed us."

"Found what?"

Green doesn't answer and instead pushes the box toward me.

"Open it."

I stare at the box.

Putting my fingers against it, I think before I open it. Green is the guy Walter claimed tried to kidnap Natalie. Minus the sunglasses and hat, it was him in the park surveillance photograph. That makes him dangerous and an enemy.

It's Finn who's a wildcard. Is he on my side or Green's? Finn isn't telling Green everything. And I think he warned me not to either.

"Okay. You're both weird as fuck. But I'll do it."

Gently, I lift the top.

There's a knife, beautiful and ancient.

Its patina is brilliant blue-green.

It's familiar. There's a faint engraving partially hidden by the colors of the patina. Straining my eyes, I examine it closer.

My heart stops.

Reflexively, I touch the knife on my belt. It's still there.

Throwing away all caution, I pick up the knife from the box and bring the handle closer. I read the engraving.

Son, be brave. Be free.

I look up at the two men in front of me. Fear and awe collide.

"How? How is this possible?"

Before either answer, a wave of images flashes behind my eyes. The sickening pressure of a non-lethal shock squeezes my veins. I drop the knife.

What's happening?

But I know. I see the photo album, Crystal's delicate fingers as they flip through the pages, her words, the stories. Natalie's eyes, her dreams, her time machine.

Memories.

Of Maverick Key, of Miami, of…

Mom and Dad.

Dr. Paulson was right.

Snap.

I fall to my knees.

Two worlds collide. My recent tactile life, as Elliot, and the more distant past of Dr. Nathan Carter. Like crashing waves, they churn and mix. I feel myself tossed and carried amongst them, moving through the ocean toward land. When they reach the shore, I touch down. And I'm something new.

Then I laugh—unhinged. Like I've lost my mind. But it's just the opposite.

"Nathan?" Finn asks. Cautiously, he walks to my side and offers me a hand.

I stare at it. Then, after a beat, take it and stand. When I meet his gaze, a flash of recognition crosses his face. He squeezes my hand harder before letting it go.

"What just happened there?" he asks.

I think carefully about what I'll say next.

"Is one of you going to explain this to me?" I ask, nodding to the knife. Of course, I already know.

Green clears his throat to speak.

Finn jumps in. "If I may, Dr. Green. I'd like to explain this to Nathan." His eyes squint when he returns his gaze to mine.

"Shortly before your disappearance, you reached out to me to inquire about my theoretical work with exotic matter." He grins. "You came to me under the guise of a hobbyist. So, as a scientific colleague, I indulged you."

He walks to a desk in the corner and pulls some papers out of his briefcase. He lays one of them on the table.

It's an overlay cave survey of Carter's Drop. But we both know it's more than that.

"So why were you so interested in exotic matter, Dr. Carter?"

"You're asking me?" I flick my gaze from Finn to Green and back to Finn.

He nods. "Go ahead."

"*Instead of the cross, the albatross*..." I mutter, then clear my throat.

"Because I found a wormhole."

CHAPTER 35

The Widow

Blue silk slides over my head and streams down my body, as cool as ocean water against my skin. Nathan will love it.

The glow from dozens of candles lights a path from the living room, through the hallway, to the bedroom and bath. Their tiny flames flicker as I pass, casting shifting shadows that make the hallway feel as if it's breathing. The floor is covered in rose petals, the thickest layer leading to the bed. On top of the dresser, chilled fruit and champagne wait among bouquets of every color. I've displayed the best photos of us across the room—big smiles and sun-kissed skin.

Belize. I smell it. I feel it.

Everything is just how Nathan arranged our bungalow on our first night.

On our Honeymoon.

I'm trying to relax, but anticipation has my stomach in tight knots. At least I know he made it through the first thermal dive in his spacesuit.

I giggle. He called me from the ship. His voice was a little… off. But it sounds like everything went as they expected for the first dive, and they made it all the way to a new chamber where they found The Towers. How many of these dives is it going to take to find answers?

But for now he's safe, and he's coming home.

Any minute now, he'll walk through the door.

I check the time again.

Smiling, I drift toward the kitchen.

Nathan's car lights stream through the windows. I look around, unsure where to stand, how to pose. I want to amaze him when he walks in. But I'm too impatient to wait, so I decide to meet him at the door. As soon as I hear his footsteps, I swing it open.

And there he is.

He's wearing crisp, light linen and looks like the archaeologist he is. My handsome genius.

I reach for his hand to pull him closer and feel something cold and hard on his finger. His wedding band. He found it.

When I meet his gaze, he's staring at me. "You're beautiful, Mrs. Carter."

Still holding my hand, he walks in and surveys the room, inspecting my handiwork. "Wow. I feel like I'm there." I tag along with him as he tours the entire house.

When we reach the bedroom, he pulls me into his arms and kisses me. The kiss is… different. More assertive, more… Nathan?

"Love you," he whispers into my ear, his chin resting on my shoulder. Then he pulls away and starts to blow out the candles.

Confused, I try to stop him. "Is something wrong?"

He smiles. "No, everything's perfect. I just don't want to burn down the house." He pauses and turns to me. I'm looking at him, dumbfounded. He knows I just spent hours getting this ready. What's he up to?

"I hope it's okay," he says, continuing. "On the drive here, I got this wild idea." He's breathless now, eyes bright.

I'm completely lost, but he looks so happy. I'll go along with it.

"There's an order you need to follow with these kinds of things. Before we take our honeymoon… I've got a surprise for you."

What's he talking about? I can feel the frustration welling up inside. I have no patience. "What is it, Nathan?"

"Ssh… I'll tell you soon."

I don't hide my frown. "I don't like to wait."

"Don't I know it. Trust me?"

Ugh. Okay.

I nod.

He spins me around, and I feel something silky covering my eyes. A mask. My skin tingles, and I can feel my heart beating even faster. I really want to know what he's about to do to me.

Then I'm airless. He cradles me in his arms and carries me outside, and I can feel the cool night air tickling my skin.

"Where are we going, Nathan? Tell me." Softly pounding my fists on his chest and giggling, I beg. "*Please*."

"Patience, you harpy."

What did he just say? I hear the breath catch in my throat and suddenly feel dizzy.

He puts me in the car and buckles me up. "Don't dare take it off." His voice is low and dark.

Despite my best efforts to sit still and wait, I can't help but wiggle in my seat and ask him where we're going over and over.

Maddeningly, he says nothing else on the drive. He just hums and chuckles when I ask him something.

Finally, the car stops.

"We're here."

"Can I take this off now?" I tug on the mask.

He covers my hands. "Not just yet." He gives me a quick kiss and carries me again. It feels like gravel, then wood. I can hear the water. Are we at the marina? He shuffles me around for a moment, then jumps. Is the floor moving?

Are we on a boat? More walking. Then I feel the softness of a bed.

"Stay still. I'll be right back."

Not knowing what he's up to is killing me. We're definitely on a boat. I can feel the launch, the low rumble of engines, and then the telltale sway of the waves.

What are you up to, Nathan?

Now there's a sense of lightness. Like that morning on Sunset Strand. The day he told me he loved me for the first time.

I hear him walk back into the room.

"Okay. So, any guesses where we are?"

"The *Adeline*?"

He laughs. "No. Guess again?"

"I don't like games, Nathan. Just tell me."

"No more guesses? I know you can do better than that."

When I answer him with a huff and a scowl, he laughs.

"All right, I'll put you out of your misery." He kisses me deeply then, pulling off the mask while my eyes are still closed. When we break the kiss, I open them, and when they focus, I recognize our bedroom.

On the *Natalie Dawn*.

"Nathan?"

"I can't create a storm on demand. But everything else…"

What? This can't be possible.

Then he smiles. That lopsided grin that's so unique to him. The one I haven't seen in almost seven years.

"But we haven't looked at that photo yet," I mutter, too afraid to believe what I'm seeing.

"It's all right here." He taps his temple.

"Nathan?"

"I'm back." He crawls into the bed with me and pulls me on top. Gazing up into my eyes, he runs his fingers through my hair and gently pulls my face down to his.

Without breathing, I wait for him to tell me.

"I remember everything."

CHAPTER 36

Maddie

"Maddie Rickter—don't you dare lift a finger. You've been cooking all day. Relax," Ms. Connor calls to me from the sink.

I let go of the pantry door and pout. "We're running low on the lemon drop cookies. They're everyone's favorite, and the holiday bonfire is just a couple of days away."

Ms. Connor glances at the kitchen table—plates of cookies, peppermint bark, and fudge covering it end to end.

"I think they're going to survive, honey." She gives me a serious look and then a squeeze. "Now rest. Really."

Christmas is less than a week away. Natalie and Scott are in the living room decorating the inn's tree, and even Ziddo is sitting next to the table drinking some of Ms. Conner's famous cocoa with a bowl of Oreshki she made just for him. Scott's been practically living here at the inn with his team while they work around the clock planning when they're not diving.

For a few short hours tonight, they've all been able to unwind and enjoy the holiday spirit instead of worrying about an environmental catastrophe. Everyone's here, everyone but Nathan and Crystal.

They're having a party of their own tonight. I smile. Crystal told me all about her plans, and I saw Nathan washing up at the inn earlier so he could spruce up before he went home. Nathan's our Christmas miracle. There's nothing else I want other than for everyone in our family to stay safe... and be happy.

Everything's just right—for now, anyway. Well, almost.

I wish Wes could have made it tonight. We're expecting him in a couple of days. Then we'll have our whole family here with us. My heart squeezes with gratitude. Before I head to the living room, I pack a few lemon-drop cookies in a container to save for Wes.

"Hand me the green one," Scott calls out to Natalie. She hands him a big, glittery ornament which he hangs near the top of the tree.

"Can we put the star on now, Uncle Scott?" She lifts the star to him. He smiles and takes it. Stretching, he tries to get it on top. A two-step stool has done the trick for everything else, but the tree is nine feet tall.

"F—" He catches himself when he looks down at Natalie. "Can't quite reach it. I'm going to need to get the big ladder."

"Here," Ziddo says, walking up from behind him. Scott steps down and lets Ziddo top the tree. I giggle as I imagine he looks just like *Bumble*, the abominable snow monster from *Rudolph the Red-Nosed Reindeer*.

"Thanks," Scott says. Ziddo nods once and heads back into the kitchen.

Yeah, everything's perfect.

♥

After everyone else goes to bed, Scott and I sit together in the living room gazing at the sparkling lights on the tree. Resting my head against his chest, I'm dozing off when I hear a soft knock at the door.

Scott jumps up to answer it.

Who's knocking at eleven o'clock at night?

Scott looks out the peephole and slings it open. "What the hell are you doing here?"

"Nice to see you too, Rickter."

It's Wes!

I rush over to him and give him a big hug. "You're early."

He squeezes me tightly, ignoring Scott's glare.

I give him a quick peck on the cheek. "It's so good to see you."

"Want a whiskey?" Scott asks. Pouring him a glass before he answers.

"Please. Neat."

Wes makes himself comfortable on the couch, and I take the chair in front of him. Scott hands Wes the whiskey and walks over to stand next to me.

Wes Harrington. In the flesh. We've kept in frequent contact while he's been in hiding, but even video calls aren't the same as seeing him in person. His presence is still magnetic.

There was a hot minute I thought we'd never see him again. For reasons neither of them has fully explained, Garrett has stubbornly held on to his guns making sure Wes stays in hiding. Relentlessly bullying him with the threat of sharing a doctored video that implies he was culpable for someone's death. It's a little extreme, even for Garrett. Wes explained to me that a caver had died in a cenote in the Yucatan. Wes couldn't save him. Curious if it was someone Garrett was close to, I asked—Wes simply said it wasn't about the man who died. It was about control.

"Spill it, Wes. Tell us about all your adventures. I'm ready to stay up all night. Start with where the heck you've been."

Turns out he's been in the Yucatan, planting trees and restoring the Maya Forest Gardens. "You must love it there. Especially to go back after what happened in the cenote."

"I do. Aside from what happened, it's the one place on this Earth where I've truly been happy." His face lights up with a memory. "I thought I could get it back."

Get it back?

I'll let that comment go for now.

"Okay. Tell us. What are *Garrett's* mysterious conditions this time?"

Wes shrugs and laughs. "Surprisingly, they're easy. He didn't even have to ask. There's going to be nooooo problem meeting them," he spits out. His eyes squint with bitterness. "He told me to stay away from…"

When he glances at the staircase behind me, his face freezes and turns a ghostly white.

I've only seen his face like that once before, when I hyperventilated after one of our dives, and he had to save me.

Until now, it was the only time I've ever seen fear on Wes Harrington's face.

His green eyes widen with shock, then narrow.

"What is it?" Worried, I turn toward the staircase.

Sid?

Her hair is styled, and she's wearing makeup and a red sundress *in the middle of the night*.

"You know each other?" I turn back. But Wes is gone.

"What the…?" Scott mutters.

The front door slams.

Wow. I turn back to Sid.

"Don't mind me. I was just coming down to say hello."

She smiles, but her eyes aren't smiling.

Thank you for reading *Tides of the Heart*. Get ready for the thrilling conclusion of the Carter's Drop trilogy with *The Heart's True North*, book three in *The Maverick Key Series*.

Want more from Maverick Key?

Join my newsletter @ margotkeene.com for exclusive content, behind-the-scenes updates and access to ***Clint & Sandy***, available exclusively to subscribers. Follow me on Instagram!

ACKNOWLEDGEMENTS

Book two is a wrap! There are so many people to thank.

First, thank you to my husband, Tony, for inspiring me every day to pursue this dream and for being there when it's hard. All of my fictional heroes are inspired by you! To my brother, John, and mom and dad, who are my biggest fans. My little girls, who will someday make their own dreams come true.

Jenn, my editor, who worked with me through the tough parts. Ashley, who created the beautiful cover and interior art.

Thank you to my beta readers: Anna, Caroline, Christal, Claudia, Lexi, Megan, Nicole, and Ruth, who read an early draft of the manuscript and offered valuable insights that helped me refine the story. And thank you to all the ARC readers who read an early copy of the finished story.

To every reader who has picked up one of my books—thank you!

As an author, it's a gift whenever a reader spends time with your work. There are so many wonderful stories, and I'm honored to share mine.

ABOUT THE AUTHOR

Margot Keene is a Florida native who turned her lifelong passion for storytelling into a full-time career. A former business analyst and project manager, she now creates swoon-worthy men, relatable heroines, and heart-stopping mysteries set amid the beauty and intrigue of the Florida coast.

www.ingramcontent.com/pod-product-compliance
Ingram Content Group UK Ltd.
Pitfield, Milton Keynes, MK11 3LW, UK
UKHW041631190726
13854UKWH00006B/2421

9 781967 133062